Eyes narrowed, with a proud lift to her head, she waded out of the water and moved towards him, seemingly not in the least embarrassed at confronting a complete stranger in her sodden petticoat.

'I trust you've had an edifying look, sir—pretending to be a gentleman, riding about the countryside on a fine horse on the look-out for poor, defenceless girls.'

Max smiled. 'You? Defenceless? Now you do exaggerate. Something tells me you are afraid of no one.' Her clenched fists and rose-tinted cheeks, the brilliance of her green eyes, told him so.

The accented voice was courteous enough, which only seemed to exacerbate Christina's temper. 'Have you nothing better to do with your time?'

'I can't think of anything more pleasurable just now than looking at you,' he replied easily. 'I was merely out riding.'

'Then you must be a stranger, otherwise you would know you are trespassing. This is private land.'

A slow, appreciative smile worked its way across his face as his eyes raked her from head to toe once more and then moved back to her furious eyes. 'A thousand apologies. I hadn't realised. But my crime—if that is what it is—was well worth it.'

Helen Dickson was born and still lives in South Yorkshire, with her husband, on a busy arable farm where she combines writing with keeping a chaotic farmhouse. An incurable romantic, she writes for pleasure, owing much of her inspiration to the beauty of the surrounding countryside. She enjoys reading and music. History has always captivated her, and she likes travel and visiting ancient buildings.

Recent novels by the same author:

THE EARL AND THE PICKPOCKET
HIS REBEL BRIDE
THE DEFIANT DEBUTANTE
ROGUE'S WIDOW, GENTLEMAN'S WIFE
TRAITOR OR TEMPTRESS
A SCOUNDREL OF CONSEQUENCE
WICKED PLEASURES
  (part of *Christmas By Candlelight)*
FORBIDDEN LORD

SCANDALOUS SECRET, DEFIANT BRIDE

Helen Dickson

MILLS & BOON
Pure reading pleasure™

First published in Great Britain 2008
Harlequin Mills & Boon Limited,
Eton House, 18-24 Paradise Road, Richmond, Surrey TW9 1SR

© Helen Dickson 2008

ISBN: 978 0 263 86286 7

Set in Times Roman 10½ on 12¾ pt.
04-1108-86506

Printed and bound in Spain
by Litografia Rosés S.A., Barcelona

at the sky, a breathtakingly beautiful blue. And in a firm, clear and defiant voice he said, 'She was mine. That child was mine. One day I will find her. I swear I will.'

Chapter One

1895

It was the sound of her ringing laughter that first drew Maxwell Lloyd to Christina Thornton. Until now only the subdued call of birds, his own quiet breathing and the lazy drone of a browsing bee disturbed the silence of the woodland. Riding slowly along the dim chequered path, he heard more shrieks and laughter, now masculine as well as feminine. He came out of the trees and on to the edge of the small private lake on Sir Henry Thornton's estate. It basked in the benign warmth of the sun and long tendrils of willow brushed the surface.

On the grass he observed two pairs of men's boots and stockings neatly tucked into the tops. Beside them were two piles of carefully folded trousers, shirts and tweed jackets. A little further apart what he saw brought a smile to his firm lips and told him much about the owner of the possessions. A small pair of leather shoes and more delicate cream stockings had been discarded with less care on the ground, and a red dress had been thrown untidily over a bush—such fine-quality material would not be worn by a servant.

Halting his horse on the edge of the trees, he surveyed the scene before him with astonishment. The sun was hot and the water looked cool and inviting and, had the lake not been occupied by three young things, he would have taken off his clothes and dove into the silent dark depths himself.

Two boisterous young men were cavorting in the water with a young woman scantily clad in what he assumed must be her petticoat. With carefree, wholesome hearts they were too absorbed in their antics to notice him, so he could look his fill.

But he only had eyes for the young woman. In those first dazzling moments he acted as any hot-blooded male would and all he could do was stare as a thrill of excitement ran through his veins. But Maxwell Lloyd was no ordinary man and he recovered at once.

Of medium height and as slender as a wand, her perfectly rounded breasts rose in two delectable white hemispheres above the lace of her petticoat. Saturated, it clung to her, outlining her body, her hips arched from her small waist, and the perfect shape of her legs. Her breathtaking beauty quickened his soul and stirred his mind with imaginings of what further loveliness lay concealed beneath her flimsy attire. Her hair was an explosion of bright, rich, dark brown curls hanging down her back to her buttocks in a tangled mass. Her face was heart shaped, her mouth like a ripe raspberry.

The two young men, one dark, the other fair, were teasing her mercilessly, splashing her with water and shrieking louder when she tried to back away and fell, dowsing the whole of her in the lake. The fair-haired young man took her hand and hauled her to her feet; not a bit chagrined, with a riotous sense of fun she laughingly threatened them with the same. In mock-terror the two young men immediately dove under the water and, when they emerged, with strong swift strokes began swimming towards the centre of the lake.

The young woman watched them go without attempting to follow. Throwing back her head, she laughed loud, with none of the ladylike posturing of other young ladies of Max's acquaintance.

'Cowards,' she called, shaking her fist high. 'You can look out. When you come back I'll get my own back. I swear I will.'

Max was riveted. Vibrant and vital, she had a freshness and a delightful simplicity that captured his attention.

Suddenly her back stiffened and she became still, like a young animal that has caught the scent of danger. She spun round and her gaze flew directly to where horse and rider stood. Eyes narrowed, with a proud lift to her head she waded out of the water and moved towards him, seemingly not in the least embarrassed at confronting a complete stranger in her sodden petticoat. There was indignation in the thrust of her chin and anger in her narrowed eyes. Stopping a short distance away, her feet were luminously white on the green grass.

How small and slender they were—like a child's, Max thought. He could see her eyes were heavily lashed, tilted, feral, and emerald green. Something that had lain dormant for many years stirred inside him. There was something about her, the boldness in her eyes, the tilt of her head that attracted him.

'Good afternoon,' she said boldly, having no idea who he was. 'We were unaware that we were being spied on.' Lifting her chin haughtily, she met the brilliant blue eyes beneath dark brows that were observing her with frank interest—far too much interest, she thought as he scrutinised her with a thoroughness that made her feel more undressed than she was. His gaze moved over her unabashedly. She stiffened with indignation. No one—especially not a man—had looked at her in quite that way before.

The man was obnoxious, she decided, although the clean-shaven face beneath his thick black hair was terribly handsome, she would grant him that. There was also an uncompromising authority in the set of his jaw and an arrogance in the tilt of his head that was not to her liking. Astride a magnificent strawberry-roan horse, his skin was as brown as if he was used to hot climes, which put her in mind of her friend's brothers, when they had come back from serving in the army in India.

Christina's pride had been pricked and she was hardly in the mood to forgive this stranger for being at hand when she was so scantily clad. With ill-suppressed ire she scowled up at him. 'I trust you've had an edifying look, sir—pretending to be a gentleman, riding about the countryside on a fine horse on the look out for poor, defenceless girls.'

White teeth gleamed in a reckless smile as Max responded. She was like a kitten spitting and showing its claws. Again his gaze slid from her moistened lips, following the line of her throat down to the tantalising orbs of flesh exposed to his view above her clinging wet petticoat. With her head thrown back and her irate breathing, they quivered and peaked invitingly, emphasising the undeniable fact that she had left her childhood behind and was on the brink of becoming an alluring woman.

'You? Defenceless? Now you do exaggerate. Something tells me you are afraid of no one.' Her clenched fists and rose-tinted cheeks, the brilliance of her green eyes, told him so.

The accented voice was courteous enough, which only seemed to exacerbate Christina's temper. 'Have you nothing better to do with your time?'

'I suppose I could find something to occupy me,' he replied easily, 'but I can't think of anything more pleasurable just now than looking at you. I was merely out riding. The day is too pleasant to remain indoors.'

'Then you must be a stranger, otherwise you would know you are trespassing. This is private land.'

A slow appreciative smile worked its way across his face as his eyes raked her from head to toe once more and then came back to her furious eyes. 'A thousand apologies. I hadn't realised—but my crime, if that is what it is, was well worth it,' the foreign voice said smoothly.

'We prosecute trespassers.'

'Really?' His eyebrows arched and his eyes gleamed with sardonic amusement, which seemed to infuriate her all the more.

'There are notices.'

'I'm afraid I didn't see them.'

'You would have, if you'd stayed on the road.'

Her tart reply almost brought Max to outright laughter. 'Then since I am trespassing and you apparently are not, I can only assume you must be related to the Thorntons.'

'Sir Gerald Thornton is my father.'

His eyes widened as a slow realisation of who she really was made its way from the wound that had been inflicted on his heart so many years ago and never healed. 'I see,' he said, giving no indication that he knew more about her that she would like. 'Forgive me if I seem surprised.'

'Why should you be?'

'It's not every day I come across a young woman cavorting near-naked with two gentlemen in the same state of undress.'

Unashamed of her behaviour and resenting his interference, she threw back her shoulders and lifted her head haughtily, unaware as she did so how the gesture lifted the roundness of her pert breasts and caused Max to experience an exquisitely painful sensation in the pit of his belly.

'One of the gentlemen happens to be my brother.'

'And the other?'

Turning her head, she looked in the direction of the lake. There was no denying the look of melting adoration when her eyes lit upon James's bobbing fair head as he continued to swim away from her.

'Oh, goodness, he—he's…'

'A close friend?' Max suggested softly.

Her head swivelled round to find his eyes probing hers. As she comprehended his meaning, bright pink stained her cheeks, her expression telling him they were in love so there was nothing wrong with what they were doing. 'Yes—yes, he is. He is also a gentleman, which you clearly are not.'

Max raised a sardonic brow at her tone and contemplated her snapping green eyes. 'That's quite a temper you have there.'

'Yes. It can be quite ferocious when I'm provoked. Now, please go away. We are enjoying the sun and minding our own business. I suggest you mind yours. You are intruding.'

'You have plenty of cheek, I'll say that,' he chuckled softly.

'Say what you like. I don't care. Just go away.'

'Hostile, too. I don't usually encounter such hostility on a first encounter.' Max looked down at this spirited young woman, her flashing eyes and defiant chin elevated to a lofty angle. He cocked a dubious brow. 'However, I would have supposed a true gentleman would not engage in this kind of sport with a gently reared young lady. I find it hard to believe your father allows such wantonness.'

Her hand pushed back the heavy weight of her hair from her forehead. 'He doesn't know; besides it's none of your business, Mr…' She shrugged for she couldn't care less who he was. 'Whoever you are.'

'Maxwell Lloyd,' he provided, finding himself unable to look away from her. In his experience, beautiful females were always conscious of their appeal and the fact that she either didn't care, or didn't know, further added to her allure. Firm hard flesh, he thought—she would be hard and soft in all the right places. Damn it! What was wrong with him? It wasn't spring, when a man was expected to have aberrant thoughts, when the wind was soft on exposed flesh after a long, hard winter—when sap was rising—and she was right. What had it to do with him?

Suddenly the sun was painfully, unbearably brilliant. He wanted to ride away. What did he care for these three young people enjoying the day and each other? And at the same time he wanted to prolong the moment, to keep the girl talking— this special girl—to fill his eyes and his ears with the sight and the sound of her.

The name was unfamiliar to Christina. She tossed her head haughtily. 'No matter. Please go away. Not only are you a trespasser, you are offensive.'

'I apologise if that's how I seem to you, Miss Thornton. But I have to say that you are the rudest, most impudent young woman I have ever come across, and I have every sympathy with your parents,' he told her calmly, 'and why they don't take you in hand I can't imagine. My father would have had you thrashed and locked in your room with nothing to eat and drink but bread and water for a week.'

For an incredulous moment Christina was speechless, then, forgetting her intention to walk away, she glared up into his far-too-handsome face, with authority and arrogance stamped all over it, her eyes two brilliant chips of ice. That was the moment she decided he was detestable.

'I can thank God he is not *my* father, who is more civilised,' she hissed. 'I am perfectly content with the one I've got. I don't give a damn who you are or where you come from—'

'You also have a dirty mouth, Miss Thornton,' Max reproached her mockingly.

Christina could feel the colour burning on her cheeks as she gazed at him with pure loathing. 'I say what I like. My only concern is that wherever it is you do come from you return there and stop bothering me.'

Max grinned affably and prepared to ride away. 'I think I like bothering you, Miss Thornton, and I shall enjoy bothering you a good deal more before I'm done.' Inclining his head politely, his eyes doing one last quick sweep of her delectable body, he said, 'Good day', and rode away.

When the stranger had disappeared back into the woods, somehow Christina managed to turn and make it back to the edge of the lake. Suddenly the brightness had gone out of the day and the breeze held a bitter chill. Stepping into the water, feeling the coldness lap at her ankles, she paused and took a deep breath and tried to stop the angry trembling inside. What a dreadful, dreadful man, even more dreadful than any man she had ever met, and she detested him thoroughly.

Suddenly James rose out of the water and splashed towards her, his lips stretched in a wide smile over his youthful face, his blue eyes laughing and so very appealing, and suddenly the warmth came back into the day and the obnoxious Mr Lloyd was forgotten.

The Thornton family had a long and distinguished history in Cambridge. In the reign of Queen Anne, William Thornton, a man who revelled in hunting and was a lover of all country pursuits, had bought several hundred acres of farmland and forests, built the magnificent Tanglewood and settled his family there.

It was so named because of the thick woodland that had to

be cleared so the house could be built. It stood at the end of a drive of beech and oak like a timeless old lady, its brooding structure of mellow stone preserved for centuries, looming out of the shadows of another time.

Having separated from James and Peter, Christina made her way to the back of the house. It would never do if Mama saw her in her bedraggled state. Hopefully she'd make it to her room and she would be none the wiser.

She entered the servants' block, with its numerous rooms housing at least fifteen servants, as furtively as any criminal. Unfortunately she had to go by the kitchen, which was the proverbial hive of industry, with extra catering staff employed to assist cook with the evening's dinner party. She would be lucky to pass unnoticed. She didn't. Holding her breath as she sneaked past the open door, she froze when Mrs Barnaby's voice boomed out.

'Miss Christina! Well, I never.'

Carrying her stockings, her skirts saturated halfway up to her waist, her wet petticoat uncomfortable beneath her dress, with her face a picture of guilt, Christina slowly turned and looked into the cavernous kitchen with its ranges, dressers and gleaming copper pans and a massive central table. Kitchen maids, preparing ingredients for Mrs Barnaby's use, and scullery maids, scouring pans at a large pot sink, paused in their work to gape open mouthed, their eyes popping out on stalks, at the young miss who resembled a drowned rat. Although it was nothing new. It wasn't the first time they'd seen her in a similar state—often much worse.

Attired in a pristine starched white apron and cap, moving towards her, her hands on her ample hips, Mrs Barnaby's eyes ran up and down her appalling appearance disapprovingly. 'Why, Miss Christina, it's plain to see you've been on one of your jaunts. I don't know what your mama will say to this.' Hadn't she seen her crossing the park in the direction of the lake with Mr Peter and his friend hours ago, their laughing faces as they larked about seeming to suggest they were up to something exciting?

Mrs Barnaby had been at Tanglewood since before Christina was born and, with the familiarity of an old retainer, felt she could say what she liked—indeed, every one of the servants and even Lady Thornton stood very much in awe of her.

Well and truly caught and in something of a fix, knowing she would have to bluff her way out of it, on a sigh and shifting restlessly from one foot to the other, Christina shrugged. 'I'm sorry, Barney,' she said, addressing Tanglewood's large and cosy cook by the nickname she'd used since she'd learned to talk. 'I know how it must look to you, but I had the most awful accident and slipped and fell into the lake. Please don't tell Mama. You know how cross she gets. Besides, I know she's got company this afternoon, so I don't want to disturb her. I don't want her to see me looking like this.'

'And I should think not. She would scold you most severely, as would your papa.'

'Papa would understand.' She smiled sweetly.

Mrs Barnaby sighed, shaking her head. If her parents couldn't stop her, who was she to interfere? 'Ah, well, I'm up to my eyes in preparations for tonight, so away with you and have Molly prepare you a bath.'

As Christina scampered off to her room, Mrs Barnaby went back to preparing the food for the evening's dinner party. Would the girl never grow up? She was seventeen and supposed to be a young lady, but there had been nothing ladylike about her just now. An image of the handsome young Mr James Embleton's sisters came to mind—sweet natured they were, always stitching samplers or dabbling in water colours or playing the piano, a trouble to no one, which could not be said of Miss Christina.

Defiant of all restrictions and rebellious of all convention, she was a complex young woman—untameable, hot tempered, truculent when she failed to get her own way, and an angel when she did. Her parents despaired of ever making a lady of her.

Molly was folding some of Christina's clothes away into drawers when Christina flounced in, crashing the door behind her and making Molly almost jump out of her skin.

'I need a bath,' she declared, throwing her muddied stockings on to the bed and kicking off her shoes. 'I'm filthy.' Immediately she began peeling off her clothes.

Molly stopped what she was doing and wrinkled her nose. For all the world her young mistress looked like a wild thing. 'I can see that.'

Molly was a first-class lady's maid. Lady Thornton had employed her when Christina was fourteen years old. She was thoroughly experienced, a first-rate hairdresser and experienced in dressing a lady and everything that appertained to her office. Molly had never met anyone quite like her mistress. In the beginning she'd been tempted to seek another position, but as she got to know her better she found there was something so appealing about her that she'd decided to stay.

'Have you seen Mama?'

'No, but I know her company left some time since.'

'I suppose she'll want to rest in preparation for the dinner party this evening.' Christina stepped out of her undergarments, leaving them in a wet heap on the carpet, from where Molly immediately retrieved them, curious as to their dampness, but deciding it would be better not to ask.

'I'll wear my sapphire blue gown tonight.' Wrapping her robe around her now naked body, Christina tied the belt tight around her small waist. 'I want to look my absolute best.'

Molly gave her a puzzled look. 'But you don't like that dress. You hate sapphire blue.'

'I've changed my mind,' she said, James having told her that sapphire blue was his favourite colour.

Sitting at her dressing table, she carefully began studying her face from every angle—which she had taken to doing frequently of late, much to Molly's quiet amusement—one didn't have to be a genius to know the cause of this sudden interest in her looks and that it had everything to do with her brother's friend.

'And you can dress my hair—all sophisticated like, with some of those glittering combs Mama likes to wear.' So James will notice how grown up I am, how pretty I am, she thought. She knew she hadn't imagined his liking for her, although as yet he hadn't told her he had any special feelings for her. He was always telling her what a good sport she was, that she was clever and interesting, and once, when she'd made an extra-special effort with her appearance, as she would do tonight, he had told her she was pretty. How she wished he would get a move on. He would have to go back to university soon. Perhaps she was going to have to make the first move.

Having brought the sapphire blue gown from Christina's dressing room, Molly was surveying it with disapproval. 'I don't think this is suitable for a quiet dinner party at home. The neckline is daringly low—far too revealing in my opinion.'

'Nonsense, Molly. It's perfect.'

'You will certainly not wear it,' came her mama's firm voice from the doorway. Lady Thornton breezed in. 'Molly is quite right. The cleavage is far too deep and will shock Mrs

Travis, the vicar's wife, who will be sitting across from you. Dear me, what would she think? The evening will be a low-key, conservative affair, so your pale yellow muslin will do nicely, so be a dear and get it out, will you, Molly? And your hair, Christina—wear it down tonight. I prefer to see you with it that way for the present. There will be plenty of occasions for your sophisticated hair-dos on more formal occasions.'

'But, Mama—'

'No, Christina, and that is my final word.' Lady Thornton smiled kindly at Molly's relieved expression, glad that she had come in time to prevent a disagreement between maid and mistress.

Christina was a constant worry for Audine Thornton. Her daughter had always been unmanageable and refused to live by the rules of polite society. It concerned her that, because of her nature, Christina would probably never form a union with a man who would be prepared to put up with her wild ways. Unfortunately Gerald, her husband, who had given Christina free rein to do just as she liked from early childhood, didn't share her concern.

'I'm going to rest for a while, but I've come to tell you to be punctual and that you must be on your best behaviour. The company will be from the local community and perhaps not as young as you would like, so, if you get bored, please remember your manners and don't let it show. There are a few additions to the invitations—Reverend Kingston and his wife—oh, and our new neighbour.'

'What new neighbour?' Christina asked sullenly, absolutely mortified that her mama had forbidden her to wear the sapphire blue.

'The one who is renting Cranworth House while Major Illingworth is in India. He took up residence a few days ago. I sent him an invitation yesterday, thinking it would be polite to welcome him to the neighbourhood. I'm so pleased he sent a note to accept.'

Christina wasn't the slightest bit interested in Cranworth House's new tenant. Turning back to the mirror as her mama went out and Molly prepared her bath, she sighed. What did she care about any of the invited guests, as long as James was there?

Mingling with the guests—twenty in all, elegant, wealthy, local people, who were partaking of pre-dinner drinks, sherry for the ladies and brandy for the gentleman—Max took a glass from the salver of a circulating servant. Of course, by now everyone knew who he was and couldn't wait to be introduced. His arrival among them had caused quite a stir—it wasn't often that a man with so colourful and mysterious a background appeared among them.

Uncommonly tall and lithe, his features strong and darkly handsome, he moved among them with the confident ease of a man well assured of his masculinity and his own worth. His hair, parted at the side, was thick and glossy black, and he had the kind of looks that set feminine hearts aflutter.

Max conversed politely, seeming to give them his full attention, but the major part of it was concentrated on the door as he waited for the daughter of the house to make an appearance. And then, as if he was seeing a dream, there she was. Everyone paused in their conversations and glanced her way. Her smile was dazzling and she seemed to bestow it on every one of those present—and did he imagine it, or did everyone resume talking with more animation than before? He smiled. Christina Thornton could lift the mood of a room simply by walking into it.

Max's whole sum and substance became concentrated on

the slender young woman. She drifted in like a butterfly in a pale lemon muslin gown, lovely and expensive, completely at odds with the young hoyden he had met earlier by the lake. The waist was tight, around which was fastened a narrow gold velvet ribbon. The skirts dipped and swayed as she glided over the smoothness of the richly patterned carpet to reveal the tips of her gold-slippered feet. She moved with a fluency and elegance that drew the eye. Her back was straight, her head tilted proudly, and her small breasts thrust forwards showed beneath the modest bodice of her gown. Her hair, a rich dark brown bordering on black, thick and gently curling, was drawn off her face and hung to her waist.

She had an individuality that had nothing to do with her beauty, which took Max's breath away. With her creamy-white complexion she was utterly feminine, but there was nothing demure about her. When in company other young ladies would keep their eyes cast modestly down—Miss Thornton showed no such restraint. Filled with restless energy, she stared directly, looking about her with a keen interest, her glance filled with anticipation and bright expectancy. When her eyes picked out James Embleton, the object of her desire, she smiled the widest smile that warmed and lit her features.

But then she saw Max. His eyes pierced her with their stead-fast gaze and her smile disappeared. Something shifted in Christina. She was most surprised to find him among the guests and curious as to how he had come to be invited, but she did not show it. Tearing her offended gaze from his and lifting her head in that unique way she had of showing her haughteur and defiance, with a deliberate snub she turned her back on him and made a beeline to where James stood talking to Peter.

They were animatedly discussing the cricket match that was to be played the following day, one that was played twice a year, the second a return match at the rival village of Farnley. Christina was swamped with dismay when they told her they were to play. She hadn't much use for cricket, considering it boring and a waste of time.

'You are to play cricket? But I—I thought we could take a picnic—the three of us, to the lake. Peter, you promised.'

James smiled an apology. 'I'm afraid not, Christina. We'll have a picnic another day. It can't compete with cricket. What do you say, Peter?'

'Certainly not. Look, there's Hal Jenkinson. He's in charge. Let's go and have a word.'

Seeing Christina's downcast face, James smiled. 'I'm sorry, Christina. Look, have Mrs Barnaby prepare a basket and we'll picnic during a break in the match—at lunch time. How about that?'

She brightened a little. 'Yes—yes, I will.'

As they were about to walk away, Peter turned back. Tall and still rather gangly, with light brown curly hair and brown eyes, he was like his mother. Sensing his sister's disappointment, he gave her a pitying smile. 'You go on, James. I'll be with you in a moment. I'd like to have a word with Christina.' Taking her arm, he drew her to a quiet corner. 'Christina— this is awkward, but I feel I must say something.'

'What about?'

'James.'

Christina stiffened, not liking her brother's tone, which was suddenly serious and more often than not heralded a telling off. 'What about James?'

'Look, I know you like him, Christina, a lot, but try not to show it quite so much. This afternoon—well—you did go over-board a bit at the lake—you know, taking your dress off and…'

'Why?' she gasped. 'You've never minded before.'

'That's because we're always alone—and you're my sister—but—you do trail after James a bit, and—well—you're too forward, Christina, by far.'

'Forward?' Her eyes snapped with righteous anger. 'I am not. I don't see James complaining.'

'He wouldn't. He's much too polite.'

'I need no instructions on how to conduct myself when I am with him,' Christina retorted crossly, careful not to be overheard as her cheeks flushed with hot indignation.

'I'm simply trying to warn you of the dangers.'

'What dangers?'

'To stop you getting hurt—as you surely will. James sees you as my sister, someone who is fun to be with, and nothing more than that.'

'Keep your warnings to yourself, Peter. I can take care of myself—and I will make him care for me.'

'He won't, Christina.' Peter's tone was sharp. 'You will be wasting your time and more than likely make a fool of yourself into the bargain. Stop it now. Please.'

When he'd gone Christina was suddenly snatched from her angry preoccupations by a voice behind her, a voice that was deep and rich in timbre—and foreign.

'Well, well, so we meet again, Miss Thornton. Who would have thought we would do so—and so soon?'

She spun round. Tall and incredibly handsome in the black and white of his evening dress, his black hair brushed to a smooth shine, Mr Lloyd towered over her.

His eyes were full of mockery when he smiled and quietly said, 'I fear my presence this evening is going to bother you some more.'

Christina straightened imperiously. 'What are you doing here?' she retorted ungraciously, with none of the manners her mama had tried to instil into her. 'How have you managed to wheedle your way into my parents' dinner party?'

'Lady Thornton very kindly invited me.' His smile widened. 'In truth, I suspect she took pity on my single state and thought to draw me into the fold, so to speak.'

'As she would a stray dog,' Christina retorted drily. 'I didn't know you were acquainted with Mama.'

'I wasn't, until yesterday when she issued the invitation. Since I am new to the area and wish to become acquainted with my neighbours, although my stay is only temporary, I accepted. It would have been ungracious of me to refuse.'

'Why? Where do you live?'

'At Cranworth House.'

Christina's lips parted in surprise and, despite herself, she felt her interest quicken. 'Oh, really—so you are the foreigner.'

'If that is what you want to call me, then please do so, although it is not a term I like. I am half-Italian.'

'And the other half?'

'English.'

'But why should you object to being referred to as a foreigner? If you are Italian—a very rich Italian, by all accounts—then surely the term is not incorrect.'

Max's mouth tightened ominously. 'And how can anyone here know my circumstances? My affairs are private. But then in a small community such as this, I suppose a stranger will be the subject of gossip and speculation. Have you done your share of speculating, too, Miss Thornton?' he asked, one sleek dark brow arched, his eyes gleaming with derisive humour.

Realising that Mr Lloyd was trying to provoke her, Christina turned to walk away. Max stepped in front of her to bar her way. Their combined movements brought them closer together. He stared at her with impudent admiration, his gaze resting for a moment on the gentle swell of her breasts before moving up to her face. His brilliant blue eyes, the curl of his well-cut lips and the lounging insolence of his long body were saying something to her she did not understand. Perplexed, instinctively she looked away. Beneath his close scrutiny her cheeks had grown pink and hot, for she was young and had not yet learned the control which comes with age and experience.

'Mr Lloyd, I would be obliged if you would step aside. I don't want to talk to you.'

Directing a glance of wry humour at her, his eyes narrowing, he said, 'Tell me, Miss Thornton. Are you normally hostile to everyone you meet, or is it just me?'

Her chilled contempt met him face to face. 'It's just you.'

'Do you mind if I enquire as to why?'

'You can ask, but I'm not obliged to answer.'

'You have certainly none of your mother's good manners,' he remarked, looking towards where Lady Thornton flitted amongst her guests in a rustling lavender-grey dress. 'She also looks so young you are more like sisters than mother and daughter.'

Christina's eyes narrowed and her lips twisted scornfully. 'What an expert flatterer you are, Mr Lloyd. Mama is still youthful, I grant you, but given the fact that she has produced two offspring, she can hardly be mistaken for my sister.'

'I see you have met my daughter, Mr Lloyd.'

Max turned and smiled at his host. Inwardly, however, he was not smiling, and he was mentally dictating a sharp reprimand, which he would deliver to the man who had masqueraded as Christina's father for the seventeen years of her life.

'I have had that pleasure—and very charming she is. You must be very proud.'

Sir Gerald beamed. He was still a handsome man, despite his balding pate and slightly protuberant belly. 'She most certainly is. And of course there is Peter, my only son, who is at Cambridge reading law—and doing well, I'm happy to say. Do you have family, Mr Lloyd?'

Max shook his head. 'Sadly, no. I have no siblings. My mother died bringing me into the world, and my father followed her several years ago.'

'Then what brought you to England?'

His expression became guarded. 'Several reasons, one of them being that my mother came from Cambridge—and I was at university here. I had a yearning to see it again—to spend some time here and look up old friends. It is where I spent many happy years in my youth.'

Christina gritted out a thin smile. 'I believe there were some Lloyds in these parts many years ago—is that not so, Papa?— and if my memory serves me correctly, a wild bunch they were, too. In fact, I do believe one of them was hanged for holding up coaches on the Cambridge Road,' she remarked airily.

The sweetness of her tone did not hide the sneer she intended. Max met it with a flicker of amusement showing on his lips, and his eyes narrowed challengingly. 'Indeed! You must tell me more, Miss Thornton. However, I do not believe it is the same branch—my mother's maiden name was Lloyd, you see, but I am intrigued by your highwayman none the less. We may have much in common. I always thought I was a direct descendent of Genghis Khan.'

Gerald smiled to himself. For one dreadful moment he thought he was going to have to intervene to defend his guest from his sharp-tongued daughter, but it seemed there was no need. He thought Mr Lloyd was quite capable of dealing with rude young women.

Failing to detect the teasing light in Mr Lloyd's eyes, Christina's eyes opened wide. 'Who is he?'

Her sublime ignorance made Max want to laugh out loud, and it took a tremendous effort to keep his face straight. 'When you have a few hours to spare, Miss Thornton, I will be happy to relate his exploits—but I will tell you he was a thousand times more formidable than your highwayman.'

'And do you take after this ancestor of yours, Mr Lloyd?' she asked in all innocence. 'And why do you use your mother's name and not your father's? Is there something wrong with it?'

'Christina,' her father said testily, shooting a sharp look of reproach at her, a look telling her not to disgrace herself. Now she really had overstepped the mark. 'Whatever name Mr Lloyd chooses to call himself by is his business, so please guard your tongue. Please forgive my daughter, Mr Lloyd. She is impulsive and far too outspoken for her own good. Those not familiar with her may take offence, but there's none meant. Is that not so, Christina?'

Christina affected an expression of smooth innocence, but neither man was deceived by it. 'Oh, absolutely.'

Quite undaunted, a dazzling smile broke the firm line of Mr Lloyd's mouth. 'I never pretend to be anything other than what I am, Miss Thornton. I do have my reasons for using my mother's name, one of them being that when I use my Italian name in England, it draws unwelcome attention to me that I can do without.'

Sir Gerald sighed heavily when he looked fondly at his daughter. 'Quite right, so no more questions, Christina. Unfortunately, I have fathered a rebellious, unbiddable child, Mr Lloyd. She was always difficult and of an unpredictable disposition. It grieves me to have to say that nothing has changed now she has reached maturity. All our attempts to discipline her have been unsuccessful, and now it's too late.'

Max's lazy smile hardened into a mask of ironic amusement as his gaze settled on Christina's rosy face. 'You have my sympathy, but it's never too late to instil discipline.'

Christina was both appalled and amused. Her tender-hearted father, always good humoured, ready to laugh and generous to a fault, had never raised anything other than his voice to her in all the years she had been growing up, and the very idea that he would start now was downright laughable. 'Yes, it is.' She tucked her hand into the crook of her father's arm when the butler announced dinner. 'I'm too old to be spanked—and Papa wouldn't do it anyway, would you, Papa?'

'Don't count on it,' Sir Gerald replied with mock gravity while patting her hand affectionately.

'Sir Gerald,' Max said quietly, his expression suddenly serious. 'I wonder if I might call on you tomorrow. There is an important matter I wish to discuss with you—you and Lady Thornton.'

Sir Gerald's brows rose quizzically. 'There is? I'm curious. Very well, although you'd better make it early—I have a cricket match to umpire, which I'm looking forwards to. In fact, I do believe they're in need of an extra player, so, if you're up for it, see Hal Jenkinson. He's the captain. Do you play cricket?'

'I most certainly do,' Max replied. 'I consider cricket as being a great part of human life and I cannot imagine what would become of the English without it.'

'My thoughts absolutely. So, will nine o'clock suit for our meeting?'

'Of course.'

Christina peered at him sharply, wondering why all the

men she knew were so fanatical about knocking a ball about a field, and she was also curious as to what a perfect stranger could have to discuss with her father.

Chapter Two

〰〰〰〰〰

Both Sir Gerald and Lady Audine Thornton, well mannered and well bred, were the ideal hosts. Whenever they entertained they liked to relax the rules. There was always plenty of amusement without any of the coarser element that vulgarises so many of the stately homes of England. They had sufficient force of character to steer clear of any such difficulties at their dinner and weekend parties.

Christina was most put out because James was seated on her side of the dining table and too far away for her to speak to him, but she was pleased Mr Lloyd had been seated further along, so she was saved the painful ordeal of having to converse with him. She did, however, study him surreptitiously throughout the meal. He seemed relaxed and comfortable as he ate sparingly and sipped his claret, completely at ease among the room full of strangers, and yet she had a feeling that beneath his relaxed exterior there was such a carefully restrained power, that a rash of gooseflesh raised itself on her forearms and a cold shiver raced along her spine.

Her parents kept up a flow of small talk. Fortunately the guests were all well acquainted and the conversation was animated and interesting, mostly about local matters. Mr Lloyd was a popular figure, everyone wanting to talk to him about Italy, and he spoke to them calmly and at length, explaining in detail what it was like.

Christina was to recall later how, on observing her parents, they exchanged worried glances and seemed unusually quiet as Mr Lloyd spoke, but she thought nothing of it just then. She realised their new neighbour was clever and keen minded as the conversation progressed, and he was evidently no stranger to the world at large. To her surprise she was anything but bored as she listened. He was so worldly and so well informed that she was fascinated and a little awed, and when he described the cities Sienna and Florence, and areas that were most dear to his heart, he seemed to sweep away the four walls and let sunshine and blue skies into the room.

Doing her best not to show her interest, she surreptitiously cast glances his way along the line of guests. At one point, without warning, he turned and she was caught in the act of staring at him. His gaze captured hers, and Christina raised her chin. A strange, unfathomable smile tugged at the corner of his mouth, and he slowly inclined his head towards her. Angrily she averted her gaze. What a conceited, arrogant man he was, and she sincerely hoped that when the evening was over it would be the last she would see of him.

When the meal was over and the ladies had retired to the drawing room, leaving the gentlemen to smoke their cigars and cigarettes and drink their port, bored out of her mind, Christina waited with considerable impatience. She was eager to talk to James, but when the gentlemen finally joined the ladies she was disappointed when he stuck to Peter and they continued discussing tomorrow's cricket match.

Standing with the vicar's wife, who was regaling her with the various stalls she had arranged to be set up the following day in the cricket field, Christina looked around her restlessly for an excuse to get away. Her gaze settled on Mr Lloyd, who was engrossed in conversation with Hal Jenkinson, who was not only the captain of the cricket team but the local doctor.

As if sensing her interest, Max turned. Their glances clashed and for a second she found herself marvelling at the colour of his eyes. They were bright blue, warm and glowing, as blue as a tropical sea, and in their depths was an enquiring look, as though to ask her what she had seen in them to arouse her interest. His eyes narrowed and his mouth lifted in one corner, and he cocked an eyebrow quizzically.

Furious with herself and with two spots of dark colour high on her cheeks, with as much dignity as she could summon she turned away.

As the evening wore on and it was clear that James was not going to come and talk to her, she flounced through the French windows on to the terrace.

From where he stood lounging indolently against the piano, on which one of the ladies was entertaining them by playing some lively, popular songs, Max's eyes narrowed, and after a few moments he followed her.

Pacing impatiently up and down the terrace, a scowl marring her perfect features, from the corner of her eye Christina glimpsed a tall figure in the shadows. Convinced he was watching her, she walked towards him. The man was standing with one shoulder propped negligently against the trellising, idly smoking a cigar, the smoke curling slowly up into the night sky as he watched her in speculative silence. Only when she moved closer still and he stepped into the light spilling on to the terrace from the drawing room did she see it was Max Lloyd.

'Why, Mr Lloyd!' she said, boldly taking the offensive. 'I might have known it would be you lurking in the shadows. You seem to have a penchant for creeping up on people.'

In no mood to be baited by the whip of her vitriolic tongue, Max's eyes narrowed and his lean face darkened. 'You're mistaken, Miss Thornton. I never creep. Like you, I was merely taking the night air and seeking privacy to smoke my cigar.' He extinguished his cigar in an ashtray placed conveniently on a low wall for those who, like himself, liked to smoke outside so as not to cause offence to the ladies.

'Please don't put it out on my account.'

'I didn't.'

Christina, momentarily distracted by the sound of laughter, was looking towards the French windows. A gentleman appeared, but after taking a look on to the terrace he went back inside. Max saw disappointment cloud her eyes and knew she had been hoping it was James Embleton who had come to look for her. Her reaction annoyed him and his temper took over.

'It has not escaped my notice that you have been watching Mr Embleton a great deal,' he remarked, shoving his hands deep into his trouser pockets. 'You have had eyes for no one else all evening.'

'And you would know that, wouldn't you,' she snapped, determined to make her escape, 'since you have been watching me?'

Max's dark eyebrows arched and his eyes gleamed with sardonic amusement. 'Don't flatter yourself, Miss Thornton. I have watched you no more and no less than anyone else present tonight.'

Christina's mouth was hard, her eyes like flint. 'How dare

you speak to me like this? You keep your nose out of my business. James is a gentleman and he treats me—'

'Like a lady? Is that it?'

He advanced towards her, and for a moment Christina felt compelled to back away from him, almost stumbling over the short train of her dress.

'What I saw you doing today were not the actions of a well-brought-up young lady,' he told her—but then, he thought, even the most naïve could see that Christina Thornton was no meek young miss who did as she was told.

Christina threw back her shoulders and lifted her head imperiously, the action saying quite clearly that she was not ashamed. 'We were doing nothing wrong,' she retorted with an insistence meant to convince him. It was as though she had resolved to justify her actions, knowing very well that if anyone else had come along—and heaven forbid it had been one of her parents' acquaintances—her reputation would have been ruined for life.

'It was you I saw cavorting near naked in the lake in your petticoat and with your hair flying loose, which no lady of my acquaintance would dream of doing,' he said accusingly, not stopping to consider why he was in such a temper and why he was intent on goading her.

Max was appalled by his own words. What was wrong with him? Why was he being like this, when all he wanted to do was talk to her, look at her? He sounded priggish and intrusive, even to his own ears, and as her expression said so clearly.

'I am different from the women you know. That's not unusual. I am a foreigner for one thing and in Italy I believe young women are—more modest, less free and easy, and I think you want to subdue me on this account.'

'It is for your parents to do that and why your father hasn't done so I can't imagine. As I told you this afternoon, I know my own would have done if you were his daughter.'

Incredulous Christina was struck speechless. For one mad moment she was tempted to slap the smile from Mr Lloyd's arrogant lips, but she knew she could not shame her parents by creating a scene in front of their friends. Forgetting her intention to escape the presence of this overbearing man, she glared murderously into his face.

'Then I can thank God I'm not his daughter,' she hissed, her chin jutting dangerously and her eyes flashing in the semi-darkness. 'I wouldn't wish the most loathsome fate of having you for a brother on my worst enemy, and I shall continue to behave as I like, however controversial that may seem to you.'

'The kind of behaviour I witnessed today would be considered both offensive and unacceptable where I come from.' He lifted one eyebrow ironically. 'You know, you really should do something about that temper of yours. You're lit up like a firecracker that's about to explode at any minute.'

'Explode? Believe me, Mr Lloyd, you wouldn't want to see my temper explode. My father would show you the door if he knew you were speaking to me like this.'

Max chuckled softly, his anger of a moment earlier abating in the face of her ire. There was an edge to her that was cutting, but beneath her glaring eyes and acrimonious tongue, he sensed the warmth and passion in her, the longing to be free, to be wild and to do as she liked when she felt like doing it. He could not blame her for that; in fact, God help anyone trying to tame her—if such a thing were possible, which he doubted—and to break that spirit of hers.

She was flushed and could barely speak because of her anger, and he had a strange feeling that her rage was directed not just at himself but at James Embleton for not seeking her out.

'Somehow I don't think he would. He would probably congratulate me for having the courage to deal with his headstrong daughter and thank me for pointing out to her her—faults.'

'Faults? Why, you unspeakable, insufferable... And I don't suppose you have any *faults* yourself, have you, Mr Lloyd?'

'On the contrary. I would be the first to admit that I have many. I am far from perfect, Miss Thornton.' His lips smiled, his teeth flashing white. 'Now, have you finished being rude to me, or are you to continue giving me a dressing down?'

Christina stared at him. He was incredulous! One minute he was reproaching her most severely for what he called her unacceptable and offensive behaviour, and the next he was treating their altercation lightly, as though it was of no consequence whatsoever. Continuing to smile, he perched his hips against the back of a bench and continued watching her intently. She did not know this man. She had never seen him before today, and yet he was watching her with a look that was much too personal—and possessive.

She became uncertain, and was beginning to feel very foolish, bad tempered and childish. In truth, he had done nothing wrong, whereas she had been ill mannered and should know better. A rueful smile lit her eyes and her lips curved softly as she responded with a spontaneity which, when she was to think of it later, would astound her.

'You are quite right. I have been rude to you—and I beg your pardon,' she uttered lightly, 'but I am the one who has had a dressing down—which is a first for me—apart from Mama, of course, but she does it on such a regular basis that it doesn't make any difference.'

Max's eyes smiled his approval at her sudden change of

attitude. 'I'm glad to see you're not angry any more,' he said quietly. 'Shall we call a truce and agree that we are even?'

A mischievous smile curved her soft lips. 'That depends.'

'On what?'

Her brows lifted in mocking challenge. 'On whether or not you can get enough runs tomorrow to save Leyton from total humiliation.'

'You are asking me to play in the match?'

'Absolutely. Since you are to reside in Leyton indefinitely, you might as well make yourself useful.'

He smiled. 'Done.'

It was a brilliant day, the summer air clear and sparkling. Christina and Molly arrived at the cricket field in a little pony carriage stacked with a heavy picnic hamper Mrs Barnaby had packed with freshly baked, mouth-watering pastries, tarts, sandwiches and delicious tit-bits. Without the slightest interest in the game, but in a love-struck state, Christina was keen to see the recipient of her unrequited devotion in action on the cricket pitch.

Enthusiastic young men in traditional white were milling about the field, waiting to start the serious business of the game in an effort to win the special trophy—a silver cup, to be presented by Christina's father. He didn't consider his participation an obligation, playing in a spirit of social duty and finding it a satisfactory bond of union with rustics and dependents. He was a true, passionate devotee of the game.

A large crowd had gathered—an amazing pleasure excursion from both villages and nearby hamlets—the women in every kind of dress and fancy hat and colourful parasols, the lads strutting about like peacocks while the young single women preened before them. Almost every patch of grass had been claimed. People lolled about or sat in deck chairs, some of the men drinking foaming mugs of ale that were being sold at one of the stalls.

There were entertainments for the children, who were playing noisily and romping about with reckless abandon. Colourful tents and booths had been erected, and even a coconut shy and archery range, and a band played a lively tune—in fact, it was more like a feast day than a cricket match.

Leaving the carriage and carrying the picnic hamper between them, Christina and Molly strode into the thick of it. Choosing a position of vantage and commanding a good view of the cricket pitch, with Tanglewood looming out of the trees behind them, to tower in magnificence over the village of Leyton and surrounding countryside, they settled themselves on the warm grass, but it wasn't long before they strolled over to the coconut shy to try their hand with the villagers.

Later, when Molly had gone to gossip with some of the employees from the house, leaning her back against a tree, Christina felt her eyes drawn to the players assembling on the pitch. One figure in particular coming through a gate at the side of the field caught her attention. He was a tall man, lithe and broad shouldered and with an easy way of walking. As he drew closer to her brother on the pitch, Christina recognised the strong dark features and proud, confident manner. It was Max Lloyd. She smiled smugly to herself, happy that he had taken up her challenge to join the team. Whether or not he could save Leyton from being beaten was another matter entirely.

Despite herself she stared at him. As if he sensed her gaze, he turned and looked at her, half-raising his hand to acknowledge her, his eyes locking on hers. The effect of that lingering gaze on her was startling. Somewhere deep inside her a tremor was awakened beneath the intensity of his gaze and she suddenly felt afraid and insecure. Quickly she looked away, searching for her father. The cricketers and the crowd were becoming restless, impatient for the game to start, but they could not begin without the umpire.

Christina got to her feet and went to ask Peter what could be keeping Papa. Mr Embleton, James's father, stepped forwards and informed everyone that unfortunately Sir Gerald was unable to take part and had asked him to stand in. After conversing with the players and a great deal of shaking of heads, they began moving into position to begin the match.

'Where's Papa?' Christina asked her brother, deeply concerned. 'He's always umpired the game. Has something happened?'

'Calm yourself, Christina. He wasn't feeling himself, so he prevailed on Mr Embleton.'

'Is Papa ill?'

'No,' he replied, beginning to move away, as impatient as everyone else to start playing. 'He's just not up to umpiring today.' Looking towards the picnic hamper, he grinned. 'I'm glad you've come prepared. No doubt Mrs Barnaby has packed enough food for the entire cricket team. Look, I'll see you for lunch. We lost the toss, so Farnley are to bat first.'

Peter left her just as James stepped up to bowl. Christina's eyes devoured him, thinking how wonderful he looked with the sun shining on his fair head and forming a halo of bright light that almost took her breath away. Seeing her standing on boundary, he waved to her, and in that moment Christina's heart soared.

And so the match progressed. Christina settled herself beneath the tree beside the hamper to await lunch. The heat and the crack of ball against bat lulled her into a sleepy state and she closed her eyes, totally uninterested now James was no longer bowling. There was a great deal of clapping and shouting as the atmosphere became loud and tribal.

Suddenly there was a stirring among the crowd and Christina was aware that there was a subtle change in the atmosphere. Opening her eyes, she saw Max Lloyd striding out to bowl. She sat up straight. It was impossible not to respond to this man as his masculine magnetism dominated the scene. There was a vigorous purposefulness in his long, quick strides that bespoke an active, athletic life. He caused an amazing buzz of anticipation around the field when he grasped the ball, and when the umpire called 'play' and he started his run in, every spectator seemed to catch their breath.

It became evident almost immediately that he had an awesome power and could dominate any kind of bowling, the very essence of a natural cricketer. His commanding presence caught the spectators' imaginations. He seemed to have a boundless energy and an all-consuming enthusiasm. His forearms were of an unusual strength and he had an impressively muscular upper body. Taking four wickets within an hour, it was clear to all that he didn't do things by halves and this was one of his attractions—it made him so compelling and irresistible to watch.

Max Lloyd was determined and clear sighted about his objectives and Christina couldn't keep her eyes off him.

During the break for lunch, as they all gathered round and munched their way through the hamper, Christina couldn't resist sneaking a look at an extremely popular Max Lloyd, and she noticed again how incredibly blue his eyes were and how attractive he was with his finely marked brows slightly raised and his hair all tousled. He was studying her closely and she was aware of the tension and nervousness in herself. A curious sharp thrill ran through her as the force between them seemed to explode wordlessly.

'Are you enjoying the match?' he asked, strolling towards her and dropping down on to the grass beside her, where she lolled against a tree sipping lemonade.

'Certainly not. I hate the game. Grown men knocking a ball into the air with a bat? What's interesting in that?' she declared scathingly. Putting her empty glass down, she drew her knees up and wrapped her arms round her legs.

'It's clear you know nothing about the finer points of cricket,' he laughed, leaning back on his elbow and stretching his long, lean body out on the grass.

'How can I? I'm merely a woman.' Christina uttered with sarcasm.

Max grinned. 'I'd have you in my team any day,' he said softly.

She looked at him with a stirring of respect. 'Why, thank you for that—but if my tennis is anything to go by, I wouldn't be any good. I rarely hit the ball and when I do it never goes where it should.' She looked at him steadily. 'You bowled well. You must have played a great deal.'

'I have, but not for a long time—not since my university days, in fact. I'm a bit rusty.'

'Then you must be quite formidable when you're on form. There's nothing wrong with your bowling arm. So far you've proved an asset to the team.'

'Enough to save Leyton from humiliation?' he enquired, the question reminding her of what she had said last night.

She laughed lightly, her small teeth shining like pearls in the brightness. 'It might very well be, if your batting is equally as good. We shall have to wait and see.'

'I will be the last to bat.'

'Then I wish you luck,' she said, suddenly becoming aware of his closeness. He looked terribly attractive in his whites, with his shirt sleeves rolled up to his elbows to show off the sunburned strength of his forearms, the neck of his shirt open to display the equally sun-browned column of his throat. 'The village plays Farnley twice a year and they're tough opposition.'

'I'll do my best.'

'How did your meeting with my parents go?'

A shadow crossed his face and he looked away. 'Why do you ask?'

She shrugged. 'I'm curious as to why Papa isn't umpiring. As a rule neither fire, famine nor flood would keep him from the village cricket match. I saw him at breakfast and he was as excited and enthusiastic as he always is before the match.' She frowned and gave him an enquiring look as a sudden disconcerting thought occurred to her. 'You must have been one of the last people to see him. You didn't say anything that might have upset him, did you?'

'I sincerely hope not.' Max looked towards the pavilion where Peter and his friends were indulging in a spot of larking about. 'Your brother and his friends are enjoying themselves,' he remarked suddenly, keen to change the subject, 'and it's clear that particular young man has turned your head.'

For the moment Christina's concern about her papa was gone and she didn't mind that Mr Lloyd knew how she felt about James. 'What extraordinary beings young men are,' she remarked grudgingly. 'Peter can't abide anything unconnected with that beastly game. During the holidays on wet days he and his friends play cricket in the gallery, without regard to furnishings and precious objects. I think it unfair that men can be so free. I envy my brother and James. They are able to do as they like, while I strain beneath the restrictions put on me by my parents and society. I do so hate it.'

'I can see how difficult that must be for one so spirited,' he remarked with mock gravity. 'Better had you been born of the male gender.'

Her eyes gently enquiring, Christina found herself quite intrigued by this stranger and their extraordinary conversation. Her mouth trembled into a smile. 'Do you know, Mr Lloyd, I do believe you're right. But I do believe it is man who keeps women oppressed.'

'I agree.'

'You do?'

'Absolutely. In an ideal world there would be equality in both sexes. But this is not an ideal world.'

'Are you a radical, Mr Lloyd?'

'I do have opinions that do not always agree with those of my friends and associates, so if that is what is meant by being a radical then I suppose I am.'

They looked towards the cricket pitch. James was striding towards the wicket to take up the batting. Tall and fine, he looked splendid in his freshly ironed white trousers and shirt. Her heart quickened.

Max watched her glance at the youth, saw the melting in her eyes, and, as he stood up to join his fellow players in the pavilion, his own were speculative.

Max Lloyd had swiftly established himself as a formidable player, and when he'd buckled on his pads, taken up his bat and begun to score runs in previously unheard-of quantities, hitting his fourth straight six, cutting between two fielders, the cheers from players and spectators were deafening. There was no other player on the field of that class. His murderous treatment of the bowlers caused them to rethink their method of attack. His finest performance, his team mates noticed, had come just before the end of the day's play when they were most needed and he steered his side to safety.

The crowd melted a pathway before him as he came off the pitch and strode through them, some giving him hearty congratulatory pats on the back. From her place on the grass Christina had a clear view of him. His face was strong, striking, disciplined and exceptionally attractive, the expression cool and unmoved by his fellow cricketers' mood of good cheer.

Unsurprisingly, the atmosphere among the locals was euphoric, and when Mr Embleton had presented the cup to the captain and people began crowding the stall for more ale to celebrate and commiserate with the losers, it was clear the celebrations would go on for most of the night.

Concerned about her father, Christina hurried home as the sky was a deep, flawless blue fading into a pool of glowing pink and red on the horizon. Against its warm, rosy colours lay the stark black silhouettes of the trees, beyond which stood Tanglewood with the lowering sun at its back.

Christina wasn't the only one to leave. In no mood for celebrating, Max slipped through the gate to walk along the path that would lead him to his house just a short distance away, there to await the outcome of his meeting with Sir Gerald and Lady Thornton that morning.

'Mama? What's happened?' were the first words Christina spoke as she hurried into the drawing room, dishevelled and with her hair all over the place, descending upon her mother like a whirlwind. Her mother was alone, sitting at her writing desk with a pen in her hand but not writing, just staring into space. 'I have been so worried. Why didn't Papa umpire the match? It must be something serious for him to stay away.'

Audine rose and faced her daughter. 'Ah, there you are. I wondered when you'd be back.'

Christina's eyes were wide with concern, for her mother's usually tranquil face was drawn and almost grey and she seemed uneasy. 'What is it? Oh, Mama, are you all right?'

'I'm fine,' she replied quickly, a forced smile on her lips— even in her hour of terror she was not going to upset her daughter. Sitting on a small sofa, she made a pretence of smoothing her skirts. 'Have you enjoyed the cricket match?'

'No, of course not. You know how I hate that wretched game—and I've been worrying all day about Papa.' Christina sat beside her mother on the sofa, facing her. Audine seemed nervous and avoided her eyes. Her hands were trembling in her lap. Christina could feel the tension in her—that strength of character which had helped her bear the burdens of life with quiet dignity seemed to have been taxed to its limits. 'Mama, you would tell me if he were ill, wouldn't you?'

'Of course I would,' she said, fingering the tassels on a cushion nervously.

'Then if he isn't ill, has his decision not to go to the match anything to do with Mr Lloyd's visit earlier? Mama, what is it? Why are you looking so frightened?'

'Oh, my darling girl, I am not frightened of anything. It's nothing, really it isn't, and your worries are commendable but unnecessary. Now why don't you go and get changed for dinner? You must be hungry after all that fresh air.'

'Where's Papa?'

'Upstairs. He'll be down shortly. After his meeting with Mr Lloyd he was—tired—that's all it was.' She smiled tenderly.

'Your papa's not as young as he was and, although he would never admit it, it's catching up with him.'

Christina didn't believe her and knew she was only trying to placate her. 'Mama, I'm not a child and I cannot ignore what stares me in the face. We both know that for Papa to miss the cricket match it would have to be something extremely serious. Please don't keep anything from me.'

'I wouldn't, not if I thought you should know. Rest assured that you papa is perfectly well.'

'And it has nothing to do with Mr Lloyd?'

For a split second Christina glimpsed in her eyes the pain of a woman deeply wounded. A cloud seemed to pass over her face and then just as quickly it was gone.

'Did Mr Lloyd play in the match?' Audine asked quickly in an attempt to divert the conversation away from her husband.

'Yes. He's quite an exceptional player—saved the day—a good all rounder, isn't that what they say? Papa would have been terribly impressed. It's a shame he missed it.'

'Yes, yes it was, but I'm sure Mr Embleton made a perfectly good umpire. As a matter of fact, Mr and Mrs Embleton have invited your father and I to visit them tomorrow and to stay overnight. I have to say that it will be a change and will do your father good to have a change of scene.'

'Are Peter and I not invited?' Christina was quick to ask, sincerely hoping they were.

'No, my dear, I'm afraid not. It's for the older generation.' She smiled at her daughter's crestfallen face. 'Don't be too upset about it, Christina. I'm sure James will find his way to Tanglewood some time during the day. You—like James, don't you?'

Christina nodded and her eyes flashed darkly beneath their ebony lashes. 'Yes, very much, and I mean to have him, if I can make him see me beyond Peter—who seems to think I'm some inept, empty-headed ninny. My heart is set on it.' Getting up, she paced to and fro across the richly patterned carpet, her cheeks flushed to a rosy glow with some inner excitement. 'I have decided that I want to marry him, Mama, and no other man will do.'

Audine disliked the wildness of her daughter's mood and was tempted to scold her, but, relieved the conversation had veered away from Mr Lloyd and the threat he posed to her beloved daughter's future, she decided to let her have her say. Never had she seen so much animation and passion in her. It seemed to permeate the atmosphere of the very room.

'And when did you arrive at this momentous decision, Christina?'

'Oh, a long time ago—ever since that first time Peter brought him home.' She tossed her head, causing her hair to shimmer. 'It occurred to me then that he was everything I wanted.'

'And what of James?' Looking into the sparkling green eyes, Audine said gently, 'Will he be willing to fall in with your plans, do you think? Do you think it will be that simple?'

'It has to be,' she replied with a wickedly radiant smile. 'He'll be delighted when I tell him about it.'

'You are still very young to be talking like this. Why the rush? You have plenty of time to think of marriage.'

'Oh, no, Mama,' Christina said, seating herself back on the sofa and frowning a little at her mother's anxious face. 'You were married at twenty and I will very soon be eighteen. James will want me, I know he will.'

'A girl's first romance always seems so enduring, so very real, but in reality the dreams never turn out that way.'

Christina jerked her head up. 'It's not like that with James and me. I know it's for real, Mama. I believe it. It may be a dream for now, but I will follow it through.'

Audine smiled resignedly, reaching out and tenderly tucking a stray lock of hair behind Christina's ear. 'Of course you will. You have character, intelligence and spirit to do that. You will never be satisfied with empty self-delusions. Whatever happens, my darling, always look life in the eye and never make compromises. But James has had sufficient time to let you know how he feels,' she pointed out gently.

'I know, but Peter's always around.' Christina smiled confidently, trusting and full of hope. 'I'm certain he is only waiting for the right moment to declare himself.'

'Then we shall have to wait and see.' On impulse Audine put her arms around her daughter and hugged her warmly. 'For now you need guidance and advice.'

'And you will always be on hand to give it to me, won't you, Mama? You and Papa.' She felt the arms about her tighten slightly, but she didn't see the bright tears that sprang to her mother's eyes.

'Yes—always,' Audine whispered, her throat constricting with painful emotion. 'But all this is still just a dream, my darling.'

'A dream not beyond my grasping,' Christina said, freeing herself from the embrace. 'I will show James how much I care for him—and before long he will be hopelessly head over heels in love with me. You see if he won't.'

Audine looked hard at her daughter's beautiful, rapt face. She would be perfectly happy for Christina to realise her dream, but with the arrival of Mr Lloyd she very much doubted it. Audine knew how stubborn she could be, how single-minded, and that she would have her way at any cost. But love? What did Christina know of love? As yet she had no real inkling of the intensity, the sheer driving force of passionate love, but when it touched her she would not deny herself the having of it.

Yet she wasn't sure that James Embleton was the right man for her headstrong, rebellious child. She needed a man with drive and a fire in his veins to match her own. A man who would curb her conceits and that wild streak in her—a man like Mr Lloyd, perhaps? Or perhaps she should call him by his Italian name and title, Count Maxwell Marchesi, who had every right to take away their precious girl.

Christina had an underlying fear that something was very wrong and her concern that something had happened to upset her parents deepened throughout dinner. Celebrating the match result with his friends at the public house in the village, Peter was absent. Her father was quiet, distracted, asking few questions about the cricket match that had always been so dear to his heart. Her mother tried very hard to act as if everything was normal, but Christina wasn't fooled.

The following day after her parents had left with Mr and Mrs Embleton, and convinced Mr Lloyd's meeting with them before the match had something to do with their dejection, she walked the short distance to the house where he was staying. The day was hot and sultry, and, glancing up at the sky, she suspected a thunderstorm threatened for later.

Of modest proportions, the old, ivy-clad house nestling in a wooded hollow, with gardens packed with an abundance of flowers and climbing plants, was a picture. Having been here many times to visit Major Illingworth when he had been home from India, Christina was familiar with the house. Inside it was beautifully decorated in peach and palest green with heavy damask hangings and tasteful furniture.

Opening the gate, she walked up the path to the door, knocking forcefully. It was opened by a man of medium height. Of slender build, with Roman features and sleek black hair, he was dressed with impeccable neatness in a black suit.

'Hello! I'm Miss Thornton. Is Mr Lloyd at home? He isn't expecting me, but I would like to see him.'

'*Si, si.* Please, step inside. If the *signorina* will be kind enough to wait a moment, I will tell him you are here,' he said, his voice heavily accented.

'There's no need, Lorenzo. I saw Miss Thornton coming down the path.' Casually attired in a lightweight jacket and trousers, his white shirt open at the neck, Max Lloyd came striding into the hall. 'Miss Thornton! Good morning,' he greeted breezily, giving her a debonair bow. His gaze briefly appraised her pale yellow gown before raising his eyes to her glare.

'Mr Lloyd!'

He frowned. 'Dear me! With a look like that, I gather you're displeased about something.'

'How very perceptive of you, Mr Lloyd,' she answered. Tossing him a cool glance, she swept past him into the drawing room, removing her bonnet as she went.

'Come in, why don't you?' he said, chuckling softly, amazed by her daring, not to mention her cheek. Looking at her retreating figure appreciatively, the small train of her dress rustling softly over the carpet, after speaking quietly to Lorenzo in Italian, he followed her and closed the door. 'Welcome to my humble abode,' he said, his mouth quirked in a half-smile.

Christina stopped in the centre of the room and turned to face him. 'There's nothing humble about your dwelling that I can see, Mr Lloyd—unless, of course, you're used to something on a far grander scale.'

'Tell me, Miss Thornton,' he said, moving to stand in front of her, 'do you make a habit of calling on gentlemen alone?'

'Of course not, but I had to come—and with good reason.'

Max's eyebrows lifted in mute enquiry.

Christina locked her gaze on his. 'Who are you really? You told me that Lloyd was your mother's maiden name and that you prefer to use it to avoid complications and to be inconspicuous when you are in this country. So, how are you known in Italy, I would like to know?'

He answered her with slow deliberation. 'Max—which is short for Maxwell.'

'I know that. And?'

'Count—Count Marchesi.'

Her eyebrows shot up. 'Count? I am impressed.'

His smile widened. 'I thought you might be.'

'And why would Count Maxwell Marchesi want to rent a cottage in this out-of-the-way little village in Cambridgeshire masquerading as Mr Lloyd?'

'I am not masquerading, and I told you I am here to reacquaint myself with old friends and to spend some time in Cambridge.'

'That may be so, but why go to all the trouble of renting a house? You could have stayed in a hotel in Cambridge.'

'I prefer the country.'

'You prevaricate, Mr Lloyd.'

'I am entitled to. It is, after all, my business where I stay. Had I wanted to stay in Cambridge then I would have done so.'

'I am convinced there is more to it than that. What is your real reason for coming to Leyton?'

'There has to be another reason?'

'Yes, I'm certain of it. What did you want to speak to my parents about yesterday? You don't know them and, as far as I am aware, you have never met them before. Whatever passed between the three of you upset them terribly. In fact, I've never seen my father so upset, or my mother for that matter.'

'Then I am sorry about that. It was not my intention to cause them distress,' he said with such sincerity that Christina found herself believing him and wondering if she was barking up the wrong tree. However, she went on regardless.

'So? Will you tell me?'

'Have you asked your parents?'

'Yes. They were non-committal.'

'So am I.'

'They dance around the issue—just like you're doing now.'

'I cannot tell you.'

'You mean you won't.'

'Both.'

'Does it concern Peter—or me?'

'I've told you, you must ask your parents. And now no more questions—and it's too nice a day to be sitting inside. Let me offer you refreshment. You are my first visitor and I would like to welcome you to my home—temporary though it is.'

Christina shook her head. 'Thank you, but I have to get back.' She was thinking that James might call and she didn't want to miss seeing him, yet she was curious to know more about Mr Lloyd—Count Marchesi.

'Nonsense. I refuse to take no for an answer. Come,' he said, striding to the door. 'Lorenzo has prepared tea and cakes for us in the garden.'

'How very civilised.'

'We Italians pride ourselves on the warmth of our hospitality.'

'But it isn't tea time.'

'Does it matter?'

'Well, in certain circles it would—but, no, I suppose you can be excused—since you're Italian.'

His chuckle was rich and deep. 'How nice of you to say so, although I'm not quite sure whether I should be flattered or offended by your remark.'

'You must interpret it as you like—but I truly meant no offence.'

They went outside and walked along a flagstone path that separated the flower beds leading to an arbour. A white lace table cloth covered a small, round, wrought-iron table on which delicate china tea things and cakes had been set out. Max pulled out a chair for Christina and Lorenzo poured the tea before excusing himself and disappearing along the path and into the house.

'That's Lorenzo, by the way, my steward, secretary and—'

'General factotum by the look of things,' Christina was hasty to add. 'He seems to know how to lay a perfect tea table as well as take care of his secretarial duties.'

Sitting across from her and resting one foot atop his other knee, Max unbuttoned his jacket and leaned back in the chair. Relaxed and comfortable, he looked across at his companion, transfixed as he stared at her seated against a backdrop of vibrant climbing red roses. Having removed her bonnet and with her luxuriant hair tumbling over her shoulders and her green eyes glowing from between the thick fringe of black lashes, she presented such a captivating picture that he was torn between the urge to shove the table and its crockery away and pull her into his lap, and the equally delightful desire simply to relax and feast his eyes on her.

He was unable to believe she was here with him after so many years. Ever since she had been taken away from Castello Marchesi, without fully realising what had happened he had carried his dream of meeting her again in his heart, and the fact that the boy had become a man had not diminished that dream.

Chapter Three

'Would you like a cake?' Max said, picking up a plate and offering Christina one of the dainty confections Lorenzo had purchased at the village bakery earlier.

Christina took one and put it on her plate. She smiled, diverted by his ever-present courteous formality, even when she wasn't being particularly nice to him. A lazy somnolence had descended on the garden and the perfume of roses—red, white, pink and yellow—was heavy and sweet.

'Why do you stare at me?' she asked, settling back in her seat and taking a bite out of her cake, finding it virtually impossible to ignore the tug of his eyes and voice.

'Because I've never met anyone quite like you.'

'Are you always so…?'

One black arched brow lifted in mild enquiry. 'What?'

'Forthright? Why do you always seem to be on the verge of laughing at me?'

'Not at you, Miss Thornton. For some unfathomable reason you amuse me—and because I happen to like you.'

'I'm surprised.'

'Why?'

'Because there have been times when I have been less than polite to you. In fact, I've been positively beastly.'

'I agree, but you're forgiven.'

'That's gracious of you to say so, but I really was quite horrid to you when we first met.' Christina glanced at him and smiled, shaking her shining head as the memory of how she had looked and what he must have thought assailed her, and when she met his eyes she saw that he remembered it too.

'You mean when you were cavorting semi-naked in the lake.'

'Yes. I was quite shameless,' she murmured, finishing off her cake and licking the sticky sweetness off her fingers, unwittingly unaware of how this simple childish gesture warmed Max's blood.

'I agree, you were. You see, life in Italy has the Italian woman living under close scrutiny of family members. Her acquaintances with the opposite sex are selected and chaperoned, and if she were to be seen swimming almost naked with two young men, her reputation would be ruined and she would in all probability see out the rest of her life in a convent.'

A note of reproach hardened his voice and Christina wondered why, but quickly dismissed it as of no importance. 'Dear me! I find that a bit extreme, but then—I'm not Italian,' she remarked airily. 'You seem very at home here, Mr Lloyd.'

'Max—please call me Max.'

'Very well. Mister Lloyd does seem rather formal, and I positively refuse to call you Count. You must call me Christina. Tell me what it's like where you come from?'

'In Tuscany?'

She nodded.

'It's very beautiful. Enchanting. Timeless. It is a different way of life altogether. You have to see it to appreciate it.'

'What is it you do there?'

'Why should I do anything? Being a count, I might be extremely rich and not have to work.'

'You don't strike me as a gentleman of leisure—no matter how rich you are.'

'You're right. I'm not. I like to be busy.'

'So, what do you do?'

'I grow grapes—as my family has done for centuries.' He went on to talk about his vineyards, of which he was inordinately proud. He was full of enthusiasm and talked vividly about the Tuscan climate and the effect it had on the grapes, and how the weather could be one's best friend or a grape grower's worst enemy, and how they prayed for warm, dry summers before the *vendemmie*, the grape harvest, in the autumn. Christina proved to be an avid listener.

'So you are very rich,' she remarked when he fell silent.

'My prosperity is largely due to my ancestors and in particular to my grandfather. He was a superb businessman.'

'I suspect you take after him.'

'I'd like to think so.'

'How interesting you make it sound.'

'It is. I—would like for you to see it,' he said, watching her expression carefully. 'Would you like to?'

She nodded emphatically. 'But it's just not possible.'

'It might be. You would be made most welcome, Christina,' he said, using her name for the first time and sending an unexplainable thrill of pleasure through her.

'Are you married?' she asked impulsively, wanting to know all there was to know about this strange foreign man who had unexpectedly appeared in their midst.

'No.'

'Are you likely to be?'

'Why?' he asked, his dark eyebrows drawing together over his incredulous blue eyes. 'Would you like to marry me?'

His question spoken in jest caused her to laugh out loud and brought a sparkle to her eyes, yet somewhere deep inside her she could feel the first stirrings of discomfort. 'Of course not. What I mean is,' she said when he shot her a thoroughly amused look, 'is there a woman in your life—someone special?'

'You're very inquisitive, Miss Thornton.'

Her eyes glowed mischievously. 'It's in my nature. I can't help it.'

'Then the answer to your question is that there are many women in my life.'

'Any one in particular?' she persisted, letting her eyes drift over his thick, smoothed-back black hair to his face, noting the Italian nobility and pride stamped on his bronzed features.

He met her eyes and the line of his mobile mouth quirked in a half-smile. 'There might be.'

She glanced at him obliquely, a warmth beginning to suffuse her face that had nothing to do with the heat of the day. His voice was low pitched and though she wasn't used to men like Max Lloyd—Marchesi, she knew it was sensual and was unsure how to respond to it. 'You're very secretive. In fact you're as mysterious to me now as you were before I met you.'

'Which adds to my appeal, I hope.'

'Appeal? Now that's a strange word to use. I don't find you in the least appealing.'

'You don't?' he asked with mock disappointment.

'No, of course I don't.'

His eyes narrowed and darkened, becoming warm and seductive. 'And you are sure about that, are you, *signorina*?'

'Yes.' Christina was glad he had called her *signorina*. It sounded alien to her, emphasising the difference between them and reducing the effect his blatant masculinity was beginning to have on her, bringing her drifting spirit back to reality. Her dawning response to him was solid enough reason to end the visit immediately. 'I think I'd better be going. I've been here long enough and there must be things you have to do.'

'Why are you nervous all of a sudden?'

His penetrating blue eyes were searching her face. She was not imagining his interest in herself. She might have no experience of men, but she was perfectly able to recognise admiration in a man's eyes. Suddenly it was like being on an obstacle course of emotions that left her confused. Without warning she had passed from the love she bore James to the more dangerous ground on to which this stranger sought to entice her.

She made absorbing work of putting on her bonnet. Until she'd come into the garden she had known exactly what she wanted, but now her dream was clouded with uncertainty. Now there was something else, something dark and secret stirring inside her that had nothing to do with James, and she didn't like it, not one bit.

'I don't know what you mean,' she said, avoiding his eyes.

'That's a pretty bonnet you are wearing. Would you like to know what I see when I look at you?'

'Not if you're going to sound like some amorous Latin lover I don't.'

He laughed softly, noting the tremulous brightness in her eyes and the way her fingers trembled as she tied the bow beneath her chin. 'We Italians are born with the ability to make love. Are you not curious to know more, Christina?'

She swallowed convulsively, her cheeks having turned a glorious shade of pink. 'Yes,' she whispered with all the honest innocence of youth. 'Of course I want to know more, of course

I want to know what it feels like to be kissed, but certainly not by some Latin Lothario.'

Inexplicably, Max threw back his head and shouted with laughter, the sound disturbing the quietness of the garden and causing startled birds to take flight. At one and the same time this delightful girl managed to be an intriguing, alluring young woman and an enchanting young girl. In the course of three days she had treated him with outright anger and rebellion, cold disdain, and now with a sprightly impertinence and light-heartedness that he found utterly exhilarating. Still chuckling, he shook his head slowly, his eyes sparkling with humour, his teeth gleaming white between his parted lips.

'I am immensely flattered that you should liken me to Rowe's libertine, but let me assure you, my dear Christina, that I am nothing like that reprobate. However, it is clear to me that I have made an impression on you and it warms my heart to know it.'

'You have no heart,' Christina quipped good naturedly, smiling radiantly, finding it impossible to be cross with him when he hadn't done anything wrong or said anything to offend. 'If you had, you would never have lured a helpless female out into the garden for tea and cakes.'

'I did not lure you and you are anything but helpless,' he told her, grinning broadly. 'However, I won't embarrass you or offend your tender ears by explaining to you what Lothario was really like, so here,' he said, pushing the plate of cakes towards her, 'have another cake.'

'I should be leaving,' she said, standing up. 'I swear the sun is getting hotter.'

'In Italy the people are content to take their ease when the sun is at its height. Won't you stay a while longer until it cools down?'

'I mustn't. I've been here for ages and if I don't show my face soon Molly—my extremely strict maid who has promised to keep a watch over me while Mama is away—will send out a search party.'

'Then we mustn't upset Molly. Come, I'll walk back with you.'

'No, you can't possibly. It isn't far.'

'I insist.'

And so Max accompanied her back to Tanglewood, and not until he'd left her did she remember the reason for her visit to his house.

To Christina's delight, James arrived at Tanglewood later in the day. Smiling in anticipation and hope, from the long window in the drawing room she watched him get off his horse. Handing it to a groom, he bounded up the steps to the house.

'Don't look like that, Christina,' Peter remarked crossly, putting down his newspaper and standing up.

'Like what?' she retorted, pretending innocence.

'Like the cat that got the cream. Since his house is full of guests for the weekend, James has come to stay the night. We've planned to do a spot of fishing in the morning. We're taking the boat out on the lake at first light.'

Christina's eyes lit up. There was nothing she loved more than fishing in the early morning when the fish were at their keenest. 'That sounds like fun to me. I'll be there.'

'No, you won't. This time it's to be just James and me. If Mama were here, she wouldn't allow it.'

'Well, Mama isn't here.'

'The answer is still no.'

'But I always go with you.'

'Not this time, so don't come trailing after us. It's

becoming embarrassing, the lengths you go to to attract James's attention, as if you consider him your personal property. He's not interested, can't you see that? Really, Christina, why can't you be like other young ladies, who sew and read romantic novels that are all the rage?'

'I hate romantic novels,' she remarked, her lower lip drooping petulantly. 'There are far more interesting things to do than read about heroines swooning over devastatingly handsome gentlemen all the time.'

'Ha! And I don't suppose you can see a similarity between that and your own silly behaviour with James. You never find his sisters hanging about like you do. Why can't you be more like them and interest yourself in clothes and fashions—?'

'For which I care even less.'

'At least they are demure, delicate and refined—and quiet.'

'And such dreadful bores.'

'Where are you going?' Peter demanded, throwing down his newspaper and striding after her.

Christina smiled back at him sublimely. 'To welcome James.'

'Christina! James is my friend and my guest. I would be obliged if you would remember that and not make a fool of yourself.'

'Fiddlesticks! Calm down, Peter. Please don't make a scene in front of James.'

'Christina!' Peter called her, but Christina was determined to be deaf. 'You will behave yourself.' She answered with a haughty shake of her head.

Christina went into the hall to greet James, an irate Peter coming after her, still ranting, but quieter now James was present. She was sorry really, for she loved her brother and hated being on the cross with him, but she found it irksome that he was for ever trying to tell her what to do, believing he knew what was best just because he was older than she was. At times he could be so tiresome, worse than Mama where convention was concerned. If only he had a more casual approach to things and didn't take things so seriously.

The rest of the day passed in a pleasant haze for Christina. Peter and James retired to the billiard room and she followed. Ignoring Peter's glower and his silent demand that she leave this male preserve so they could play the game and drink their port in peace, she took a seat in the window bay and settled down to watch. She would have loved to challenge them to a game, for she was rather good at it and often beat Peter when they were alone, but that would have been taking things too far and have Peter physically marching her out of the billiard room and packing her off to bed.

Sneaking a glass of port when they became absorbed in the game, she sipped it slowly, feeling her body relax as the alcohol warmed her stomach. She never drank anything stronger than wine weakened with water, which was all her mama would permit. She wasn't sure she liked the taste of this rich, fortified wine, but if James liked it then she decided there could be nothing wrong with having a glass.

She sat and watched him lean over the table, the large gaslights above the table shining on his golden head. When Peter went out to get another bottle of port, she stood up and sidled over to where James was chalking his cue. Her face was flushed with the wine and her head felt woolly.

'Peter tells me you're taking the boat out on the lake in the morning, James.'

'That's right, Christina. First thing.'

'You won't object to me going with you, will you, James?'

He smiled, trying to hide his discomfort. Much as he

liked Christina and always found her fun to be with, he wished she'd stop seeking his attention all the time. He wasn't stupid or blind and knew in which direction her thoughts were leading her, but if she was waiting for him to declare himself, then she was in for a long wait. She might be the sister of his closest friend and very beautiful—anyone looking at her could not deny her that—but when he decided to settle down to wedded bliss, it would be with a woman with a far gentler and easier temperament than Christina Thornton.

'I'm sorry. Better not, Christina. Not this time. Peter—'

Sudden anger flashed in her eyes. 'Oh, bother Peter. You want me along, don't you?'

'Well—I—I…'

He looked beyond her and Christina saw relief flood his eyes when Peter came striding in carrying a bottle of port. Peter looked at his sister accusingly. She put her chin up defensively in the face of his scowl, and with a flare of temper and feeling more than a little sick from the port, she turned and flounced out of the room.

Christina slipped from her bed when dawn was breaking, the sky a faint and rosy pink on the horizon. Careful to avoid the domestic quarters, where sounds of industry coming from the kitchen could be heard already, she let herself out of the front door. Running through the woods to the lake beyond, she hoped to be there long before Peter and James and was prepared to wait. With a bull-headed stubbornness that afflicts those who love, she was convinced that when they saw her they would capitulate and let her go with them.

Disappointment swamped her when she saw that the boat was already bobbing gently in the middle of the lake, both

Peter and James oblivious to her standing on the bank watching them cast their lines into water.

Anger hot and fierce consumed her. How could they? How could they be so cruel? Peter was the worst kind of beast and James didn't care for her after all or he would have stood up to Peter and not done this.

What was wrong with her? Why wasn't he attracted to her? Was she plain, was she ugly? What? Compounded out of vanity and complacent confidence that she could make him love her, she had wanted him to notice her so much.

Her heart and her quick, intelligent mind now realised that she had made herself look a fool, running after him the way she had, and her heart quailed contemptuously at her forward conduct. The enormity of it all hit her like a rock and stung her to new rage, rage at herself with all the fury of thwarted and humiliated first love.

Blinded by tears, she whirled about, knowing only that she must get away from the lake. So lost was she in her anger and self-chastisement that she didn't see the horse and rider coming towards her. A voice calling her name startled her. She jumped, not expecting anyone to be in the woods at this hour. She stopped and stood very still as the powerful figure of Max Lloyd drew level and he dismounted.

'Christina? I didn't expect to see you at this hour. You're out and about early.'

'I can see I'm not the only one.'

'I like to ride early.' He looked concerned as he studied her tear-stained face and the droop of her slender shoulders, re-alising she was in the grip of some powerful emotion, for there were tears of rage and misery in her eyes. 'Is something wrong? You look upset to me. You have been crying.'

'I'm perfectly fine,' she retorted, averting her eyes while

realising she must look a mess. She took a deep breath, trying to stifle her rising embarrassment. Max Lloyd had caught her at her most vulnerable. Anger at being so surprised made her voice tremble and her eyes gleam like two hard green stones as she said coldly, 'Please excuse me. I'm—in a hurry to get back to the house.'

'Then I'll walk with you.' Taking the reins of his horse, he walked beside the irate young woman, matching her quick strides with his own. Turning his head, he looked at her for a moment, touched by her obvious youth and perhaps also by some private scruples. As she moved she had the animal grace of a young thoroughbred, yet at the same time a warm, vibrant femininity that touched a deep chord in him.

'You'll probably resent me saying this, but you look more than a little out of sorts. What, I ask myself, is so important as to drag you from your bed at this hour and make you cry?'

'Fishing,' she snapped. 'And I'm not crying.'

He arched a brow. 'Fishing? You like fishing?'

'I do.'

'Alone?'

'No. Peter and James have taken the boat out on to the lake.'

Max was beginning to understand. Concealing the irritation he always felt when James Embleton's name was mentioned, he said, 'And you wanted to go with them.'

'Yes. They refused to take me.' She sighed, her face crestfallen. 'I was too late anyway.' Turning to look at him, she saw the blue eyes laughing in the tanned face and amusement tugging at the corners of his firm lips, which quickly rekindled her ire. 'Don't you dare laugh. It's in very poor taste.'

'Why should I laugh?'

'Because there is no more foolish sight than a woman who

makes a fool of herself over a man who does not want her—the way I have done over James Embleton.'

'So the unimaginable has happened.'

She nodded. 'It looks like it.'

'I think you are more upset with your own behaviour than James Embleton's rejection of you. So he isn't as susceptible to your charms as you would like him to be.'

'You don't understand. You'll never understand,' she blurted out before she could stop herself.

'I can understand only too well. You seem to have got yourself into quite a pickle, as you English say, over this young man. You are very young, Christina, and have much to learn.'

Christina stiffened with childish fury. How dare this impudent foreigner say these things to her? 'I'm not obliged to discuss my feelings with you. It's always the same assumption. Can no one think of me in any light but as a silly naïve girl?'

A slow, lazy smile swept across Max's face, and Christina braced herself for him to say something mocking, but his deep voice was filled with admiration and teasing. 'You are a delightful girl, Christina, who has a habit of doing without thinking first. Like I said, you have much to learn about life—and men.'

She stopped abruptly and glowered up at him. Not for one second was she deceived by his tender concern. 'And who will teach me these things? You?'

He smiled and his eyes shone with a roguish gleam. 'I would like to.'

'Is there something wrong with me? Am I not attractive to look at?'

'You worry too much,' Max said, his eyes held by the pale, graceful figure. The lights in her glorious hair changed colour rapidly in the light that filtered through the upper branches of the trees, from the deepest brown to a rich mahogany. A kind of anger welled up inside him against James Embleton for causing her distress. 'Take it from me, there is nothing wrong with the way you look. James Embleton must be blind. He doesn't know what he's missing.'

'He doesn't?'

'No.'

'Then—would you like to kiss me?'

Max frowned and looked away. She didn't know what she was asking.

Christina misinterpreted his response and continued to walk on in a huff, her hands clenched and her chin thrust out. 'There, I knew it. There is something wrong with me.'

Striding after her, Max took her arm and spun her round to face him. 'Have you never been kissed?'

She shook her head sullenly.

Cupping her chin in his hand, Max looked deep into her eyes, his own intense and gentle at the same time. 'One day I will kiss you, Christina. That I promise you, and when I do you will want me to go on kissing you. But not now, not when you're all fired up and thinking of someone else. When I kiss you it will be because it is me you want. Do you understand?'

Max was attired in snug-fitting calf-coloured breeches and tan riding boots, bottle-green jacket and a rakish cream silk cravat around his neck and she looked at him hard, as if for the first time. His magnificent physique was displayed in a way that made her throat go dry. With a thick lock of black hair drooping across his brow and his incredible blue eyes, she thought how terribly attractive he was, the most attractive man she had ever met, and there was no point in denying it.

With the quietness of the woods all about them, for a moment she was held by his gaze, unable to drag her eyes from the ones that commanded her attention. It was as if he searched out her very soul, and he had a way of making her feel consumed by that heated regard. His fingers still cupped her chin and his touch excited her, warmed her, but her mind shied away from going any deeper than that, for it seemed obscene to even consider she might have feelings for any other man but James. He seemed to sense her discomfort; his smile became positively wolfish.

'You must think me stupid,' she retorted, taking a step back so that he had to release her chin. She looked away and stiffened her spine. Max's dark brows drew together over incredulous blue eyes.

'No, I don't. You decided that.' For a moment he studied her with heavy-lidded, speculative eyes. 'Perhaps I will kiss you after all.'

Christina found she was unable to move when his hand suddenly cupped her cheek. 'Look at me,' he said in a low, velvety, unfamiliar voice that sent apprehensive and exciting tingles darting up her spine. She raised her eyes to his tanned face. Although no one had ever attempted to kiss her before, she took one look at the slumberous expression in his eyes and was instantly wary.

'Are you really going to kiss me?'

A slow, lazy smile that made her heart leap worked its way across his face and Christina was unable to drag her eyes from his hypnotic gaze. 'Yes, I am.'

Terrified of what would happen next and that she would make a complete idiot of herself, she whispered, 'I—don't think you should. It doesn't matter—really…'

Ignoring her protests, Max tilted her face for a kiss. Lowering his head, he touched her lips with his. Then he looked at her to assess her reaction. 'Well?'

Christina's eyes were wide with bewilderment—and disappointment. 'Was that it? Is that all there is to kissing?'

Max looked down at her, gazing into the wide, luminous eyes of this unpredictable girl, and tenderness began to unfold within him. 'No,' he murmured. 'There's much more.' Placing his hands on her shoulders, he puller her towards him, so close that her breasts pressed against his chest and the rest of her body fitted perfectly into his. Her question, spoken in complete innocence, caught Max completely off guard. Every feminine ploy in existence had been used on him in the past, but without success—and yet this artless child-woman, her candour combined with her upturned, beautiful face and alluring body pressing against him, acted like a powerful aphrodisiac.

Lost in a confusion of apprehension and yearning, suddenly Christina saw something primitive and alarming kindle in his eyes, and so lost was she in her own thoughts that it took a moment before she realised that his gaze had dropped to her lips and that he meant to kiss her again.

'You don't have to—'

Without hesitating for a moment, with desire surging through him, heating his blood and sending it singing through his veins, Christina Thornton became an alluring and incredibly enticing woman. Ignoring his conscience, which suddenly reared up with acid disgust to remind him that he was deliberately seducing a gullible child, Max thrust it away and smothered her objections with another kiss, completely different to the one before. It was long, tender and devouring, and at first Christina didn't know what to think of it, and then as his lips began to move over hers, coaxing, fiercely tender, determined, her body jerked and she tore her lips from his, struggling like a young animal caught in a trap, until she felt his large masculine hand curve round her nape, his long fingers sliding into her hair, and his breath warm on her parted lips.

His mouth claimed hers once more, his lips insistent and moving with inflaming expertise over hers. Dizzily, Christina slid her hands up his chest, feeling the power of him, the sheer strength packed into the hard muscles beneath her fingers as she yielded her lips to his, parting them beneath the sensual pressure, and the moment his tongue slid between them, invading her mouth and taking possession of her, she became lost in a sea of pure sensation.

Melting against him and moulding her body to his length, she clung to him for support, unaware of how this innocent action triggered an instant reaction from Max. His arms tightened around her, his hand caressing her spine as he deepened his kiss, his parted lips moving over hers and crushing them with hungry ardour.

In his arms Christina moaned softly, and the sound somehow penetrated his aroused senses. Releasing her lips and raising his head, he gazed down into the intoxicating, slumberous green eyes, unable to believe the passion she had unexpectedly evoked in him. Her cheeks were soft and flushed a delightful shade of pink, and her lips were swollen from his kiss and trembling. His arms slackened, but he did not release her, and when Christina saw his firm, sensual mouth twist in a grim smile, she had the impression that he was struggling for composure.

'Well, Christina? Was that kiss more like the one you were expecting?'

'No—I wasn't expecting anything quite like that.'

'And? What was your opinion?'

Disentangling herself from his arms, she stepped back, her emotions roiling from his kiss and implacable attitude and trying desperately to match his casual mood. 'I—I can't say because I have nothing to compare it with. I confess that I am confused, but what I will say is that I know better than to let you kiss me again.'

A smile touched the corner of his sensual lips. 'Very wise. Who knows where the next kiss might lead? Although I assure you, I am not in the habit of seducing innocents.'

'But I was *not* in danger of being seduced,' Christina stated proudly.

Lazy mockery gleamed in his narrowed eyes. 'And you are sure about that?'

'Absolutely. At least now I will know what to expect when anyone kisses me in the future.'

'James?'

She looked perplexed as she considered his question. If she were honest, she would have to admit that at the moment, with the taste of Max's kiss still on her lips, it wasn't James she was thinking of. She just happened to want Max to kiss her again, more than anyone—even James. That thought sent her mind into chaos. How could she have responded so wantonly to Max's kiss when she had only ever yearned for James?

'I've only ever thought of James,' she told him honestly.

Max's expression hardened when she spoke the name of the youth who held her heart—and Christina's female intuition told her that she had touched him.

'I know,' he said, his voice harsh.

They walked the rest of the way in silence. By the time they reached the house, with her sharp mind and clever brain, Christina was in control and her powers of reason had returned. James might have broken her heart, but not her. Where Max was concerned, that was another matter entirely. His kiss had stirred her body to such heights that it had refused to listen to reason, and in no time at all he'd had her melting and pliant. There was no doubt at all that it had left her disturbed and strangely excited. In his arms she had been swept away to the edge of an abyss, beyond which her instinct told her her life would change, and she was too afraid to find out more.

Aware that it was not as bright as when she had set out for the lake, she looked up at the sky. It was the colour of a mussel shell, the lowering clouds snuffing out the sun, and in the far-off distance she could hear the rumble of thunder.

'There's a storm in the air,' she said. 'I can hear the thunder. Perhaps it's as well. This heat of late has made us somewhat complacent. I only hope Peter doesn't stay out on the lake too long.'

'I'm sure your brother is old enough to take care of himself.'

'I know he is, but if the trout are biting he'll stay out there until the bitter end.'

'Will you be all right?'

She smiled up at him. 'Yes. I'm fine now. Truly. In fact, suddenly I'm ravenous. Would you care to share breakfast with me? Mrs Barnaby, our very efficient cook, always provides enough eggs and bacon to feed a regiment of soldiers.'

Max would have, but, his bland expression fading to one of grim displeasure as he forced himself for the first time to face what had happened to him when he had taken her in his arms, and deciding it would be inappropriate under the circumstances, he declined.

'Thank you, but perhaps some other time, Christina. I have to get back. Do you ride, by the way?'

'Yes, often.'

'Then perhaps you would care to accompany me some time—with your parents' permission, of course.'

'Yes, I'd like that.'

'When do you expect them back?'

'Some time later this morning.' She gave him a questioning look. 'Why, do you want to see them?'

He nodded. 'Perhaps tomorrow.'

Christina watched him mount his horse and ride away
before going into the house. Unable to put his earth-shattering kiss from her mind, she felt a lightness of heart and found
it strange that she was no longer angry that Peter and James
had gone fishing without her. Remembering his easy, smiling
attitude when he had released her, her stomach wrenched as
she compared her own gullibility and innocence and stupidity
to his sophistication and worldliness.

Having no intention of waiting for Peter and James to
appear for breakfast, Christina ordered hers to be sent to her
room. Washing and tidying herself up, after eating her breakfast she curled up in a chair and tried to read. The heavy
thunder in the distance was moving closer.

Continuing on his ride, Max thought of Christina with fascinated interest, amazed by the ease with which she had in-
sinuated herself into his heart for the second time in her
seventeen years. He had thought of her often, knowing that
one day he would come looking for her. Having grown up in
total ignorance of who she really was, she was fresh and
alive—and totally spoiled.

He thought of her bold request for him to kiss her, and the
incredible surge of hot desire she had ignited in his body. He
smiled. Christina Thornton was full of surprises, full of
promise, and her allure was deep and abiding. Her finely
sculpted features were flawless, like a jewel that, against the
proper background, would outshine all the rest.

As he followed the path that would take him to Cranworth
House, he remembered the moment when he was ten years

old and his step-grandmother had told him that before Christina had been taken to England, the Thorntons had consented to the betrothal between the two of them. He had never abandoned the dream that he would meet her again, and now he had he was not disappointed.

The air was oppressive and there were flashes of lightning like violent silver demons hurtling across the sky, and then there would be a pause before it flashed again. Tired of trying to read, feeling restless and vaguely disturbed and apprehensive—although she couldn't think why because storms had never bothered her before—she got up and went to the window. Great drops of rain were beginning to fall out of a sky that had grown much darker, with flashes of lightning ripping through, and for an instant the earth was a blinding silver blue. The wind had risen and was whipping the trees into a frenzy. It was so strong that an old oak on the edge of the wood came crashing down, its roots exposed in a tangled mass. She thought it fortuitous in that it would provide them with plenty of good logs to feed the house fires, but then another thought struck her—that it was an omen of something worse to come.

The heavens opened and rain began to come down in sheets, lashing the window panes. Her concern that Peter and James might be caught up in it out on the lake was alleviated when she saw two figures emerge from the trees that bordered the gardens, and make a dash for the back of the house, carrying their catch in a wicker basket, which they would present to a delighted Mrs Barnaby, who would no doubt serve it up later.

Another fusillade of thunder shook the earth. The storm was right overhead. It was late morning when it finally abated and the sun came out with a brilliance and warmth that made the land steam beneath its heat. James left to ride home. Christina joined Peter in the drawing room, retiring quietly to a corner of the room to read. He gave her a queer look, for this was most unlike her. No doubt he thought she was sulking because he'd refused to let her accompany them on their fishing trip, but it couldn't be further from the truth.

Hearing carriage wheels grind sharply to a halt in the drive, Christina hurried into the hall to welcome her parents home. They came in together, the soft murmur of her mother's voice as she spoke to her husband drifting to Christina and lifting her heart. There came with her the faint scent of roses, which seemed to emanate from her body and the folds of her clothes, a fragrance that Christina would always link to her mother. Having worried about them travelling back in the storm, she was glad they were home.

There was something about their manner and the way they kept looking at each other that gave her a feeling of unease. When her mother had removed her hat and handed it to a servant, she turned to her daughter, and Christina thought she looked tired and anxious.

'Is something wrong, Mama?' Christina asked. She got the impression her parents were avoiding her eyes. 'I'm surprised you made the journey in the storm.'

'Your father and I wanted to get back. We'll go and change and have some tea, and then we would like to talk to you, Christina—you and Peter.'

'What can be of such importance that made you brave the storm?' she asked.

'We'll tell you shortly,' she said, smiling softly and patting her cheek in passing to the stairs.

* * *

Fifteen minutes later the four of them were in the drawing room, Christina and Peter seated together on the sofa facing their parents. Christina looked at her mother with concern. Her eyes were red, and Christina was sure she had been crying. But why? She had never seen her mother give vent to tears in her life. Suddenly both her parents looked old, frail and vulnerable, with no trace of their cheerful happy selves. It was plain that something was terribly wrong, but although her mother dabbed at her eyes with her handkerchief, she had a steadfast look about her. Christina was afraid—she had never felt so afraid in her whole life. Never had such feelings of dread swept through her as they did now.

'Mama, will you please tell us what is wrong?' Peter prompted.

'It—it concerns Christina. We—have things to tell you, things you have a right to know,' she said, fumbling on the seat beside her for the support of her husband's hand as she prepared to divulge the truth to her beloved daughter about her birth.

And she did just that. As tenderly and as carefully as she could she told her, and so acute was Audine's guilt that she could not lift her eyes and look into those trusting green eyes.

Christina stared from her mother to her father's bowed, grey head. 'Adopted?' she echoed in bewilderment.

Raising his head he looked at her directly. 'Yes, Christina. You are our adopted daughter.'

She stared at him for a long time through eyes huge with horror and disbelief. 'But—I can't be. There has to be some mistake.' She looked at her mother, willing her to tell her it was not true. 'Mama?'

Her mother nodded. 'What your father says is true, Christina. I'm so sorry. All your life we have kept it from you, but circumstances have changed and we have decided you must be told the truth.'

Christina swallowed the tears that had risen in her throat and threatened to choke her. She glanced at Peter. She couldn't see him properly, but his mouth was tight and she knew he was struggling to come to terms with the shattering revelation that she was not his sister.

'But—I don't understand—any of it.'

'Oh, my dear,' her mother soothed, 'in time you will, and come to terms with it. Everything is going to be all right. It is going to be difficult, I know, but hopefully you will come to realise that it changes nothing. You have a great deal to live for and you are still our beloved daughter, Christina.'

'But I'm not,' she cried, feeling as if her heart were breaking. 'I never have been. Oh, Mama, Papa—how could you keep such a terrible secret as this from me all these years?'

'Because we have always looked on you as our true daughter, but we knew we would have to tell you some time. Your—your real father's family imposed—'

'Don't,' Christina interrupted fiercely, springing to her feet, her eyes blazing with the belief that the less she knew about the people on that other side of her, they would not become real. 'Don't tell me about him. I don't want to know. It—it's all too much to take in.'

The shock that had blessedly anaesthetised her up until now began to dissipate and she realised that this was not a dream, nor a nightmare from which she might wake. This was real and she had to face it, acknowledge it. For the first time in her life she faced a crisis and was unable to rely on her parents or her brother or anyone else to shield her from the pain of it. But how could she survive this when her whole world had been torn apart?

It was the knowledge that the two people she loved most weren't her true parents that hurt. They were everything to her. It was devastating to know this and that they had kept it a secret for all these years. She stared in silent astonishment, neither speaking nor moving for some seconds.

'I don't know what to say to you,' she said at length, never having felt such wretchedness. Putting her hand to her head, she shook it dejectedly. 'I need to think about it. Right now I can't deal with it.' Tears started to her eyes. 'It—it's so hard.'

'We want what's best for you, Christina. We always have.'

Christina stopped pacing the carpet and looked at her brother, who had remained silent since coming into the room. She could see that he had the best of both his parents, but there was a strength in his features that was lacking in theirs. For the first time in her life she realised how very different she was from her brother, not only in colouring but in temperament. Why hadn't she noticed it before? But then she'd had no reason to, wrapped as she had been all her life in a beautiful, uninterrupted dream.

But all that had been wiped out in a moment and now, as she looked at her brother, with tears not far away Christina found herself feeling strangely isolated and different, as if she didn't belong. From his expression it was plain that Peter was as anguished as she was, as bereft as she was.

'Peter, I realise how difficult all this must be for you also. One minute you have a sister who has grown up with you, and the next—'

'I still have a sister, Christina,' Peter said fiercely, springing to his feet, close to tears himself. 'Nothing has changed— and despite our differences I love you dearly. This is your home. It always has been and it always will be, and I will support you in whatever decisions you make regarding your future.' Seeing the tears glistening on Christina's lashes, he held out his hand. 'Come, you are upset, and rightly so.'

Ignoring his hand, Christina straightened and flung her head from side to side. 'Upset? Peter, you can't possibly know how upset I am. I am devastated.' Wiping her cheeks with the back of her hand, she turned from them. She had to be alone. Another minute and her control would crack. 'I'm going to my room. I must be by myself. I have to think.'

When she turned and darted for the door in a flurry of skirts, Peter was about to go after her until his father also rose and gripped his arm.

'Let her go, Peter. You know what she's like. Christina's headstrong, impetuous nature has always given us cause for concern, but she is sensible and I know she will go away and think deeply about what she's been told. Do as she says. Better that she is left alone for now. Later we will discuss the implications of her birth.'

Peter stared at him, bewilderment clouding his eyes. 'Implications? You—you mean there is more?'

His father nodded gravely. 'Oh, yes, there is, Peter—a great deal more; if you think her reaction to being told she is adopted is severe, then what we have to tell her is far worse and I fear how she will take it.'

Chapter Four

With her mind stumbling over itself and her head spinning, Christina rode her horse hard in an attempt to make sense of what she had just been told. Emotionally confused, she didn't know how to deal with the enormity of what had transpired and she needed to be alone so she could keep a firm grip on herself the only way she knew how, for if she did not she would go completely to pieces. She couldn't stand the pain of it, knowing the two people she loved and trusted most in the world were not her parents. The situation was not to be borne. The problem was insurmountable.

The countryside was drenched with the earlier rain and sparkled beneath the heat of the sun. Lazy white clouds in the blue sky were being carried along on a slight breeze. The ride helped and she began to feel better, but the hurt and pain in her heart was still sharp and she knew it would be a long time, if ever, before it would leave her. Slowing her horse to a trot, she found herself heading in the direction of Max's house.

Max Lloyd had a strange and strong effect on her—he invaded her consciousness, and took over her mind. She found it hard to explain because it was something she had never experienced before. The way he had of looking at her, and the way he had kissed her, was a new and very powerful and profound thing. That something was happening against her will she knew, but with this new devastation she had ceased to think about Max Lloyd since her parents had arrived home.

Always one to be in control of her emotions, she fought her feelings, telling herself she didn't want to see him, even going so far as to ride in the opposite direction from his house when she reached it, but there was some strange and mysterious pull drawing her back. When Lorenzo opened the door and let her in, when Max Lloyd gave her that knowing look of his and half-smiled at her, the resolve melted away.

They looked at one another across the hours that had gone by since they had parted—to Christina, after all that had transpired in the meantime, it seemed like an age. His dark hair was smoothly brushed back and he was freshly shaved. He smelled of cologne and, casually dressed, he looked immaculate.

Max studied her face, feeling a *frisson* of alarm as she looked up at him with a haunted, wild expression, and he sensed that tears weren't very far away.

'Come in, Christina. I am surprised. I wasn't expecting you.'

'How could you?' she said, clutching her riding crop in her gloved hands. 'I didn't mean to come...'

He looked at her. 'Then why did you seek me out, Christina?'

'I—I don't know—not really. I—like being with you, I suppose. You seem to know what I'm feeling. Perhaps that was why.'

Max noticed that she was measuring her words, and he began to realise that she had not come to him on a whim. 'Thank you. That's compliment indeed.'

'There is something else. I—I have to talk to someone,' she told him touchingly.

'And you thought of me.'

'Yes. I hope you don't mind. I—know this is highly irregular, but I was desperate to get out of the house. Will—will you ride with me?'

'I could do with some fresh air myself. Wait a minute while I saddle my horse.'

'I'll come with you.'

Max sensed she wanted to be with him on common ground, adult ground. Something was wrong. He could sense the change in her.

'Come,' he said, mounting, having saddled his horse while she had quietly waited. 'I like open spaces. We'll ride away from here.' *Away from our thoughts and far too many emotions,* he thought, *all of them ungovernable while he was with Christina.* He kicked the horse and cantered ahead of her along the path that led to the long sweep of open countryside beyond Tanglewood. There they gave their horses their heads, deriving tremendous satisfaction in the freedom of the ride.

'Max, wait,' Christina called when they had been riding for about fifteen minutes. 'I find it difficult keeping up with you. My horse is more docile than your powerful stallion and I've already almost ridden her into the ground.'

Like a man in slow motion, when Max heard her call out he wrenched his horse round and waited for her to catch up, not realising he was so far in front.

When she drew up alongside him, Max gave her a worried look. 'Christina, when are you going to tell me what is troubling you?' He smiled wickedly. 'It doesn't by any chance have anything to do with what happened between us earlier, does it?'

She flushed and averted her eyes. 'No, of course not, but—something has happened.'

'Would you like to share it with me?'

Walking her horse on, she said slowly, 'I suppose everyone will know soon.' She looked at him directly, trying to hide the pain. He rode beside her, sitting easy in the saddle, as if resigned to a difficult discussion, but his gaze did not waver from hers as he waited for her to continue. 'Max, have you ever lost someone—someone you loved very much?'

He nodded.

'When?'

'Once—when I was a child.' His voice was very heavy suddenly. 'It was a long time ago, but for a long time I thought about her every day. Contrary to popular opinion, I find that the passing of time and the dulling of grief have very little to do with one another.'

'I'm sorry. You see, we have something in common. I'm glad you feel comfortable enough to tell me.'

'I told you, I was a boy and I learnt to live with it, learnt what to do with the pain. Time does help, if not heal.'

'Did the person die?'

He shook his head. 'No, she was taken away.'

'Then if you knew you were never going to meet again, that in itself must be like a bereavement.'

'Yes, I suppose it was. But what is this, Christina? Have you lost someone close to you?'

'In a way—you see, my parents have just told me that I am adopted, that I am not their daughter at all.' She forced herself to sound calm and lucid, trying to keep a tight hold on her emotions.

Max's eyes softened with understanding, and also something else that Christina couldn't comprehend just then. 'I see. I'm very sorry. I can understand how difficult it must be for you, knowing that.'

'Do you really?'

'Yes, but it shouldn't change the way you feel about your parents.'

'No, but knowing what they have done has hurt me terribly. I came to see you because you are the only person I could think of who has nothing to do with this—this unbelievable deceit that has been practised by my parents throughout my entire life.'

Apart from a tightening of his features, Max's expression didn't change, but inside he was feeling like the worst kind of fraud, for wasn't he himself complicit in the deceit she spoke of? 'Christina, would it not be better to discuss all this with your parents.'

'No—not yet. I need to calm down first.'

'Did they tell you anything else—apart from the fact that you are adopted?'

She looked at him sharply. 'No. What else could there be? What could possibly be worse than that?'

He shrugged. 'Why did they tell you now? Do they give a reason?'

'No. All they said was that the circumstances had changed and I had to be told the truth.'

'Then don't you think you should have asked them what these circumstances are? Knowing you, Christina, you probably left with your rage flying high and with the story only half-told. For instance, did they tell you who your real parents were?'

She scowled darkly. 'No. I don't want to know.'

'But you will have to—at some time. Better to get it over with, don't you think? Once you have talked about it you can put it behind you and move on. Besides, have you given any thought to how your parents might be feeling now? Pretty wretched, I imagine.' Watching her closely, he rode on in silence for a moment, letting his words sink in before he continued. 'At this moment you are thinking only of yourself but, in fairness to your parents, I suspect they are blaming themselves for not telling you sooner. Giving you this dire news cannot have been easy for them, and I imagine they have been carrying a great burden of guilt with them for years.'

She felt herself drowning in remorse as the mere thought of what her parents might be suffering nearly broke Christina's fragile grip on her control. 'I never thought of it like that,' she said bleakly.

A faint crooked smile curved his lips. 'That's understandable. It's natural that you would have been in shock at the time. I feel that the sooner you speak to them in a reasonable frame of mind, the better.'

Feeling better for having talked to him, Christina sighed. 'Thank you, Max. Listening to some common sense has helped. I feel better already.'

Max looked at her for a long time, then he smiled. 'How wise you are, Christina, for one so young. Come, we will ride a little further and then I will escort you back to the house.'

Something in his expression was warmly intimate and made Christina feel alarmingly alive in a way James had never made her feel. That was when it occurred to her that for the past few hours she hadn't given James a thought, and that it no longer mattered.

Dusk had faded into twilight when Christina next saw her parents. They didn't come down to dinner, but sent a message telling Christina and Peter they would take coffee with them in the drawing room afterwards. The meal was a subdued affair between brother and sister—which is how they still thought of each other and always would. Nothing could change that.

When Christina's parents joined them, immediately she crossed to them and hugged them both, full of remorse and desperately wanting to make amends for her behaviour earlier.

'I'm so sorry about earlier. I shouldn't have left you like I did, but I was terribly shocked by what you told me. I could never have envisioned anything like this—how could I possibly?'

Overcome with emotion, her father patted her shoulder and led his wife to the sofa, where they sat side by side, ignoring the coffee the maid poured for them before leaving them alone.

'It's just that I found it hard coming to terms with the fact that you were not who I thought you were, without being told about my real parents—who they were or where they came from. I didn't want to know—not ever. They gave me away, so they mean nothing to me.'

Her father nodded slowly. 'They didn't give you away, Christina, but I can understand your reluctance to think about the people who shaped your life before we stepped in. Now you've had time to digest what we told you, have you become curious to know about your roots?'

'A little.' She shrugged. 'I suppose I shall have to know some time. But no matter where I came from or who my real parents were, I shall always look on you as my mother and father. Nothing will ever change that.'

'Why did you adopt Christina?' Peter asked, wanting to get everything out in the open in order to understand it. As yet he was unable to take in the enormity of all this and what it would mean for Christina and the future.

'After being blessed with you, Peter, your mother found she was with child once more. Having promised ourselves a trip to Italy to visit Lydia, Audine's sister, we decided to go before the baby was born. But your mother had an accident—she tripped, falling down some stairs.'

'Were you very badly hurt?' Christina asked, full of concern for her mother.

'Yes, I was,' she said quietly. 'Unfortunately I went into labour before my time and I lost the child—a girl—and I had to come to terms with the fact that there would be no more children.'

'Understandably your mother was devastated and quite inconsolable,' her husband said, taking his wife's hand and holding on to it tightly. 'Her sister—your mother, Christina—had also given birth to you, but tragically she died soon afterwards. She died before Audine had the chance to see her.'

Christina felt her mother's anguish as if it were her own. 'I didn't even know you had a sister, Mama.'

'No, we never told you or Peter. We thought it would complicate matters and lead you to ask questions we would find difficult to answer.'

'When my real mother died, what happened to my father? Was he Italian?' Her father nodded. 'So, I am half-Italian. I don't think I look Italian.' Christina looked down at herself, as if she might have changed somehow. 'Why did I not remain with my real father?'

'There were—complications. When your mother saw you and held you in her arms, she wanted to keep you—we both did. When we expressed a desire to bring you back to England there were no objections, but…we had to adhere to certain conditions—one of them being that your true identity must not be kept from you.'

'We agreed to the conditions,' Audine told her daughter, 'but as time passed we could not bring ourselves to tell you.

You were as much our child as if I had conceived you, and every day we have lived with the knowledge that one day something would happen—that—someone, would come to claim you—to take you away. But as time went by and nothing was heard—we began to hope. Please don't be angry, Christina. Your father and I loved you from the beginning. We were devoted to you, and that devotion has never faltered.'

Christina frowned. Something they had said puzzled her. 'Why were you afraid that I would be taken away? Who did you expect to claim me? Who were you afraid of?'

'Christina,' her father said, suddenly uneasy, 'there is something else we have to tell you, but we are waiting for a visitor. There is one other person who should be here—someone who insisted on being present.'

Before Christina could voice a question the door opened and Max Lloyd entered the room. Christina's eyes widened in surprise and she stared at him, bewildered and curious as to why he was present.

He inclined his head. 'Lady Thornton, Lord Thornton. I apologise if I've kept you waiting.' His gaze briefly settled on Christina where she sat beside her brother, the graceful folds of her simple dark blue dress falling about her. Her face was pale and lovely and her gleaming dark hair had been pulled back into a fat chignon, her skin held tightly against the beautiful bones of her face. With the absence of bright colours, the severity of her dress and hair gave her a grace and serenity he would never have thought her capable of when he had first seen her cavorting in the lake.

'Mr Lloyd, earlier today Christina learned that she is our adopted daughter. My husband and I have also told her about her parentage—that her father was Italian. Since you expressed a wish to be present when we told her of her inheritance, we thought it best to wait. Thank you for coming at such short notice.'

Christina looked bewildered. 'But, Mama, what has any of this to do with Mr Lloyd?'

'Please listen, Christina. It—will all become clear to you.'

Dressed in black, Max strode across the room to stand against the French windows and stood looking out over the gracious sweep of green lawns. He had his back to them and his tall body and broad shoulders threw an ominous shadow across the carpet. Christina had the uneasy thought that he was like a large predatory hawk in the midst of a gathering of tame birds.

'Mama, this has come as such a shock. It is the most wretched time of my life. I cannot imagine what can possibly be worse than what I have already been told. What happened to my real father?'

Her mother looked at Max Lloyd, who hadn't moved from his stance by the window. As if on cue he turned, his face taut and expressionless.

'Your father was called Roberto Carletti. He died recently,' he told her flatly.

Christina looked at him. Something dark and not to her liking began to form in her mind and a wave of alarm swept over her. Something was amiss in all of this, something that didn't make any sense. She sat up straight, as if her posture could restrain her hurt and rising discomfort—as if her dignity could restrain the enormity of this.

Cautiously she said, 'I see. Max, why are you really here? Somehow I don't think it's a coincidence.'

'No.'

He turned his head away and she stared at him with sudden, heartbreaking clarity as all the bizarre puzzle that had bewildered her about Max Lloyd, about his arrival in Leyton, his meeting with her parents before the cricket match and their distress following this, all fell into place, gruesome and complete—or was it? Was it possible that there was more? A rock settled where her heart had been, cold rage where there had been trust and, she had thought, a growing friendship.

With all her senses heightened sharply by her growing awareness of Max's menace to her future, a spark of self-preservation ignited within her, and unable to keep the accusation from her voice, she said 'You! You knew about me, didn't you, Max, before I told you?'

Max turned and a pair of piercing blue eyes locked on hers. 'Yes,' he confirmed, his expression grim. 'I am very sorry. It was not for me to tell you, Christina, but now you know, you must be told the whole of it.'

Gerald stood up, straightening his body, as if he were about to withstand a physical blow. 'The fault lies with us.' His eyes were on Christina, silently pleading for her understanding. 'We should have told you, Christina. I have dreaded this moment of reckoning ever since we discovered Mr Lloyd's true identity, that he is, in fact, Count Marchesi. Now that the time is here, it is worse than I ever imagined.'

Furious that Max Lloyd had reduced her beloved father to this pathetic, pleading man, and that her beloved mother was in a state of such distress that her knuckles were white as she twisted the folds of her gown, she shot to her feet. With her fists clenched and her scornful green eyes hurling daggers across the distance that separated them, she was physically trembling with rage and a craving for justice and retribution.

'It was you my parents were afraid of, wasn't it, you they feared would come and take me away? Of all the despicable, treacherous, underhand people I have ever met, you are by far the worst.'

'Christina! Please stop this,' her father uttered brokenly as he tried to preserve some modicum of order over a situation that was rapidly beginning to disintegrate. 'Mr Lloyd is our guest and I will not have you being rude to him.'

'I'm sorry, Papa, but Mr Lloyd is not the sort of guest one invites into the home of decent, respectable people.' She turned back to Max. 'How could you? Oh, how could you do this to my family?'

Deeply moved by her outburst, Max took a step towards her and then stopped. 'Christina, I am not your enemy.'

'No? Then what are you?'

'Your betrothed.'

A silence fell on the occupants of the room that could be sliced with a knife. Christina stared at him through eyes huge with horror and disbelief. 'Your betrothed? Now you are being ridiculous. That's impossible. How can that be? I don't ever recall being asked.'

'It was decided before your mother and I brought you to England,' her father told her. 'One of the provisos was that you would return to live in Italy when you reached eighteen.'

'And the second?'

'That you marry this young man, Max Marchesi.'

Wildly, Christina shook her head, her mind already realising what her heart couldn't bear to believe. 'Are you telling me that all this was decided, that I was pledged to this—this man without considering what my feelings might be when I reached eighteen—that I might not want to live in a country that is completely alien to me—married to a man I might even despise?'

Her obvious distress brought Peter to his feet. 'Christina, please calm yourself. You are upset,' he said, placing a restraining hand on her arm.

'Upset?' she flared, shaking away his hand. 'Yes, Peter, I

am upset, but I am also furious.' Suddenly the roiling pain and rage erupted inside her and she whirled around on Max in a frenzy of fury. 'Who struck this cruel bargain to which I would never have agreed had I been consulted from the outset—and for what reason? You would have been a child yourself at the time, so who was it and why?'

Max watched her intently, taking in every detail of the girl he had agreed to take as his wife to unite two old Tuscan families. 'Your paternal grandmother. She was married to my grandfather and lived at Villa Marchesi, which I inherited on my father's death. Now the death of Roberto Carletti, your father, has been confirmed, you are her heir, Christina, and she very much wants to see you. Your grandmother is a wealthy woman in her own right, with her own vineyards and olive groves that border my own. You stand to inherit all her property and wealth when she dies.'

At last a glimmer of understanding dawned on Christina. It was as if a window had been opened in a darkened room to let in the light. She held her head high and met his bold stare. His body was instantly alert and his bearing more upright. She could almost feel the attitude he had adopted—that of a predator ready to strike at its helpless prey.

'Now I'm beginning to see what this is all about,' she said slowly, clenching her hands so tightly that her nails dug into her flesh. 'Whoever marries me will stand to gain a great deal. You, it would seem.' Her eyes, glittering with outrage, narrowed as the insult to her pride hit home. 'What a cold-hearted villain you are turning out to be, Max. Is that why you are here? To check things out? You came to take a look first, didn't you, masquerading as Max Lloyd so that if you found someone ugly and with buck teeth, you could have crept back to Italy and I would have been none the wiser?'

'I never creep and that was never my intention.'

'No, you are arrogant and controlling and stride around as if you own the world and everyone and everything if it. Well, Count Marchesi,' she flared, 'if you are here to claim your bride you have arrived several months early.'

'You will very soon be eighteen,' he pointed out sharply.

'Not for another eight months. I thought you were my friend, when all the time you saw me as nothing more than a means to an end—that you only want me for what I would bring with me should I agree to be your wife. Well, the situation is not as cut and dried as you seem to think.'

Max's whole body had tensed into a rigid line as her harsh words pierced the armour of his calm composure. His jaw hard and tight, he was looking at her intently, as their eyes parried for supremacy in a silent battle of unspoken challenges. It was as if no one else existed in the room.

'You have no choice, Christina,' he stated coldly.

'Yes, I do. How could you do this to two people who never did a thing to hurt you? In hurting them you have hurt me, so go away, Max whoever you are, back to where you came from, and whatever your reason for coming here I do not want to know. I am not interested. I am not going to Italy and I am certainly not going to marry you. The very idea is ludicrous.'

Max moved closer to her and leaned forwards. He said very slowly, 'Mark well my words, Christina—the matter is not open to discussion. You may not think it so very ludicrous when you know all the facts. There are a great many explanations to be made, questions you will want to ask that only I can answer.'

'My parents can do that,' she countered fiercely.

'Not really. You see, your true parents lived in Italy—in Tuscany. Sir Gerald and Lady Audine have little knowledge of the events that shaped your life all those years ago. They know very little about your Italian relatives.'

'And you do, I suppose. You were there.'

'For some of the time, yes, I was.'

'I don't want to know. I don't want you to tell me...' Cracked with emotion, her voice failed and she could not go on. Suddenly it was all too much. Fighting back the scalding tears that rushed to her eyes, she didn't see the anguish in his. Turning, she ran blindly to the door, past where her parents whose faces were haunted and grey, now stood.

For a long moment there was an awful, ominous silence when the door had closed on Christina, and the very air seemed to crackle with tension. Max made a move towards the door.

'I will go to her and explain.'

Peter, extremely worried about the effect all this upset was having on his parents, stepped in front of him. 'No, please, I must ask you to keep away from her just now. Later you can speak to her. You must understand how this must look to Christina right now and in her present mood it would be a great mistake to press her.'

Max stood looking at the closed door through which Christina had disappeared, fury emanating from every inch of his taut, powerful frame. How could her parents have kept the fact that she was not their child from her—and the fact that she was betrothed to him? They had promised they would tell her the truth, promised they would tell her who she was, about her real parents, and not raise her in ignorance. For Christina to have found out in this unfortunate manner had forced her into a position to oppose him, and he had no doubt that she could become a very determined adversary.

Feeling the need to get out of the house, he turned to Sir Gerald. 'I apologise for this. It was not my intention to cause upset. I don't think anything is to be gained by my presence here, Sir Gerald. When Christina is more herself, I will speak to her.'

'Yes—yes, I think that would be for the best.'

With a curt bow to Lady Audine, he left the house.

After walking along the path from Tanglewood with ground-devouring strides as the wind rose once more and whipped the trees into a frenzy, Max let himself into his house and ordered Lorenzo to pour him a large brandy. Lifting the glass, he frowned into the contents. Christina had reacted as he had expected she would on being told of their betrothal, and she had turned the full force of her anger on him. But if she thought to change his mind and force him to bow out of the arrangement, it was out of the question.

He had been raised with the knowledge that one day, following his marriage to Christina, the Marchesi and the Carletti estates—two of the oldest and richest estates in Tuscany—would be united and run as one—by him. Already he was impatient to have everything completed, and he'd be damned if he'd allow Christina to defy him and ruin everything.

She had been left to run wild with no firm parental guidance all her life. Recalling how quickly she had melted in his arms and returned his kiss with such ardour, he did not have the slightest doubt of his own ability to lure her into his arms again. A few weeks under his domination, her spirit would be broken and he'd have her purring like a kitten. And yet, he thought, staring down into his glass and unable to suppress the smile that curved his lips, her courage and her spirit was what he admired most about her, and God help him if he did anything to destroy that. She was also a natural-born temptress with the smile of an angel. She would never bore him, he was certain of that.

However, he could not pretend that he was not concerned about the dissension that had blown up between them, so tomorrow he had to find a way to make amends.

After leaving the drawing room, Christina ran up the stairs in her tear-blinded haste to seek refuge in her room. Once inside she leaned against the closed door, her head thrown back and her teeth clamped tight and she struggled for control of her rioting emotions.

Her beloved parents' faces, contorted with pain and deep distress, appeared before her tightly closed eyes and she moaned aloud with sick remorse. She could not find it in her to lay any blame at their door for any of this. Yes, they should have told her, but she understood why they hadn't. It was Max she blamed. If he had not come here, she would have continued to live in blissful ignorance of who she really was, whereas now she realised she was nothing but a pawn in a game played by two selfish Italian families and Max arrogantly believed he held all the aces. How could this have happened without her knowledge or consent? How could her future be threatened like this? It was hardly believable, ridiculous—in fact, it would be laughable if Max weren't so determined.

Suddenly the walls of her room seemed to close in on her, the atmosphere becoming more and more claustrophobic. Pushing herself away from the door, she scrambled into her riding habit. If she stayed inside another minute she would go insane.

As she made her way to the stables, the weather was no longer gentle. Rain was beginning to lash down once more and the wind ran high to match her mood.

Christina was already galloping away from the house when Peter saw her from the drawing-room window. Now what was she up to, the little fool? he thought crossly. As if they didn't have enough to worry about without her riding off into the dark with another storm brewing. Not wishing to alarm his parents, he excused himself and went after her.

After an hour of searching, soaked to the skin, his horse exhausted, he went back to the house, cursing vociferously when he found she had not returned, then in desperation, turned his horse in the direction of Max's house on the off chance that some mad scheme of hers might have taken her there.

Max was pulling on his boots before Peter had finished telling him of Christina's escapade, and in a matter of minutes he was riding in the direction he had ridden with her earlier that day, Peter going back to the house to see if she had finally returned.

The wind was strong, driving the rain into Christina's face as she headed back towards Leyton, realising how foolish she had been to rush out into the wild elements. Unfortunately the clouds obliterated the moon and the night was almost pitch black, so she didn't see the low overhead branch of the tree at the side of the track. Her head slammed against the branch and a white flash of pain burst in her brain as the reins were jerked from her hands and she fell out of the slippery saddle. When a clap of thunder shook the earth, her terrified horse bolted, leaving her lying semi-conscious in the mud.

Fighting the darkening shrouds of oblivion, she rolled and tried to rise to her feet. Groaning and holding her head, she stood up; the ground around her swam and dipped with a sudden lurch. She looked around for her horse, straining her eyes in the gloom. It was nowhere in sight. Knowing she had no choice but to try to make it home on foot, she tried to walk, but the pain in her head tore at every nerve in her, sapping her strength and her will to go on. Seized by a great weariness and hampered by the buffeting wind and rain and water-filled ruts, she made slow progress.

Her boots squelched in the mud, but, undeterred, she stumbled blindly on until ahead of her she could just make out the village. Lamplight in the cottage windows twinkled in the darkness and she could just make out the ghostly shape of the church near the crossroads. She didn't hear someone call her name above the noise of the wind. The first sense of being followed was a crawling of the hair on the nape of her neck, yet there was nowhere she could retreat to hide.

She was only aware of another presence when someone grasped her shoulder. She spun round, her hair a wild, wet tangle sticking to her face, beneath which her eyes peered out like an animal from its den, blood oozing from the cut on her head mingling with the rain.

Trying to run from the threat, she stumbled and fell. She saw the shape of a man as if through a long tunnel, his cloak flying wide behind him until he resembled a great bird swooping down on her. When she felt strong hands grasp her and pull her to her feet, with no idea who her assailant might be, she struggled wildly, clawing at him, her nails raking his face, in her effort to escape.

'Get off me. Let me go.' Like a vixen she fought against the hands that held her. 'Let me go,' she cried again, but she could not fight against the force that had her in its grip. Her body went limp as she felt the fight go out of her. The rain clung to her eyelashes like tears, and her cloak hung heavily, like the shroud of someone found drowned.

'Let me go,' she cried helplessly. 'Please let me go.'

But Max Lloyd picked her up into his arms and held her

against his chest, his face distraught as he looked at her lovely hair streaming across her face like wet seaweed. Somehow he managed to hoist her into the saddle and climb up behind her, and as he headed for Tanglewood his heart went out to her.

Christina sighed and closed her eyes as a strong, steel-sinewed arm went round her and held her close. Her cheek lolled against his chest, and even the fear that she might be in the clutches of some wild beast receded when she smelt the familiar spicy tang. She was in Max's arms.

Reaching Tanglewood Max kicked at the door, which was flung open by Peter, who had been waiting impatiently. Then Molly was there and what seemed like a houseful of anxious servants.

'What on earth has happened to her?' Peter asked, shocked by the bedraggled sight of his sister being held by Max Lloyd, her head resting on his shoulder.

'I found her in the lane beyond the village. She's taken a tumble from her horse and is in quite a state.'

'I can see that. Good God, the little fool. To go riding out on a night like this was suicidal.'

'We'd best get her to bed,' Molly said, shocked at the sight of her young mistress, with blood streaming from a cut on her brow.

'Show me,' Max said. 'And get the doctor to take a look at her.'

He followed Molly up to Christina's room and placed her gently on the bed, over which a protective cover had been hastily thrown. Forced to give up his burden to Molly and another maid, who was already producing fluffy white towels from a drawer, for one agonising, soul-wrenching moment,

Max took one last look at Christina before he left. Her eyes were closed and her face was whiter than death.

Downstairs Peter handed him a brandy. 'Here, you look as though you need it.'

Max took it gratefully and swallowed it in one. When Peter offered him another he shook his head.

'Do your parents know that she went out?'

'Yes. I had to tell them. They have been informed that she has been found and will go and see her. Mama is quite distraught, and rightly so. I'm afraid that being told she is not their real daughter seems to have tipped Christina over the edge.'

Max was inclined to think it was the betrothal that was the cause of that, but he did not contradict Peter.

Peter sighed tiredly, running his fingers through his hair. 'What a mess. I've sent someone for Hal to take a look at her. Maybe he'll give her a draught of something to make her sleep. She needs rest.'

'I'm sure he will.'

Peter's blue eyes narrowed in a slight frown, a pensive expression as he studied their handsome neighbour.

'Do you mind if I ask what your relationship is to Christina?' Peter asked.

'None. My grandfather married her grandmother.'

'And did you know Christina's mother?' Peter asked. 'I'm curious to know what she was like—this aunt I never knew I had. Is Christina like her?' He smiled. 'It has always been a mystery to us where she got her wildness from. Perhaps you will know.'

A faint smile touched Max's lips. 'Christina is very much like her mother, who was hot headed, yet warm and giving—and she could be as stubborn as a thousand mules.'

Peter laughed. 'Then that explains it.'

* * *

Christina opened her heavy-lidded eyes, closing them quickly when they were assaulted by bright sunshine filtering through the curtains. A dull ache throbbed in her head and she felt strangely depressed and melancholy. Her foggy mind refused to function and, instead of forcing her thoughts to the surface, she opened her eyes, preferring instead the anaesthesia of watching the shifting shadows on the ceiling.

Turning over, she tried to understand the bitter desolation that held her in its grip, pulling her down to despair, and in that instant she remembered the scene in the drawing room the night before. She also recalled her anguished, pain-racked flight on her horse. Most of what had occurred was hazy. She remembered being knocked from her horse and also she recalled with bitter irony Max Lloyd bringing her home. With so many people living in Leyton, it had to be he who found her.

Gingerly touching her head, she felt the small dressing Hal had put there, and feeling quite wretched, a tear found its way down her cheek. She tried to shut out the reality of everything that had happened, but it was too awful, too painful to be ignored. Unable to bear it, to dwell on it, she dragged herself up to a sitting position and drew her knees up. Wrapping her arms around her legs, she rested her forehead on her knees.

'Oh, Mama, Papa,' she whispered brokenly. 'Why didn't you tell me? Why did you let me believe all my life that I am Christina Thornton, your daughter?' Tears threatened, but she didn't break the dam of her self-control. She had to be strong, to get through this, and she would be, she had to be, and the sooner Max Lloyd realised she had no intention of becoming his wife and he had gone back to Italy, the better.

Deeply concerned about her daughter, Audine insisted—on Hal's instructions—that Christina remain in bed for twenty-four hours.

The following morning, bathed and seated at her dressing table and feeling much better, Christina was brushing the tangles out of her hair when Molly came to inform her that Mr Lloyd had arrived and was asking to speak to her.

Christina put the brush down with a clatter and turned to face Molly, her face as black as thunder. 'I don't want to see him, Molly. We have nothing to say to each other. Please go and tell Mr Lloyd that I am not up to seeing anyone. Papa can have a word with him.'

'He's been closeted with your parents in the drawing room for the past hour. He is now installed in the library with your brother, who has asked for coffee to be sent in.'

'Then let Peter entertain him. I'll stay out of the way until he's gone.'

'He will not leave until he's spoken to you. You know, you gave us all such a fright the other night. When I think of the state you were in when he brought you home, it was lucky he found you.'

'Yes,' Christina murmured with bitter sarcasm, 'wasn't it.'

'He came twice yesterday to see how you were, so he must be concerned. Don't you think you should see him and thank him for helping you? From what I've seen of Mr Lloyd, he'll keep coming back until you do.'

'No, Molly, and I won't be browbeaten into doing so—besides, when he found me I didn't want helping,' she said ungraciously.

Knowing this was not the case, but that it was no use

arguing with her when she was in this mood, and with her chin adamantly set, Molly went downstairs to tell Peter.

It was fifteen minutes later when Peter came himself to ask Christina to see Max. 'He's determined, Christina,' he informed her.

'I don't care. I don't want to see him.'

'Now you are being deliberately evasive,' he reproached sharply. 'As far as I can see Mr Lloyd has done no wrong and you are being unfair to him. You will have to see him some time.'

In the end Christina gave in, knowing Peter would give her no peace. Pausing with her hand on the drawing-room door handle, she took a deep breath, lifted her chin and quietly swept inside.

Chapter Five

Max was standing with his back partially to her, impatiently slapping his thigh with his gloves while he gazed out of the window overlooking the gardens. Beneath his exquisitely tailored tweed jacket his shoulders were squared and his jaw was set with implacable determination.

'You asked to see me,' Christina said crisply.

For the past half-hour Max had been kept waiting. Expecting a cold reception, he had told himself on his way here that no matter what she said to him he would be patient and understanding, but, the longer he was kept waiting, it was all he could do to bridle his temper and stop himself going to her room and dragging her out.

At the sound of her voice he turned, unprepared for the young woman who stood with her hands clasped in front of her. Dressed severely in a dark blue dress with a high neck, with her hair drawn from her face and neatly arranged, her head was held high, her back straight, and if her mama were to come in and see her she would have been proud, for, at last, all the training both she and her governess had tried to instil into this young girl was there to see. But Christina Thornton's eyes were not the eyes of a woman who was drowning in regret. These eyes were hardened green eyes chilled to chips of ice.

'Thank you for seeing me.' Max made no move to go to her.

Infuriated by his imperious tone, Christina raised her chin another notch. However, she was momentarily stunned when she saw the scratch marks down one cheek. 'I didn't want to. It was Peter who persuaded me. You are rather difficult to get rid of. Did I do that to your face?'

He nodded, his expression cool. 'No matter. You were distraught.'

'Yes, yes, I was. However, I do apologise. I don't usually go around hurting people.'

'I hope you aren't suffering any ill effects from your night ride, Christina.'

'Apart from the cut to my head I am fine. Unfortunately, I didn't anticipate being knocked off my horse. Peter told me it was found in the village and brought back yesterday morning. It was pretty scared by the thunder. It—all became too much that night. I had to get out of the house.'

His expression softened. 'I do realise that—and I understand.'

'Do you?'

Max sighed and took a few steps towards her. 'Yes, of course I do.'

'I don't believe you. No one can understand how I'm feeling.'

'I realise how difficult this is for you; since you're looking for someone to blame, then it might as well be me. I have a strong back, Christina. I can take it. Can you not at least have the common courtesy to listen to what I have to say?'

'You should have done that at the beginning—especially the bit about our betrothal, about which I knew nothing.'

'I couldn't do that, not without your parents' consent. You must see that.'

'They are not my parents,' she stated calmly. 'Whatever you have to say to me now, you will be wasting your breath, so, you see, your visit has been pointless. I told you that I am not interested in anything you have to say to me. I would like you to leave now.'

Max moved closer until he stood just two feet away from her. 'I know you would,' he said quietly, 'but I'm not going anywhere until you hear me out. Are you angry with your parents for deceiving you all these years?'

'No, I'm not angry with them. I'm not sitting in judgement on them either. And of course I want to know, to understand how it all came about, to know the whole sorry story, but not now. I can't bear it, you see.'

Although her eyes were glaring defiance at him, they were sparkling with suppressed tears. Max was moved by her outburst of feelings. 'I would like to help you bear it, Christina, if you would let me.'

Christina gave a hard, contemptuous little laugh. 'What? To help me know who I am? No one can do that. All my life has been a lie. I feel like a trespasser—with no roots, no rights in this house. The man and woman I have known all my life as my mother and father are not and never have been. Now I look at myself and ask—who do I look like? Whose eyes have I inherited? I always believed my character was an even mixture of both my parents. Now I feel fragmented— like a broken vase that won't fit back together. For the first time in my life I have been forced to look at myself and ask—who am I?'

'I can tell you. These are things you have a right to know, things you should know.'

'You expect me to submit to being told about a family who threw me out?'

g every aspect of it, and then he was gone,
behind him.

od there, holding the package, fragmented
misery. She stared down at the small package
ents before peeling off the wrapping. To her
t at all what she had expected, she saw it was
all brown fluffy bear with green beads for its
ort of thing babies had.

e in her throat and tears stung the backs of her
she thought back to the conversation they'd had
gone riding, that was the moment she realised
Max had loved and lost had been herself.

e window, she watched his departing figure.
been so shattered a few moments ago when he
e was going back to Italy? Why had she felt so
she believed she might be saying goodbye to
Was it because a grudging friendship had grown
, nourished by a teasing repartee?

way from the house, Max was unable to believe
ome to this. A wrenching stab of pain and loss
s innermost being, when, only a few weeks ago,
so confident that it would end with Christina ac-
him back to Italy, or arrangements being made
vel at a later date.

e thought this was the end then she was mistaken.
nce aside, from the moment he had seen her cavort-
ked in the lake his baser instincts had been stirred.
enough of her since that day to realise she had many
ributes, and he thought with pleasure of the children
produce—plus an heir for Castello Marchesi.
ack of it all he wanted the Carletti estate, and one

A look of irritation flashed across his face. 'Be sensible, Christina. They did not throw you out.'

'But this woman, my grandmother—I have formed my own opinion of her and it is not favourable—didn't want me, otherwise she would not have let me go. Why did she, and why, after all these years—when not a word has been heard from her, no enquiries into my education and my general well being—does she expect me to leave everything I know and love and go to live in Italy, as your wife?'

Blithely Max chose to ignore the bitterness that laced those last three words. 'It was all part of the arrangement she made with your parents at the time.' His lips curved in a slow, almost conspiratorial smile. 'I confess she is a bit of a tyrant.'

'Then if she is such a tyrant, why do you put up with her?'

'Italians are passionately loyal and protective to both friends and family. The family is of central importance in the fabric of Italian society.'

'Not, it would seem, where I was concerned.'

'I consider you part of my family, Christina—just as much as your grandmother.'

'For God's sake, Max,' she snapped viciously, 'I cannot just embrace her as though nothing has happened. What utter selfishness. Although perhaps it turned out for the best for me, because I've been raised by two wonderful people who have always loved me unconditionally.'

'Then you have been blessed indeed,' he said quietly, his face grave but calm. 'Christina, when I came to England I came solely because of you. I do care about you, you must believe that.'

'Because of me? I thought you came to be reacquainted with old friends,' she scoffed.

'I lied.'

'And now you have found me I suppose you are going to drag me back to Italy with you.'

'Had I any intention of dragging you to Italy,' he said tersely, 'I would not have come all this way to see you first. I would have ordered you to Tuscany on your eighteenth birthday.'

Christina could hardly contain her bitterness and animosity. 'I find a betrothal between the two of us outrageous,' she insisted angrily.

'Why is it?'

'Because you care only about yourself and what *you* want. I don't want to marry you.'

His eyes hardened. 'That's too bad. There is nothing unusual in our betrothal. In Italy it is often how things are done in families of note. And—I want a wife.'

'At any price, it would seem,' she bit back angrily. 'Will you not release me from the bargain that was made between my grandmother and my parents?'

'No, I'm afraid not.'

'Then please don't insult my intelligence by pretending to care for me, when we both know the real reason why you want to marry me. I promise you that if you force me into this, I will make you a cold wife.'

One black brow flicked upward in a measuring look. 'Are you threatening me, Christina?'

'Of course not. I'm merely pointing out how things will be and that my feelings won't change.'

'You are certain about that?'

'Absolutely.'

'This is a difficult time for you, I realise that. When you have had time to adjust, to think about everything, then arrangements can be made for you to travel to Tuscany.'

'I do not want to go,' (anger, but he seemed no

'If there is anything y(Italy tomorrow, I will not

Christina could not ex and nor did she care to anal and any hope for a reprieve her shoulders drooped in d

'Then—this is goodbye'

'For now.' His gaze feast fragrance of her perfume di was seized by a strong year he had when he had found he what I have said without ar Christina. Have the courage do not foolishly refuse what

Turning from her, he cross he seemed to remember so package off the table where come in, he carried it back to

'I almost forgot. I have a pres too late, but better late than nev

'If it is from my grandmothe

'I promise you it has nothing

Taking it from him, Christi 'What is it?'

'Something I wanted you to away from Castello Marchesi. It to the most beautiful little girl h what you will, Christina. It is you

Bidding her a formal and stilt door where he turned. His gaze li

was memorisin closing the doo

Christina st into splinters o for a few mom surprise and n an adorable sn eyes, just the s

A lump ros eyes, for when when they had that the perso

Going to t Why had she had told her l desolate whe him for ever? between ther

Striding a it had truly penetrated h he had been companying for her to tr

But if sh Her inherita ing semi-na He had seen pleasing att they would

At the b

way or another he wanted Christina Thornton. If she didn't create too much fuss, he would come out of it well.

Christina spent the rest of the day in her room. With her entire future hanging by a thread, it took supreme effort to sit through dinner and to ignore her parents' apprehensive glances. She knew their earlier meeting with Max had concerned her, and she wondered at the outcome. Impatient to know, she desperately wanted to speak of it, but noting the tired lines on her father's face and the dejected droop of his shoulders quelled any questions that sprang to her lips.

The moment dinner was over, she excused herself and went to her room. It wasn't long before her mother followed her, her features composed into a sympathetic smile. Christina, who was beside herself with worry, sprang up from the window seat where she was gazing bleakly out over the darkening landscape.

'Mama! I'm so glad you've come. Please tell me what the meeting was about between you and Max earlier. He actually intends for me to marry him, but he can't force me, can he?'

'Come, sit down.' Audine drew her daughter down beside her. 'Oh, my darling, of course Mr Lloyd can't force you to marry him.'

'You're quite certain?'

'I'm positive,' her mother soothed, smoothing the hair back from Christina's brow.

'And you won't make me?'

'No. Your father and I would not do that. We only want what is best for you, but—I think you should consider the consequences if you do not marry him.'

'Mama? What do you mean?' she questioned in helpless confusion, scrutinising her mother's non-committal face.

'What consequences? No one considered the consequences to me when that cruel bargain was struck, so I don't feel the slightest need to consider the consequences to Max Lloyd if I refuse to marry him. Besides, arranged marriages are so old fashioned. It isn't me he wants. It's what I will bring to the marriage when my grandmother dies—a vineyard and olive groves, apparently. It's all so degrading and insulting.'

'Try not to see it in that way, Christina.'

'I can't see it in any other way. And why on earth she doesn't just leave it all to Max is beyond me. I don't want anything from her, and it would save a lot of trouble and heartache if she did. And as for uniting two ancient Tuscan families, surely she did that when she married Max's grandfather.'

'Unfortunately, Christina, it doesn't work like that. Your inheritance—Casa del Sole—comes from your father. Your grandmother does not have the power to dispose of it; besides, she always lived in the hope that Roberto would return and work the estate. Now he is dead it will pass to you.' Reaching out, she took Christina's hand in hers and smiled gently. 'Would it really be so terrible if you married Mr Lloyd? It became obvious to me and your father when we spoke to him earlier that he has developed a great affection for you. He—is quite taken with you.'

'But, Mama,' Christina murmured blankly, 'I just feel that this is wrong.'

She looked with desperate appeal at the woman who had raised her, while in her mind she saw Max as she had come to know him, the Max who had patiently listened to her when she had told him how devastated she was to learn her parents were not who she thought they were, the Max who had kissed her with both tenderness and passion, wiping all thoughts of James from her mind, and the Max who had searched for her in the storm and given her comfort as he carried her home. How different that Max was to the Max who was determined to marry her at any cost—a ruthless Italian nobleman who considered property and the uniting of two old Tuscan families more important than he did her feelings.

'It may seem like that now, Christina, but you will have plenty of time to think about it. Your father and I agreed to the terms of the proviso your grandmother insisted upon. Had we not, she would never have allowed us to raise you here at Tanglewood—which I know Lydia would have wanted. Your—real father couldn't cope. He went away, so it was left to your grandmother to decide what was best for you.'

'In all these years, did she ever enquire about me?'

Audine sighed, shaking her head slowly. 'Sadly, no. You cannot condemn Mr Lloyd for wanting to marry you, and arranged marriages may be old fashioned, but they have been a custom in the best families for centuries—especially in Italy.' Gently she placed her fingers beneath Christina's chin, tipping her downcast face to hers. 'Can you honestly say you haven't felt a liking for Mr Lloyd—even against your will?'

There was no challenge in her mother's tone to justify an argumentative denial, and Christina's innate fairness, especially in the light of that devastating kiss, prevented her from speaking harshly. She shrugged awkwardly and looked away. 'Sometimes.'

'And against your will?' Audine teased.

In spite of herself, Christina smiled. 'Always against my will—and my better judgement.'

'Mr Lloyd will be leaving for Italy shortly so you will have plenty of time before you reach eighteen to consider what you want to do.'

'Mama, can I ask you something?'

'Of course. Anything.'

'Do you and Papa want me to marry him?'

'Only if it is what you want.' Her eyes clouded and she said tentatively, 'It—will make things very difficult for us if you don't, but if you're completely certain that you don't want to marry Mr Lloyd, then—we will support your decision.'

'Difficult?' Christina echoed in bewilderment. 'How will it make things difficult for you? Is there something else you haven't told me, because, if so, then you must.' It came to her in a wave of alarm sweeping over her that there was something amiss in all of this, something that didn't make any sense at all. Then slowly it began to penetrate what it was. Cautiously, she said, 'Has it anything to do with money, Mama? Is that it? Did my grandmother *pay* you to look after me?'

Audine didn't reply at once. She could feel Christina's nerves stretched taut, close to breaking, but she had weathered one storm and she was sure she would weather the next. 'Yes,' she whispered, 'yes, my darling, she did. So, you see, your papa and I—we are indebted to her. She has provided for you throughout your life on the basis that when you reach eighteen you will return to Italy and marry Max.'

'And if I don't?' she whispered, with sudden, heartbreaking clarity.

'If you refuse to honour the betrothal agreement, your grandmother will naturally demand that we repay the money.'

'But—Papa is very rich…'

'Only because your grandmother has made him so, Christina. We could never repay the amount of money she has given us over the years. We—just don't have that sort of capital.'

Suddenly the picture was complete, in every gruesome, horrendous detail. Drop by precious drop Christina felt all her confidence draining away. A wave of sick disgust swept over her. This was too much. She saw her mother through a bleary haze of scalding tears. Dragging air into her lungs from the thick knot of emotion in her chest, she said, 'So everything that I have—the clothes I am wearing, my horse, even the food I eat—that woman has paid for?'

Audine nodded.

'Then it is I who am in her debt. What kind of woman is she who can do something so vile, to organise my entire life as though I am nothing but a piece of property? She has left me with no other choice but to marry Max. Unless—perhaps there is someone who could advance Papa the funds—a purely business arrangement…?'

'No, I'm afraid not. Unless—we sell Tanglewood—'

'Sell Tanglewood?' Christina was horrified that such a thing should happen. 'No, Mama. I would never ask you to do that.' Her heart screaming her resentment, looking down at her hands she tried to think, tried to find some way of escape, but there was no loophole and no way out for her. Seventeen years ago her parents had agreed to the betrothal and her return to Italy in good faith and it would reflect badly on them if they reneged on their word. Raising her eyes, she looked directly into her mother's face. It was anguished, understanding, soft as Christina had never seen it before; also plain for her to see was her mother's love for her.

Audine put out her hand and took her beloved daughter's, and when she spoke her voice was torn with sorrow, and yet what she said she felt was right and true. 'Max is a good man, Christina. I really do believe that.'

'Do you, Mama? I hope so, because if not it will be unfortunate for me and hard to live with.'

'But you will. He will not harm you, Christina, for you will not let him. You have spirit. You are strong. Lydia was strong, and you are so like her. Make this decision and be proud. Make him love you.'

'I don't know if I care to have his love, but I will marry him.' She sighed and shrugged her shoulders. 'What does it matter?'

Christina lay in bed in the semi-darkness. The night was still and humid, with only the slightest stirring of the curtains. When she heard the clocks strike midnight she climbed out of bed and went to the window and opened it wide. The moon and stars illuminated the ground and trees and she peered down at the garden, feeling as though she had been born anew. Anger still simmered quietly in her breast, anger at her grandmother and Max.

But beneath that was the need to know who she really was, whose child she was, because until she knew she would never feel entirely complete. Tomorrow Max would leave and she would not see him again until she was eighteen. Did she not want to know about Italy? Her family? Her real father? The Carletti family? Despite the shocking way her grandmother had assumed complete control over her life, did she not want to know about all this? Yes, she had to admit that she did. Very much.

The following morning found her standing uncertainly at Max's door. It opened before she could knock.

'Signorina Thornton,' Lorenzo said in his heavily accented voice, seeming pleased to see her. 'How very nice it is to see you again.'

'Hello, Lorenzo. I know how busy both you and Mr Lloyd must be, but do you think I could see him?'

'Come in—please. Mr Lloyd is busy—we have to catch the train for London this afternoon, you understand, but I know he will spare the time to see you. It will be a pleasure. Would you please wait in the garden and I'll go and tell him you are here.'

Christina entered the quiet, scented garden through the French windows, wandering deep in thought, absently touching flowers, then sitting on a bench in a small arbour.

Max came to the open glass door and paused, arrested by the sight of her, by the sheer beauty of the picture she made surrounded by clambering pink and white roses. With her hair falling in a glorious tumble about her shoulders and her chin tilted with a quiet pride, she seemed alluring and elusive, and lost and lonely and vulnerable, and he was going to miss her like hell.

Sensing his presence, Christina turned her face towards him. Instantly all her anxieties returned and she blamed herself bitterly for disregarding them. Standing up, she waited quietly and calmly for him to reach her, her eyes enormous in her pale face. With his black hair and white lawn shirt and cream trousers, he looked incredibly attractive, and as he strode towards her she noticed his limbs were strong and toned, his flesh radiating the healthy luminescence of having enjoyed many long hours beneath the Italian sun. Despite how hard she struggled against it, each moment she spent with him she grew closer to him emotionally, and her mind fiercely warned her to draw back.

Max's eyes looked directly into hers, his expression unreadable, neither warm nor cold. The torment in Christina's mind showed on her face and, seeing it, he guessed at the questions there.

'Christina! I am surprised to see you. I thought we'd said our goodbyes yesterday.'

His direct, masculine assurance disconcerted her, but she was determined not to show weakness. 'We did, but there is something else that must be taken care of before you leave—an important matter that has a bearing on my decision about marrying you.'

'And what is that?'

'I now know that my grandmother has provided for my up-bringing. Mama told me last night. You can have no idea how that has made me feel.'

'I think I can.'

'No, you can't,' she broke out furiously, her eyes gleaming like two hard green stones. 'It would seem I am under obligation to marry you. I owe my parents a debt of gratitude—I am indebted to my grandmother for different reasons. How dare she place me in this position—and you, because by agreeing to the betrothal you condone what she has done and that makes you just as bad.'

'Christina, listen to me—'

'No, Max, you listen to me. If I refuse to fall in with her plans, what will she do? Demand her pound of flesh and force my parents to return the money, knowing they can't and would be forced to sell their beloved home or face life in a debtors' prison?'

His expression hardened. 'Stop it. Now you are being ridiculous.'

'No, I'm not. I will not let that happen, so I will agree to the marriage, even though I am against it and it feels like I am signing my own death warrant.'

His eyes narrowed and darkened angrily. 'I do not like your tone, Christina.'

'What you like or dislike is a matter of supreme indifference to me, Max,' she said cuttingly. 'I really do not care.'

'I appreciate that you have had a severe shock and that you are suffering the aftermath of it and I am prepared to be patient. I cannot condemn you for your reaction.'

'Don't you dare, and do not patronise me either.' Her natural resilience began to reassert itself. She shook back her long dark hair and glared at him. 'From the moment my real mother died I have been a pawn to be used by my grandmother. I am the one who is in her debt, not my parents. I will marry you, Max, because I have been left with no choice, but I will not marry you a day before I am eighteen. How it is done is up to you, since it is all part of the deal you struck with my parents. But I shall have a say in what happens after that.'

'I am happy with your decision, Christina.'

Christina knew by the sudden gleam of triumph in his eyes that he knew that he had triumphed. 'Don't look so smug, Max.' she retorted contemptuously. 'I haven't finished.'

'No?'

Disliking his easy manner, Christina looked at him with growing annoyance. She moved closer to him. 'Far from it. I know that a debt is something which cannot be dismissed with a click of one's fingers—and yet I know it is a debt that my grandmother is prepared to wipe away at the stroke of a pen on the day I become your wife—and it would be a pity if her generosity was not appreciated or accepted,' she said sarcastically.

Max's jaw tightened and a glint of anger showed in his eyes. 'You are being unnecessarily hard on your grandmother, Christina. Perhaps when you come to know her you will feel differently.'

'I don't want to know her—the woman who is the architect of all my wretchedness, who planned my future with utter disregard for my own feelings in the matter? I don't think so. I cannot forget that. From the very start, unbeknown to me she has had complete control over me and has called the tune. Now it is my turn. Yes, Max, I will marry you, but I will not be a true wife to you. I will be your wife in name only.'

Max smiled inwardly. He wasn't unduly concerned about her announcement, for he was securely confident in the knowledge that he would have no difficulty in luring her into his bed when she was his wife. He put a finger under her chin and tilted her face upwards. For a moment she resisted him and then she raised her eyes and looked him straight in the face. He laughed gently, his lips curling mockingly, but there was a fire in his eyes that told her all too clearly that her resistance excited him.

'Have it your way for now, Christina, but remember this. I know how you feel when you are in my arms, I have seen it in your eyes and felt how you reacted to my kiss, and if you think you can stand against me indefinitely you are mistaken. When you bear my name I will have the right to do what I will to my own wife. You will be mine body and soul—you and your possessions—so let that be an end to the matter.'

There was a warning underlying the lightness of his words and Christina knew that he spoke in all seriousness. Max Marchesi was a man who must conquer whatever the odds against him and she knew she could expect no mercy from him and that his passion would never be satisfied until she had surrendered herself to him absolutely. The deep timbre of his voice reverberated in her breast and she gave up trying to discern what his faults might be.

Dropping his hand, he stepped away from her. 'Now that is settled, tell me, did you like my gift?' he asked, with casual dismissal of everything that had been said and expecting her to do the same without further argument.

'Yes,' she replied tightly, still struggling with her resentment. 'Thank you for the bear. It's so sweet.'

'I'm glad you like it. I'm happy to have given it to you after all this time. So,' he said, with tender gravity, 'is there something else that has brought you here?'

'I did want to thank you for the bear, but—I—you said I should come if I—I wanted to talk…' She paused, hoping he would say something to help her, but he remained silent, watching her. Drawing a long breath she said, 'I would like to talk.'

Max's dark blue eyes looked at her with piercing intensity. 'So, what do you want to talk about, Christina? Have you changed your mind about wanting to know about your family?'

She swallowed and nodded. 'Yes—I mean no…' She sighed, shaking her head miserably. 'In truth, I don't know what I want. I'm so confused about everything. All I know is that nothing is the same any more, and when you go back to Italy I'll—I'll not be able to ask you about—things, and there is no one else to tell me.'

'And are you sure you want to know about your family— about your grandmother?'

She nodded. 'Although I cannot understand the kind of woman who would hand her grandchild over to someone else to raise and pay them to do so.'

'That someone else did happen to be your real mother's sister, Christina, so it was not so very bad. Your grandmother did not forget you, she merely got on with her life. Come, sit down and I will explain.'

They sat facing each other on the bench. Max casually propped his ankle on the opposite knee, his gaze settling on her face. He gave her a long slow look, a twist of humour around his beautifully moulded lips. She was quiet, thoughtful, but beneath it he could sense her anger and resentment bubbling away. He wished to put her at her ease, so let the smile build about his mouth, creasing the hardness of his jaw.

'No matter what you tell me,' Christina murmured, 'I want you to know that my parents—the two people who loved and raised me—will always be my true parents. No one can ever take their place. I would like to know something about my real father. My mother has told me about Lydia, but she did not see much of her after she went to Italy. Did you know her?'

'Yes, I did. She was several years older than me. I liked her very much.'

'Do I look like her?'

'Yes, the resemblance is startling. She was very beautiful— at least I thought so. I was only a child, but I remember thinking how lovely she was—lovely and carefree, with an enormous capacity for having fun. She was also courageous— with a rebellious nature, spirited, forthright, honest and caring—and she had dark hair and brown eyes.'

'Mine are green.'

He smiled softly. 'I've noticed.'

'Did my father have green eyes?'

'Your father? Yes, I believe he did.'

'Did Lydia love him very much?'

Max slanted her a soft smile. 'I think she must have done, don't you?'

'I'd like to think so.'

'If I tell you something of how things were back then, it will help you to understand. Your grandmother was a respectable widow woman—wealthy in her own right after her husband Signor Carletti died—and a close neighbour. My grandfather was a widower and they married. Your mother and Roberto—your grandmother's only offspring to her first marriage—married and lived at Casa del Sole—it has been the home of the Carletti family for generations. When your mother died you were brought to Castello Marchesi to be cared for by your grandmother.'

'And my father? What was he like?'

'He was a quiet man, living his life very much in his mother's shadow. He loved your mother deeply—in fact, he simply worshipped her and they were devoted to each other. When you were born he was so happy—they both were—and when she died he couldn't quite believe it. No one could. She died suddenly, quietly, one week after your birth. The doctor said it was a blood clot that killed her.

'Your father was consumed with grief, and then he was violently angry. He withdrew into himself. He couldn't bear being near anyone. And that's why he arrived at Castello Marchesi with you.'

'Did he blame me for my mother's death?'

'I think he did, but he also blamed the midwife and anyone else who was close to Lydia at the time.'

'How did my grandmother react to him?'

'Characteristically she told him to pull himself together and get on with things, which is her way. One day he left and never came back. That was the last anyone saw of him, until a letter came from a captain of a merchant vessel, informing your grandmother of his death just two months ago. Apparently when he left Castello Marchesi he went to France and found work in the dockyards in Marseilles.'

'How very sad. How I wish I could have known him. Perhaps if my grandmother had been of a more caring nature, he would not have left.'

'We will never know, Christina. One thing you should know about your grandmother is that she is a strictly controlling character. She comes from a long line of rigidly upright people with impossibly high standards for themselves and everyone else, people who despised weakness in any form.'

'And my father was a weak man, it would seem. Little

wonder he went away—I would like to believe it was not me he was running away from, but his domineering mother.'

Observing the pain in her eyes, Max's heart constricted with an emotion so intense that it made him ache. 'You were a beautiful baby, Christina. I would go to the nursery every day to see you. Rosa, your *bambinaia*—your nursemaid—adored you. She was inconsolable when you were taken away.' His eyes became clouded with memory. 'It was a great blow to us all. One thing your grandmother insisted upon was that you were to be told of your true parentage. She was most insistent and would not let you go otherwise.'

'But why?'

'Because you were the Carletti heir. It may surprise you to know that she even put some small items belonging to your mother into a box to be given to you when you were older.'

Christina stared at him in puzzlement. 'She did that? Then—the box must be in the house somewhere. I'll ask Mama.'

'There may be something there that will make you feel close to your real mother—a bond, perhaps, that will offer comfort.'

Christina sighed and looked at Max. He was watching her, totally relaxed. 'Were you lonely when you were growing up at Castello Marchesi?' she asked suddenly. 'I recall you saying that you have no brothers or sisters and that your mother died when you were born, so what about your father?' When she saw his expression stiffen she thought she was treading into forbidden territory, but she went on anyway. 'Were you close to him?'

He shook his head and a deeply rooted bitterness darkened his eyes. 'Sadly, no. My father was rife with every kind of weakness your grandmother despised. He drank too much and squandered money. He never worried about tomorrow and didn't give a damn about anyone but himself—not even his own father when he was alive. He died at a drunken party in Rome, where he had taken his latest lover for the weekend.'

'I'm sorry.'

He gave her a wry smile. 'Don't be. I learned to live with it. Without your grandmother there would have been nothing left. Her icy demeanour always seemed inhuman to me and even as a child I disliked her, but as I grew older and saw my father sink into degradation, I came to respect her and her will to overcome. In fact, I have come to admire her very much. She sets terribly high standards for everyone, but at least she *has* standards. Knowing she couldn't change my father, she handled his wild, philandering ways the only way she knew how—by holding her head up as best she could, getting on with what had to be done and pretending she didn't know what was going on.

'She was there when I needed someone very badly. When my grandfather died and with my father absent for most of the time, until I finished my education she kept things running. So you see, Christina, despite the harsh treatment you think she meted out to you by sending you away, I owe her a debt of gratitude—you also. Because of her you grew up safe and secure with people who love you.'

'And now it's time for me to repay that debt,' Christina said, unable to conceal the bitterness she felt. 'No doubt she expects me to return with you to Italy.'

'She knows that going to live at Castello Marchesi as my wife will be a big step for you and expects you will want to wait until you are eighteen.'

Christina got to her feet and looked down at him. 'Yes, it is. But don't worry, Max. I shall adhere to my decision to marry you. I have given you my promise.' She tucked a lock of hair that had slipped over her cheek behind her ear. 'I think

I have kept you long enough. You must have things to do if you are to leave this afternoon.'

'Lorenzo has everything in hand. We have plenty of time before we have to journey to Cambridge to catch our train. Come, I'll walk back with you.'

As much as Christina resented the way she was being manoeuvred into marriage, she was strangely reluctantly to part from him and didn't try to dissuade him from accompanying her.

'So,' Max said as they walked slowly along the quiet, leafy lane towards Tanglewood, 'how do you feel now you know how things were when you were born?'

Christina was quiet for what seemed an age, and then she looked at him, unable to disguise the trauma in her startling green eyes. 'I feel so many things, but mainly I feel both furious at the way I am being manipulated and yet sad—especially for my real father. How unhappy he must have been. If only people didn't keep secrets, life would be so much simpler. I'm—also afraid of the future.'

'Don't be. You have courage, Christina. You will come through this. You're a fighter.'

She gave him a wry smile. 'Mama said something like that. I wish I had your confidence.'

'You will survive. Nothing lasts for ever.'

'I truly hope not. Just now I feel as though I'm being pulled in several directions and I resent it bitterly. I resent you. I'm going to have to be strong to come to terms with what's happened—discovering who I am and not who I thought I was, to adapt to the fact that I am not an English girl, but half-Italian. It's like gaining a whole new identity—but I don't want to lose the identity I have always had because it would mean losing the very essence of myself. Can you understand that?'

'Yes, yes, I can, and if she could see you now, Lydia would be very proud of the way you have turned out.'

She laughed lightly. 'Even though I'm terribly spoiled, too proud for my own good and terribly wilful?'

'Traits she would have recognised in herself.'

They walked on a little way in silence. Max turned and looked at her profile, tracing with his gaze the classical lines of her face. She was quite extraordinarily lovely. He had never seen the like of her. She had an untamed quality running in dangerous undercurrents, a wild freedom of spirit, just below the surface. For Max Lloyd, Italian nobleman, she represented everything most desirable in a woman.

'When you come to Italy, to Tuscany, you will like it, I know.'

'And Castello Marchesi? Is it very beautiful?'

'I think so—but then it is my home so I am biased. It is the estate's showpiece—once a medieval fortress with a colourful history. It stands in rolling countryside of olive groves, cypress trees and vineyards, overlooking villages and the villas of my neighbours.'

Having reached the bottom of the drive, Christina stopped and turned to him. 'I'll be all right now. You had better go back.' Thinking that he would go and leave her, she was about to turn away, but he wasn't finished yet.

'Not before we have said goodbye.'

Max took her hands and drew her towards him so that his hips leaned hard and flat against her skirts. Christina swallowed nervously. She wasn't used to men like Max Lloyd. His powerful masculinity was an assault on her senses. He was standing very close. She had to look up to him. Impatiently she tried to shake off the effect he was having on her. Why had she allowed him to walk back with her? Why had she allowed herself to be attracted by him—and why, oh, why did she want him to kiss her when he was one of those responsible for all her misery?

As he bent his head, his firmly chiselled lips began a slow, deliberate descent towards her. At first he kissed her lightly, as he would a child. She tried not to show surprise or emotion, but that first touch was exquisite. His lips were warm, his kiss soft, and he kissed her long and lingeringly, a compelling kiss that made her head swim, and in that moment when Max felt her lips soften involuntarily, the girl in his arms became an enticing woman, and he realised that leaving her today was going to be harder than he'd imagined. Without realising what he was doing, his arms went round her with stunning force and he deepened his kiss.

That was the moment when Christina's mind went blank as his sensual mouth seized possession of hers in an endless, long drugging kiss that quickly built to one of demanding insistence and shook her to the core of her being. The world began to tilt as he crushed her tighter to the hard length of his body, parting her lips and exploring the honeyed softness of her mouth. Whether from fear or desire, Christina moaned softly. She clung tighter to him, raising her arms and sliding her fingers into the crisp hair above his collar.

By the time Max finally raised his head, Christina's weakened defences crumbled completely. She felt dazed and her body quivered with all the raw emotions and the mindless pleasure he was capable of arousing in her.

He tipped her chin. 'Look at me, *caro.*'

That deep, husky voice calling her darling was almost capable of making her do anything. She dragged her wide, wary gaze up to his smouldering blue eyes.

'Now do you accept that you will marry me?' he murmured huskily.

Abruptly Christina recollected herself. She knew exactly what he was trying to do—to shatter her defences and make her pliant to his will. Her body had responded eagerly, then mingled rage at his impertinence and horror at her own reaction caused her to break away with a violence that brought her staggering back. The spell was broken.

'Max, stop it. Don't touch me. How dare you do that? Kissing me in so cavalier a fashion—as if you already own me.'

He smiled lazily, his white teeth flashing from between parted lips. 'Come now, Christina, you are being unreasonable.'

'Unreasonable? Because I don't want you to kiss me?'

'But you do. Be honest with yourself and admit it.'

The amusement in his tone made her blood boil. She faced him squarely with her elbows akimbo and her eyes hurtling daggers at him. The memory of that burning kiss, and the dark, hidden pleasure it had stirred in her, roused her to fresh paroxysms of anger.

'You think I am so easy, don't you? Well, you are wrong. You may force yourself on me now if that is your desire, but I will be no more yours after we are wed as I am now. I will not be bullied. Never again will you treat me casually. And remember what I said. Until I am eighteen this is my home and I will not leave until that day. So be gone, Max—back to your castle and cool your heels. Leave me in peace.'

Before Max could stop her, with one final glare she whirled and stamped her way up the lane towards the house.

Shaking his head and smiling to himself, Max turned and headed back the way he had come. He turned and looked back when he came to a final bend in the lane, unable to resist the view of swinging skirts and trim back he was afforded. Even as he watched her march on, he counted it strange that the memory of that one kiss should return to warm his body so strongly. It would seem they were caught up in something that could not easily be cooled, and he doubted distance or the eight months before they would meet again would have any effect on the heat of their emotions.

Chapter Six

Over the weeks and months that followed, Christina was forced to grow up quickly and found it increasingly important that she should keep herself occupied. But beneath her calm exterior she endured a sickening turmoil of inevitability, knowing that very soon she would have to part from the two people who had given her a sense of worth and for whom she had borne a real and unselfish love.

She was unable to still the confusion of thoughts in her head, to still the tempest of her emotions Max had stirred in her. He had aroused her, angered her, made her think and feel, and when he had gone he had left a vacuum in her life that nothing and no one could fill. The disruption his arrival had brought to Tanglewood affected everyone, and they became resigned to the fact that Christina would soon go to Tuscany and marry Max.

The house was quiet for most of the time. There were few social events, although family and friends continued to call frequently. Peter was in his final year at university and came home at every opportunity. Christina saw very little of James, and she was surprised how this didn't bother her any more.

Her eyes no longer sought him out and her heart no longer stirred when she was in his presence.

The box her grandmother had asked to be given to her, the box Max had told her about, her mother gave her. They opened it together. It was a poignant moment for them both, and it was a while before Christina could bring herself to look inside.

It was small and tied around with a blue ribbon. Inside there was nothing of value, just an assortment of small trinkets, simple things a girl would have. They meant nothing to Christina, but they had to the young woman they had belonged to: a comb adorned with colourful beads, a hair pin with a flower, a lovely brooch of fine filigree gold set with bright red beads and a black bead in the centre—a poppy, the rich colour twinkling when it caught the light. There was a narrow ring—a twisted silver rope—Lydia's wedding ring, her mother told her, and, most touching of all, at the bottom of the box was a rosary and a prayer book.

Despite the resentment she felt towards her grandmother, Christina was deeply touched by the thought she had given to organising the box—an indication that the old woman had at least one redeeming feature. Placing the ring on the third finger of her right hand, she found it to be a perfect fit, and, taking some small comfort from having it there, she placed everything else back in the box.

As time went on she became restless with a sense of fore-boding. Despite herself she had been counting the days, and as her eighteenth birthday drew near she wondered which one would herald the Italian count. When the day finally arrived, there were still no words of his intended arrival.

Returning to the house from riding out with Peter and having left him at the stables, she was met by one of the servants.

'Your parents are in the drawing room and there's a gentleman with them, Miss Christina.'

'A gentleman?' Christina enquired, removing her hat and placing it on the hall table.

'I don't know what he's here for, but he's come all the way from Italy and he's been sent by Count Marchesi.'

Christina took a long steadying breath and smoothed her hair. 'Then I'd better see why he's here.'

As she entered the room, a gentleman seated conversing with her parents came to his feet. A large leather case was on the floor beside his chair.

'Christina, this is Signor Benito Massa,' her father said in introduction. 'He's a lawyer sent by Count Marchesi.'

Rising, Signor Massa bowed his sleek dark head. 'It's a pleasure to meet you, Miss Thornton,' he said, expressing genuine delight at meeting Christina. He was a man in middle age with skin tones approaching a deep mahogany from his endless summers beneath the hot sun, and despite his near perfect English he was clearly Italian.

'You have come a long way, Signor Massa,' Christina said politely, while feeling a tightening of apprehension in her chest.

'From Sienna. Count Marchesi went to some length to tell me about his visit to England and his betrothal to you, but he failed to inform me of your youth and that you are a very lovely English lady.'

'You obviously see things differently to Count Marchesi,' Christina replied drily. 'But tell me, how do you know Max and what has your acquaintance with that gentleman to do with your visit?'

Signor Massa was confused by her veiled sneer and politely explained. 'I have been associated with the Marchesi family for a good many years, and my father and grandfather before that.'

'Signor Massa is here to arrange the details of the marriage, Christina,' her father informed her.

'I see,' she said. 'And you have a letter from Count Marchesi?'

'I have more than that,' he replied, hastening to produce some documents from his case.

'And the bridegroom? When is he arriving?'

'He isn't, I'm afraid. Count Marchesi has been—inconvenienced—and is unable to make the trip to England, which is why he has sent me. I bear his proxy and together with Father Whitfield—who, I believe, is your parish priest—we will perform the service in Count Marchesi's absence. It simplifies the matter since you are both of the Catholic faith.'

Christina stared at him through a haze of red. Never had she heard the like. 'Do you mean to tell me that Max can't even be bothered to turn up for his own wedding?'

'I told you, Miss Thornton—he has been—inconvenienced.'

'Has he, indeed! Well, Signor Massa, I am tempted to send you straight back to your client to tell him to—'

'Christina,' her father said sharply, getting to his feet. 'Signor Massa is here for no other reason than to see that the wedding is carried through efficiently, without delay and any drawbacks. I think we would all appreciate your co-operation in this, since one way or another it has to be done.'

Christina looked at him, longing to argue and shout her resentment, but she held on to her self-control and tried to see the logic of it. She knew from experience that to confront Max now would lead to argument and strife, and it was probably best, for the moment at least, to avoid any confrontation with her errant fiancé. But the disappointment she felt by his absence from what should be the most poignant and important moment of any girl's life was real and the pain went deep.

'Very well. But of all the men in all the world, only Max

Marchesi could manage to obtain a bride and marry her while she is on one side of it and he on the other—to exchange vows with a woman who has no other choice,' she exclaimed bitterly. 'It's a strange kind of marriage and bodes ill for the future.'

'I sincerely hope not, Miss Thornton, and I am deeply sorry if Count Marchesi's absence causes you any distress. The marriage will be legal and binding in any court of law,' Signor Massa told her, having been warned by the Count himself of the young woman's stubborn independence and trying to soothe her ire as much as possible.

'I am sure it will be, Signor Massa. Max will have been sure to block any loophole that might offer me a way of escape.'

And so, in the absence of her bridegroom, Christina uttered her vows before Signor Massa and a priest with that strange sensation of helplessness and fatality which one sometimes has in a dream.

Christina, now Countess Marchesi, and an excited and well-organised Molly—who had jumped at the chance to go with Christina to Italy as her companion, accompanied by Signor Massa, who was to escort them to Tuscany—left Tanglewood for London on the first stage of their journey.

The parting from her parents and Peter was painful and it was difficult tearing herself away, to leave behind her all the happiness she believed she had ever known.

In London the hotel where they spent the night was close to Victoria Station, from where they caught the boat train for the Continent the next day. From Paris they travelled to Italy. Although singularly uneventful, it was a long journey and an exciting one. The train puffed its way through villages and towns and beautiful farmland threaded with rivers. It was early summer and the weather still reasonably pleasant for travelling.

The Alps were an awesome, splendid sight and had a strange, solemn beauty. They were highly picturesque, with effervescing springs rushing down the mountainsides into the valleys below, the lofty peaks reaching up into a cloudless clear blue sky. On reaching Turin the hotel they stayed at was both solid and respectable, the perfect place to enjoy the taste of luxury after the long and tiring train journey south. Leaving Turin, Sienna was their destination, where they arrived a day ahead of schedule. Largely surrounded by its medieval walls, Sienna was considered one of Italy's most enchanting cities.

Having read about it on the train, Christina was keen to see some of the places of interest the city had to offer, in particular the Duomo, Sienna's great black-and-white cathedral, and stroll through the Piazza del Campo, which was reputed to be one of the loveliest public spaces in the world, but Signor Massa was keen to travel on to Castello Marchesi where he could relinquish his charge. After one night at the hotel, the morning found them seated in a hired carriage, their luggage strapped to the back, riding out of the ancient Italian town. The driver headed in a westerly direction across a beautiful and constantly changing landscape.

'Is Castello Marchesi very far?' Christina asked, while Molly sat demurely beside her, observing the scenery in wide-eyed silence.

'Some considerable distance—approximately ten miles,' Signor Massa told her, his leather satchel containing the precious marriage documents on the seat beside him. 'We should arrive before dusk.'

'What is it like?'

'Very grand and very big. You will be impressed, I promise you. It also produces some of the best wine in the area.'

Christina settled back to enjoy the ride. The afternoon was

peaceful, the air heavy with the perfume of blossoms and the drone of bees. The track they were following reached a junction marked by a shrine—a beautiful little statue of the Madonna in a niche with fresh flowers at her feet.

Taking the right-hand track, they continued up a hill with hawthorn hedges dripping with blossom on either side. Multicoloured butterflies flitted in the warm sunshine, and the birdsong was most pleasant. The hills offered wonderful vistas of the countryside—of vine and pasture, a lush forest in between, crags and terraced stone-walled hillsides, cypress groves and lofty castles and Romanesque churches and farms, of which there seemed to be hundreds devoted to the grape and the olive.

Signor Massa talked intermittently, telling her the names of the villages that clung to the hillsides, places of interest and the people of character who lived in the places they passed.

As they neared Castello Marchesi, Christina wondered what to expect. For the last few miles her trepidation about meeting Max again increased. Seated with his back to the driver, Signor Massa turned and stared straight ahead at something in the distance. When he turned back to his companions there was a faint smile playing about his lips. Christina looked ahead to see what he had been looking at, and her eyes widened with awe at the incredible beauty spread out before her.

Directly in front of them, decked out in golden splendour, lay a valley dotted with farms and neatly tended fields and olive groves and a picturesque village. And on a wide plateau stood a castle, with soaring turrets and glass windows glinting in the sun like so many jewels.

'What is that, Signor Massa?'

'That, Countess, is Castello Marchesi.'

Christina was awestruck. The structure was arrogant and strong—just like its owner—menacing in a way, but utterly beautiful and imposing. She found it difficult to withdraw her gaze from it.

'But—I never imagined it would be quite so grand.'

The closer they got, Christina continued to admire the splendour and symmetry of Castello Marchesi. Dark cypress trees marked the skyline, along with chestnut and oak. Terraces, walkways and bowers where wisteria thrived lay on either side of the drive. Several smart carriages were lined up in front of the house. Christina was nervous about entering this immense establishment unexpectedly. She looked to her escort for help.

'Max has guests. I can't possibly go in when there are other people.'

'Yes, you can.' He smiled kindly, having become inordinately fond of this young woman the more he had got to know her. 'You are his wife and mistress of all this. If you can't enter, then who can?'

'I know, but how can I?' Her voice pleaded with him. 'I'm hot and dusty and my dress is creased and dishevelled from the journey.'

Signor Massa laughed at her. 'Don't worry. Take it from me, Countess, there is nothing wrong with the way you look. If you walk in with enough assurance, you will convince everyone that you have a right to be there—which indeed you have—and no one will see the defects.'

Christina hesitated. She did have a perfect right to be there, but it didn't stop her from being nervous. 'How I wish I had your confidence.' Looking at the impressive closed double doors at the top of a short flight of stone steps, she took a deep, determined breath. 'Well, here goes. Wish me luck.'

Signor Massa paused to have a word with the driver, and Molly hung back to help supervise the unloading of the luggage.

Reaching the doors, Christina hesitated for a moment before tugging at the bell pull. In that brief time the door was opened by the imposing figure of a rather sombre footman dressed in black. She asked to see Count Marchesi and was surprised when he also replied in near-perfect English. Nervous and forgetful of her title, she gave her name as Miss Thornton.

Feeling very much the foreigner, Christina was overawed by the interior of Castello Marchesi. After leaving the temporary haven of the carriage, she stepped into a hall filled with flowers and light, her feet sliding silently on a floor of black-and-white marble mosaic. Corinthian pillars, tall white marble statues and magnificent furniture were displayed under massive glittering chandeliers dripping with crystal. A wide staircase carpeted in deep-blue rose from the centre to the upper floor, where it split to form a graceful gallery on either side. Through an open door she could see into a room with a large table surrounded by people sharing a meal, the hum of laughter rising and mingling with the conversation.

One particular dark-haired woman, exquisitely dressed in an ice-blue gown with diamond earrings flashing against her cheeks, said something to the dark-haired gentleman sitting next to her, and then she laughed, her laughter as light as a balloon sailing up into the sky. The man was unmistakably Max. He looked so poised, so debonair. A half-slow smile curved his lips. The two were easy with each other—familiar.

Christina's breath suddenly caught between her teeth and she was unprepared for the painful thrust to her heart—and also something else that was decidedly unpleasant, and if she were to analyse it she would discover it was something akin to jealousy. When the servant bent and spoke quietly to Max, he raised his fine, dark eyebrows and finally looked in the direction of the door. Excusing himself, he quickly left the table.

Christina carefully refrained from gazing at the masterpieces displayed on the walls, for suddenly there he was, Max, striding quickly towards her to receive his bride, his heels clicking on the marble floor. He was achingly familiar and just as she remembered: keen features, fine-boned face, taut, bronzed skin and deep blue eyes, his thick black hair brushed smoothly from his forehead. Suddenly and inexplicably Christina's heart gave a joyful beat.

The vision awaiting Max made him pause in his stride. In her white dress and with her back to the open doorway, Christina looked like a heavenly apparition, a radiant silhouette with the sun behind her. A world of feelings flashed across his face—disbelief, surprise, happiness, but only fleetingly. As he came closer his expression cooled.

'Christina, what is this?' He was unable to conceal his surprise. 'I expected to be greeting my countess, not Miss Thornton.' His voice was soft, though his smile was knowingly chiding.

'You are. I forgot. I haven't had time to get used to it.'

'Where the devil have you sprung from? I was not expecting you
until tomorrow.'

As Christina stepped forwards with a quaking reluctance, clutching her bonnet in her hands, her lips curved in an uncertain smile. Drop by precious drop she felt her confidence draining away, especially when those thoroughly blue eyes locked on her and slowly appraised her. In some strange way they seemed capable of seeing right inside her. It was all she could do to face his unspoken challenge and not turn and flee.

'We arrived ahead of schedule, I'm afraid. Signor Massa was impatient to get here.'

The silky smoothness of her voice sent a tingle down Max's spine as he remembered that same voice in England, raised in anger, when they had parted all those months ago, and now he found the green eyes smiling at him with warmth. He couldn't describe how he felt for her because he didn't have any words. All he knew was that he felt strange, different from anything he had expected to feel or would ever feel again when he'd left her. Seeing her in Castello Marchesi, he felt as if she had always been there, or as if he'd spent his entire life waiting for her to be there.

'I—I hope you don't mind.'

'Mind? It's high time you were here. Welcome to Castello Marchesi—your home. Allow me to compliment you. You look very well.'

The formal tone and stiff manner of this polite, uninterested and incredibly handsome stranger threw Christina off balance. She had in the very least expected a light kiss on the cheek by way of greeting—which was not unusual when a man met his wife for the first time, but he made no move to approach her. Stiffened by pride, with a tremendous effort she managed to dominate her disappointment.

In spite of his cool welcome, she was suddenly overwhelmed by a warm rush of tenderness. She was suddenly so sharply conscious of her deep attraction for him that she had to make an effort not to throw her arms about his neck. But Max was not a man like any other. The impulses that would have been so natural to an ordinary mortal must be mastered until it suited his pleasure. It began to dawn on her that this was a man different to the one she had known in England. He had been an intrusion into her life. Now his manner bore an odd touch of threatening boldness.

'I know my arrival has taken you by surprise, Max, but you might at least look pleased to see me,' she said tersely.

He gave a short laugh. 'I am delighted to see you, Christina—and you have your maid with you, I see.' He cast a glance at Molly, who was hovering in the doorway with a bag in each hand. He gestured with a flash of his eyes to a servant to relieve her of her burden. 'I hope you didn't find the journey too arduous.'

'Oh, you know me, Max,' she said airily, 'I was never one to be afraid to meet new challenges. And Molly is my companion, not my maid. The journey from Sienna took us longer than expected. There was so much to see we had to keep stopping on the way, and Castello Marchesi is very beautiful. Why didn't you tell me it would be like this—and so big? Why, it's like a palace.'

Max smiled easily for the first time. 'Why should I spoil this moment of pleasure at seeing the sheer amazement on your face?' he countered.

When a burst of laughter disturbed the quietness of the hall, Christina looked uneasily towards the door where he was entertaining his guests. 'I'm sorry. I'm intruding. You have guests.'

'It makes no difference. Come now. It will give me great pleasure to introduce my wife to everyone.' He held out his hand to her. 'Then you can eat with us, although perhaps you would like to freshen up first. Rooms have made ready for you and your companion, and then you can come and join us. They're a nice enough bunch—business associates, neighbours.'

Christina hung back. 'Business associates?' She swallowed as though she had something stuck in her throat. 'I know nothing about business—and my dress is soiled and crumpled from the journey and I don't speak Italian.'

Hearing the panic that sharpened her voice, Max smiled in

an attempt to reassure her. 'Christina, relax. My friends will adore you. You look wonderful.'

'Rubbish. I feel as tattered and unkempt as a street urchin.'

'Then you must have some fascinating street urchins where you come from. Not all my guests are Italian, and they speak English—at least some of us do. I know they would like to meet you.'

'I'm sure they would, but I would appreciate a little time to adjust before meeting everyone.' Christina could hear the rustle of taffeta as someone came up behind him, but all she was aware of was his eyes scrutinising every detail of her face.

'Max,' a husky female voice said from behind him, continuing to speak in English though heavily accented with Italian. 'I didn't know you were expecting more visitors. We would have waited to begin eating had we known. Please introduce me.'

Max turned, and, holding out his hand, drew a woman out of the shadows towards him, a woman whose presence Christina hadn't been aware of until then. It was the dark-haired woman she had seen seated next to Max at the table. Tall and supremely confident, she was about twenty-five with a mature figure. She was not beautiful, or even pretty, but alarmingly arresting. Christina suddenly felt extremely gauche. Oh, why did Max have to look so devilishly handsome—and why did this woman have to be so alluring and provocative? In comparison she felt immature, girlish and completely unsophisticated.

Christina absorbed the stranger into her conscious thought. Whatever she had expected, nothing had prepared her for the remarkable presence of another woman. As though out of a fog she heard Max speaking to the woman in Italian and then, taking Christina's hand and drawing her closer to his side, in English, he said, 'If you will permit me, Francesca, it gives me great pleasure to present to you my wife, Christina.'

The woman, Francesca, turned her gaze on Christina for a moment and her eyes changed from the warm devotion they had bestowed on the man beside her, to the implacable frost of one who knows she is looking at a rival. Openly hostile, she studied Christina, as if she were the enemy she had heard about and needed to devise a strategy fast. Then she smiled.

'Of course—if she is indeed your wife. Max has told us of his marriage. I am considering the frenzy you will create when he presents you to everyone else.'

The tone, lightly contemptuous and at the same time suspicious, made Christina's spine stiffen. With that feminine intuition that recognises what is in another woman's mind, what she saw in the Italian woman's eyes was more than dislike, more than jealousy. The woman's body harboured a silent hatred. For her? Why? She was sure that in time she would find out, but for now she had other things on her mind to deal with. However, a small surge of anger momentarily diverted her from her own predicament and helped regain her self-command.

'Francesca is the daughter of Don Cantoni, who has a large estate across the valley,' Max explained.

'And we've been friends for many years,' Francesca was quick to add, moving closer to Max.

For one awful moment Christina was seized with a passionate dislike for the other woman, which was so unexpected. She was clearly very well acquainted with Max. How well? What was she to him? His mistress? Suspicion was doing all kinds of things to Christina's self-esteem at that moment. She told herself angrily she was being oversensitive to read so much into so few words, but, if the woman was Max's mistress, she didn't know how she was going to bear the humiliation. For one reckless moment she wondered if she could possibly summon up the nerve to turn away, but she knew that she could not. It would be incredibly bad mannered. And this was Max's house—the real and very present Max Marchesi.

'Oh, I see,' Christina remarked—and she did see. Very well. Suddenly she was feeling uncomfortable and didn't want to be there. Molly came to stand beside her and she turned to her, which gave her a moment to collect her thoughts and to hide her face for a moment. She would not show how much Max had hurt her. She would not show how much she cared.

When she turned back to them, her eyes were sparkling and her lips curved in a smile. 'This is Miss Chesterton—my companion.' The cool tone of her voice pleased her.

Francesca's uninterested gaze slithered over Molly and she bowed her head like a queen bestowing a regal favour upon a lesser mortal, before she brought her eyes back to Christina.

If Christina was disconcerted by Francesca's abrupt manner, she hid it under a mask of formality and responded with a dismissive smile that she hoped would make her more mysterious than scatterbrained. Having no wish to remain in the hall any longer, to beat a hasty retreat, she said, 'I hope rooms have been prepared, Max. I would appreciate a hot bath and something to eat.'

'Of course.'

They were interrupted when Signor Massa hurried in carrying his leather satchel. Beaming brightly and relieved to have completed his mission successfully, he crossed to the Count, who greeted him warmly.

'It's good to see you, Benito. I hope your journey was uneventful.'

'It was. I have some important documents to give you and then, if you don't mind, I will return with the carriage to Sienna.'

'Will you not stay the night?'

'Thank you, no. Some light refreshment, perhaps, and then I must return to my dear wife who will be waiting.'

Max spoke sharply in Italian to a footman in dark livery and then looked at Christina.

'The footman will show you and Miss Chesterton to your rooms, Christina.' He turned to Francesca. 'Please return to the other guests, Francesca, and make my apologies. I wish to have a word with Benito in private.' His gaze slid back to Christina. 'When you have bathed and eaten, if you have no wish to be introduced to my guests, I know your grandmother would like to see you. I'll come and see you shortly.'

Christina smiled sweetly. 'I would appreciate that. I don't want you to put any pressure on me, Max. I would like time to settle in, to familiarise myself with people and places without being swamped by attention—which will be in-evitable, I suppose, when they know your wife has arrived from England.'

After saying farewell to Signor Massa, Christina allowed the footman to conduct her up the grand staircase adorned with a gilded rail of wrought iron to a large and spacious beau-tiful room.

It was tastefully furnished and done up in pale peach and white. Christina looked around the room. She had always lived in luxury, but this house and this room went beyond her wildest imaginings. It was not only the hangings of white brocade em-broidered with the Marchesi crest, the polished, graceful Italian furniture, the soft satin cushions, the velvet chair covers, the pictures, the gilt-framed mirrors and thick rugs, it was also the little ornaments and vases that decorated the room, and she was convinced each one was worth a small fortune. French windows opened on to a wide balcony overlooking the splendid gardens and the vineyards and olive groves beyond.

With two maids to do her bidding—although communication was difficult since neither of them spoke a word of English—Christina bathed and changed into a lavender gown and enjoyed a relatively restful repast before Max appeared. After a sharp knock he entered without being told to, which Christina objected to, but decided to let it pass, for nothing was more obvious to her at that moment than those eyes that immediately took in every detail of her appearance. The greatest compliment he bestowed on her was to smile admiringly.

'You look lovely, Christina,' he said, looking at her with obvious pleasure. She had bloomed since he had last seen her. The heat of her bath had tinged her cheeks a warm pink, her eyes sparkled more than before, and he wanted to linger over her full red mouth. 'Lavender suits you. I trust the room is to your liking?'

'Yes—it's lovely—and such a beautiful view,' she replied, having no notion of his amorous thoughts. 'Have you come to take me to my grandmother?' He looked at her and she questioned innocently, 'Or did you have some other matter you wished to discuss with me?'

'I have something to give you, but in truth, Christina, there is much we have to settle between us.'

'If by that you mean our sleeping arrangements, I thought we ended that discussion in England.'

His jaw tightened. 'Do not be mistaken, Christina. The discussion is far from settled.'

'So, what is it you have to give me?'

'This,' he said, opening a small brown leather box he carried in his hand and taking out a ring. 'The wedding is not complete without this.' Lifting her left hand, he slipped the glowing gold band on to her third finger. 'I sincerely hope this ring never leaves your finger, Christina.'

'A wedding ring,' Christina whispered, staring at it in disbelief.

'What did you expect? Is it so strange for a husband to give his wife a wedding ring—a token of his devotion? I apologise for the delay, but now you have it.'

'It—it's a perfect fit. How did you know?'

'Your mother told me before I left for Italy.'

Christina looked up at him. 'You really have thought of everything, haven't you, Max?'

'If I had thought of everything, Christina, you would not be sleeping alone.' Abruptly he turned away from her. 'Come, I will take you to your grandmother.'

'She won't mind being disturbed?'

A slow smile touched his lips. 'She'll never forgive me if I don't.'

'But—she may be asleep,' Christina said in an attempt to put off the dreaded moment of meeting her formidable grandmother.

'Then we'll wake her.'

'Won't she be angry if we do that?'

'Not when she knows the reason.' He looked at her sharply. 'Nervous?'

'Terrified,' she confessed.

'Don't be. She's looking forwards to meeting you at last.'

Christina followed him along the landing, up a short flight of stairs and then along another landing, off which, in addition to more grand salons, the dowager Countess Marchesi had a suite of rooms.

Max knocked sharply on the door and, on hearing someone call out for him to enter, opened the door and ushered Christina inside. A maid bobbed a curtsy and indicated a half-open door. Christina followed Max into a sitting room, where the woman who had orchestrated her life with such cold and calculating precision sat reading, a branch of tall white flickering candles at her side. Attired in a black silk dress and her silver hair secured in a neat bun at her nape, she raised her head.

'I've brought someone to see you, Grandmother,' Max said, striding briskly towards her, and, bending his dark head, placed a light kiss on her cheek. 'It's Christina. She arrived in Sienna ahead of schedule and here she is.'

Christina sensed that the affection between them was a natural thing and that her grandmother had devoted all her time and energy on the motherless Max when he had been growing up.

Clasping his hands behind his back, Max went to stand by the open French doors, propping his shoulder against the frame. Folding his arms across his chest, he settled his eyes nonchalantly on Christina, his gaze never wavering from her.

The faded blue eyes that looked up at the visitor were unclouded, penetrating and inquisitive. 'So, you are Christina,' the dowager said, getting up and waiting for Christina to come to her. 'I am very happy to welcome you to Castello Marchesi, and I hope you will look on this house as your own.'

The voice was a splendid contralto, deep and warm and heavily accented, but she spoke perfect English. Of medium height, slim, straight and regal and not at all what Christina had expected, the dowager Countess Marchesi could, when she pleased, be awe-inspiring. This was one of those moments. Almost without her conscious volition, Christina's feet carried her forwards. Step by step they carried her nearer to the woman who had taken charge of her life.

'Thank you. You are very kind,' she said stiffly, wondering vaguely how she should address her.

Sensing her dilemma, the dowager Countess said, 'I am your grandmother. That is how I would like to be addressed.'

'I must offer you my deep apologies, Grandmother, that Max and I should impose ourselves on you at this hour, but he was most insistent we should come.'

The dowager Countess looked slightly surprised and Christina was aware that Max was looking at her intently.

'Max knows me so well and that I would have been most put out if he hadn't. Besides, I rarely go to bed before ten o'clock.' Quite suddenly she relaxed and her tone became warm. 'So, you are Roberto's daughter—oh, you are still but a child. And an outrageously pretty one at that. Max did not tell me.' She held Christina's gaze as, unafraid, Christina looked back, her eyes never wavering. 'You resemble Lydia. And, by all the saints, you have green eyes—just like your father and your grandfather. Did you ever wonder where they came from?'

'No, not really. In truth, I never thought about it much.'

'Didn't your aunt and uncle tell you about Roberto?'

'No—and I always believed they were my parents. That is how I still think of them and always will.'

The old woman nodded. 'Your loyalty does you credit, but they should have told you the truth nevertheless. It would have saved you a lot of heartache.'

'Max told me all about the conditions you imposed on them.'

'Then I won't go over them again. The most important thing is that you are here now and that you are Max's wife— at least, I hope you are. I trust Signor Massa conducted the marriage ceremony according to your instructions, Max?'

'Yes, he did,' he replied.

'And how do you feel about that, Christina? What do you think of your husband?'

Christina cast the gentleman in question a sharp glance, before looking again at her grandmother. 'I shall try to make do with him, I suppose, since I have little choice in the matter.'

The older woman found it hard to suppress a smile. 'I see you are a sensible young woman as well as a beautiful one. The two don't always keep company together, but in your case I believe they will. You were resentful when you were told about the betrothal?'

'Yes, I was. Who would not be?'

The old woman chuckled and cast the gentleman they were discussing an amused look. 'There are many *signorinas* hereabouts and beyond who are fondly hoping for his favours, *signorinas* who would be both honoured and deeply flattered if they were to find themselves betrothed to Max.'

'Having seen the magnificence of the house and with a weighty title to go with it, I am sure they would, but I would have preferred to choose my own husband. However, I am not one to shirk my obligations,' she said, still on her dignity.

The old eyes scrutinised her again, a spark of admiration in their depths. 'Or to speak your mind, I see. I like that.' The thin pursed lips spread into a smile of heartbreaking tenderness. It was the kind of smile that would have melted into forgiveness anyone she might have offended, but it did not melt Christina. 'But what are we doing standing, when we could be sitting down and having a quiet chat?' She looked at Max. 'Don't you have guests to entertain, Max?'

'What you really mean is that I'm not wanted,' he remarked, pushing himself upright and crossing to the door. 'Very well. I'll leave you ladies to gossip in private.'

When he'd left the room the dowager Countess lowered herself into her comfortable brocade chair. Christina sat in a matching one at an angle to it. It was quite obvious that her grandmother was now relaxed and ready to talk to her on almost equal terms, but Christina was not entirely mollified.

The older woman seemed to sense this and impulsively she put out her hand and laid it on Christina's.

'I think,' she said, 'that you are angry with me because of the way I have ordered your life. You are resentful, and I cannot say that I blame you. Is this not so?'

Christina nodded. 'Yes, it is. It was difficult coming to terms with things I knew nothing about. My life was changed overnight.'

'I understand, but please don't let it affect you too much. Whatever you may believe, I only ever had your best interests at heart. It was a difficult time for me when your mother died and your father... Well, Roberto went to pieces.'

'Did it matter to you that he married an English woman?'

'Not, not at all. Besides, Lydia was strong and wilful. Roberto was not. He needed someone like Lydia. It was a tragedy that she should die so young. I see you wear her wedding ring. Audine gave you the trinket box I made up for you.'

'Yes. I—I was much moved by it. Thank you. I shall treasure it always.'

'The things were not of any value, but they were precious to Lydia. It was right that you should have them. I am so pleased you have returned to Italy.'

Christina met her eyes and when she spoke her voice was laced with bitterness. 'To marry Max and to unite two of Tuscany's oldest families.'

The dowager sighed and withdrew her hand. 'How cold and unemotional you make it sound.'

'It wasn't very flattering to know the man I was to pledge my life to was not marrying me for myself, but for my inheritance. If I had refused, would you have insisted that my parents repay all the money you gave them for my upbringing?'

She smiled slowly. 'No, Christina. I may be a formidable old lady, one to fear, I have been told, but I am never cruel.'

'So—what you are saying is that I need not have married Max?' Her voice was trembling as the realisation hit her with a mighty force.

'The betrothal was part of the arrangement and I'm happy that the two of you have married, but if one of you couldn't stand the sight of the other, then, no, the betrothal would have been cancelled.'

'But Max said…' Understanding that Max had played her false, and beginning to realise that she had done her grandmother a terrible injustice, Christina's eyes narrowed and ire flared in their depths. 'Why, that cold, calculating, arrogant… He had me believing I had no choice but to marry him. It is a case of the most wicked deception I have ever heard. Oh, what I will say to that man when I see him. He must have wanted my inheritance very badly.'

The dowager chuckled softly. 'Believe me, my dear, when Max wants something he will move heaven and earth to get it. He has told me that for the time being, since the two of you are virtually strangers, your marriage is to be in name only.'

Christina stared at her in astonishment. 'He actually told you that? Is nothing to be secret in this house? I will not change my mind. He will just have to wait until I'm ready.'

'Do not be so certain of that. This marriage is very important to Max and he is not noted for his patience. He can be very persuasive when he chooses, and very determined.'

'So can I.'

The dowager's smile was one of understanding. 'Be patient, Christina. One day it will all come right. I know you will be happy—happy enough to forget what brought you and Max together.'

Christina looked at her. Her grandmother spoke the words she wanted to hear, words that were attuned to her own pathetic craving for the man who had made her his wife so dispassionately. But her grandmother knew and had been impelled to say the words. Christina met her eyes and she saw real and sincere concern and friendship, the sort of friendship one woman offers another, and this gave her a feeling of security, a good warm feeling.

She managed to smile. 'Thank you,' she said simply. 'But how am I to stand seeing him day after day—to have him watching me—waiting for me to…' Her face flushed crimson and she turned her head away in confusion, for she had quite forgotten for a moment who she was talking to and that her grandmother was still a virtual stranger.

'Then I may be able to help you. Tell me, Christina, how do you feel about living here—at Castello Marchesi?'

'I find it terribly daunting. It's so vast and—intimidating. Rather like its owner.'

'I couldn't agree more.' She sighed as memories of another time assailed her. 'It's not at all like Casa del Sole.'

Christina looked at her with sudden interest. 'Casa del Sole? Your old home?'

The dowager nodded slowly, becoming preoccupied. A thought occurred to her, which took hold with such force that she could not set it aside. In fact, it was quite delightful, and the more she thought about it the more she liked it. She knew that if Christina took after her mother and grandfather—her own dear first husband—then she was a young woman of passionate feeling. And she would be good for Max. She also seemed to know her own mind and had the temerity to stand up to him. That boded well for future happiness.

A definite twinkle entered her eyes as they again settled

OFFICIAL OPINION POLL

ANSWER 3 QUESTIONS AND WE'LL SEND YOU
2 FREE BOOKS AND A FREE GIFT!

0074823 ||||||||||||| ||||||||| ||||||||| FREE GIFT CLAIM # 3953

YOUR OPINION COUNTS!

Please tick TRUE or FALSE below to express your opinion about the following statements:

Q1 Do you believe in "true love"?

"TRUE LOVE HAPPENS ONLY ONCE IN A LIFETIME."
- ○ TRUE
- ○ FALSE

Q2 Do you think marriage has any value in today's world?

"YOU CAN BE TOTALLY COMMITTED TO SOMEONE WITHOUT BEING MARRIED."
- ○ TRUE
- ○ FALSE

Q3 What kind of books do you enjoy?

"A GREAT NOVEL MUST HAVE A HAPPY ENDING."
- ○ TRUE
- ○ FALSE

YES, I have scratched the area below.

Please send me the 2 FREE BOOKS and FREE GIFT for which I qualify. I understand I am under no obligation to purchase any books, as explained on the back of this card.

2 FREE BOOKS AND A FREE GIFT

H8KI

Mrs/Miss/Ms/Mr   Initials

BLOCK CAPITALS PLEASE

Surname

Address

Postcode

Chapter Seven

On leaving her grandmother's room, Christina was so pre-occupied with her thoughts and the suggestion she had put to her that she took a wrong turn. Descending a flight of stairs, she suddenly realised this wasn't the way Max had brought her. Finding herself in the hall, she was about to climb the grand staircase she had taken on her arrival when a voice rang out in Italian. Turning, she saw a gentleman she assumed must be one of the guests striding towards her.

'I'm sorry,' she said. 'I—don't speak Italian.'

He grinned. 'I do—but not like a true Italian.'

Christina brightened, her relief evident. 'Oh—you are English.'

'And so are you, which means you must be Max's wife.'

'She is,' Max said, seeming to appear from nowhere, his tall, imperious figure coming striding towards them, Francesca following close on his heels.

Christina met her silently assessing gaze with quiet composure. The Italian woman's nonchalant walk and feline movements she thought were irresistibly reminiscent of a cat. She didn't like Francesca Cantoni—brittle, sophisticated, conceited stranger, who resented her intrusion into their select society.

The gentleman inclined his head without removing his eyes from Christina. 'I am enchanted to meet you, Countess,' he said, smiling into her eyes in a way that told her she'd just received a compliment. 'Max told us he was expecting you, but I had no idea you were already here.'

'Christina arrived earlier this evening,' Max explained. 'I didn't expect her until tomorrow.' He looked down at his wife. 'Francesca you have already met and Guy Saunders is a close neighbour of ours, Christina.'

'And also a long-time friend of your husband,' Guy was quick to add. 'Italy has been my home for many years.'

'Then I expect I shall be seeing more of you, Mr Saunders.' Already liking their neighbour, Christina found herself smiling at this engaging gentleman. He was a young, reasonably attractive man, not tall but of strong build, with well-groomed fair hair and friendly brown eyes.

'You most certain will, and please feel free to call me Guy,' he said, his dancing eyes passing over her face lightly.

'And you must feel free to call me Christina.'

Max scowled his disapproval to see Guy's appraisal of his wife, to watch the appreciation in his eyes as they regarded her lovely laughing face, the slim length of her softly rounded form, the fullness of her breasts and the simple elegance of her gown.

'Don't allow this reprobate too much freedom, Christina. Give him an inch and he'll take the proverbial mile.'

Guy smiled broadly. His teeth shone white and even in his brown face, his fair hair flopping over his brow. 'I am sure Christina will have much to do settling in, and if she would like to see more of the place where she is to live, it will be my pleasure to show her around—should Max be too busy, you understand. I shall make myself available.'

'I don't think so, Guy,' Max said tersely. 'Besides, I would have thought you had enough to do at Villa Candido.'

'Nothing that can't be put aside for a very beautiful young lady,' Guy replied in undaunted spirits, his eyes gleaming devilishly.

Christina bestowed on Guy her sweetest smile. 'Thank you, Guy. Despite what Max says, I do appreciate the offer.'

'And will take me up on it, I hope.' He flashed a wide grin. 'Should you ever grow weary of your husband's ogre-like disposition, be aware that my house is a close haven. Indeed, I would be sorely tempted to lure you away from this moody friend of mine.'

Christina's responding smile hinted of a certain distrust. 'And I am certain that when a gentleman makes such a scandalous suggestion in front of a lady's husband, one doesn't mean one word of it.'

'It's when he begins seeking you out in private that you must be more wary of his motives,' Francesca murmured mockingly.

Guy chuckled, eying Max with much humour. 'I know Max is a crack shot with a gun. Sneaking after his wife behind his back could be life threatening.'

'Quite right,' Max drawled. 'Francesca is right to tell you to be wary, Christina. My good friend's intentions are to dishonour every female who is foolish enough to fall for his silken tongue.'

Guy accepted this light riposte with a long, heartfelt sigh. 'Ah, well, you can't blame a man for trying.' Observing Max's ominous frown, he hid his amusement behind a mask of genteel imperturbability. 'But shame on you, Max,' he mockingly reproached. 'When Christina arrived you should have sent the lot of us packing. Apart from Francesca and myself, Countess, you will be happy to know everyone else has left—so now your husband can give you his undivided attention, although I'm sure the others would have liked to meet you.'

'I was unable to persuade her to dine with us,' Max told him.

'Which was quite understandable, Max. I was quite exhausted after the journey and desperately in need of a bath.'

'Oh, dear,' Francesca purred. 'I hope for Max's sake you don't have an aversion to meeting his friends and that you do not intend keeping yourself in seclusion.'

Christina stared at her. She was angry at as well as nervous of her own ineptitude with this self-confident woman; whatever she had expected at Castello Marchesi, she had not bargained on finding someone like Francesca Cantoni, who was adroitly putting her in her place.

'On the contrary. I am looking forwards to meeting all Max's friends.' She smiled at Max. 'The sooner the better.'

Francesca looked at Max and said something soft in Italian, her eyes flashing a blatant message, making Christina very much the foreigner. Feeling a shock of disbelief at this blatant innuendo, she lifted her chin in a small gesture of defiance.

'I'm sorry,' she said. 'I don't speak your language, but I fully intend to learn. Did you say something to Max that you don't want me to know about? A private joke, perhaps?'

Detecting his wife's underlying sarcasm, Max shot her a look of displeasure. 'Francesca was merely thanking me for a wonderful evening, Christina.'

'Really?' Christina remarked, her heart beating with rapidity at the Italian woman's cheek. How dare she try to undermine her confidence? This woman had known Max a long time, she was certain. Had she shared intimacies with him and were those intimacies still continuing? After all, it was inconceivable that a virile man like Max had lived all his life at Castello Marchesi without knowing and loving women. 'I'm sure it has been, Signorina Cantoni, and that Max has been the perfect host.'

'We have all had an enjoyable evening,' Guy was quick to say in an attempt to diffuse the unpleasant situation that he could sense developing between Christina and Francesca. 'Next time it will be so much better. Your presence will definitely enhance the occasion, Christina.'

'Thank you, Guy. Now,' she said, taking a deep breath, 'it is late and it has been a long day, so if you will excuse me I would like to retire,' she said, uncaring now if it was considered bad manners or not to say so.

'I do apologise if we have outstayed our welcome. I quite understand that newly married couples find lingering guests tedious,' Guy said, chuckling softly, 'so I won't suggest that we stay for another coffee or a brandy—that really would be an abuse of your hospitality.'

'You're right. It would,' Max stated flatly.

Christina felt a sudden rush of fullness to her throat at Guy's well-meaning remark, and wondered what he would say if he knew that Max didn't love her, that their marriage was all a sham.

Guy turned away. 'Excuse me, I'll just go and see where my carriage has got to.'

'I think I should leave also, Max,' Francesca murmured when Guy had left.

'I'm sorry your father was unable to come. I hope he's soon feeling better. Give him my good wishes and tell him I'll call on him soon.'

'I will. Knowing I would be among friends, I knew you wouldn't mind if I came alone. Although—I was relying on you to take me home, Max,' Francesca murmured. 'You know how it is. When I arrived I sent the carriage back home rather than have the driver hang about indefinitely.'

Christina couldn't believe what she was hearing, that Francesca fully expected Max to offer to drive her home. She suspected that this was what Francesca had been waiting for all along. She felt as though her marriage to Max meant nothing to this flamboyant Italian woman, who seemed perfectly at home and comfortable at Castello Marchesi. In fact, the more she listened to Signorina Cantoni and watched her sensuous bodily movements, the more convinced she became that she was Max's mistress. Her cheeks burned with the realisation.

'Of course,' Max replied. 'I'll order the carriage.'

'Why, thank you, Max.'

Christina stared at him. His face was expressionless, his voice polite enough and she couldn't help wondering just how often his movements were engineered by this clever woman. Christina was certain she could detect a look of triumph in Francesca's dark, glowing eyes.

'Oh, dear,' she purred. 'I do so hope you will forgive me for dragging Max away. I do promise not to keep him away too long.'

'I really don't think there is any need for Max to take you home, Signorina Cantoni,' Christina found herself saying. 'Guy, would it be out of your way to escort Signorina Cantoni home? It would save Max the trouble of having the carriage brought round.'

Guy could see what was happening and grinned, a willing participant. 'Happy to be of service, Countess.'

'But Guy isn't going anywhere near my home,' Francesca objected firmly.

'Francesca, it really is no trouble,' Guy told her, his eyes warm when they settled on her face. 'I would be delighted.

In fact, I absolutely insist. I can't think of anything I would enjoy more than a tête-à-tête with such a gracious and lovely lady in the moonlight.'

Christina looked at Francesca, whose carmine lips had settled into a pout as she scowled darkly at Guy. 'There you are. Problem solved,' she quipped airily.

They walked across the hall to the door, Christina and Guy a few steps behind Max and Francesca.

'Don't let her provoke you, Christina,' Guy murmured to her surprise. 'I hope you don't think it impertinent of me to say that I consider Max a very lucky man.'

'I do not think such a charming remark impertinent, Guy. I only hope Max agrees with you.'

'Despite everything, I hope the two of you will be happy.'

Christina's heart suddenly plummeted. Despite everything? So Guy knew about their arranged marriage and the circumstances behind it, and if he knew, then Max must have told him, she reasoned. And if Guy knew, then who else knew. Francesca? The entire neighbourhood? When she considered the implications of this, it brought a bitter taste to her mouth.

'I hope so too,' she said softly, and she really did.

'Of course you do. Max deserves to be happy, after everything he's had to endure. First his mother, and then his father dying in so shameful a manner.' He turned and looked at her, suddenly alarmed in case he'd divulged a confidence she knew nothing about. 'He has told you about that?'

'Yes, he has.'

Relieved, he smiled. 'You will bring a breath of fresh air into his life. I can see that.'

Christina blinked up at him, beginning to feel better when she realised it was Max he had been referring to and not her marital affairs. It wasn't in his nature to do that and if she wasn't careful she was in danger of becoming obsessed with the reason why Max had married her.

'I can see you are a good friend to Max, Guy, and his happiness is never far from my thoughts.'

As she bade Francesca a cool goodnight and watched Max give her the dutiful kiss on both cheeks, she refused to let herself be filled with self-pity at the role in which she found herself.

Christina followed Max as he strode purposefully across the hall, having to almost run to keep up. He was angry, that was plain. He nodded curtly to a servant, who opened a pair of double doors with ornate brass handles to a luxurious study. It was lined with books behind richly carved recesses of polished wood. When the door had closed Max stopped in the centre of the room and spun round and looked at her with undiluted anger.

'Do you mind telling me what all that was about? What do you think you were playing at, trying to embarrass me in front of my friends? Just what did you hope to achieve by being rude to Francesca?'

Fury, full bodied and fortifying boiled up inside Christina at the injustice of his accusation. 'Me? Embarrass you? Why, of all the arrogant, hypocritical remarks I have heard you utter, that has to be the worst,' she burst out angrily. 'How dare you lecture *me* on decorum and reprimand me on my lack of it,' she fumed, pointing a quivering finger at the door, 'when I had to stand out there and be introduced to your—your paramour—who was insufferably discourteous to me, I might add, and her manner such that I truly thought *her* to be mistress of the house.'

Max's brows rose. 'Paramour? What the hell are you talking about?'

'Signorina Cantoni—that's who I'm talking about.'

'Francesca is not my paramour, as you so charmingly put it, nor is she mistress of this house.'

'No? Then perhaps you should inform her of that, because when a woman sidles up to a man the way she did to you, then that is where she wants to stay.'

'Now you are being ridiculous.'

Christina's ire at his condescending superiority was almost more than she could take. 'You are taking me for a fool, Max, and I will not stand for it.'

'Christina, I think you should go to bed before I forget myself. You are beginning to sound unpleasantly like a jealous wife.'

'Wife? Yes, I am your wife—a very valuable wife—and you couldn't even be bothered to turn up for the ceremony so you sent someone else to do it for you. You are just as impossible as I remember and I am seriously beginning to wish I had never come here.'

'You came because you had no choice,' he stated bluntly. 'You were obligated to come some time.'

'Obligated?' she flung back, planting her fists in the small of her waist. 'Cajoled, coerced—and almost seduced by you into coming, more like. Forgive me if I don't feel married. Had I been given any other choice I would not be, but you left me with no alternative. You see, Max, I was such a gullible fool that I listened to you.' She saw his head jerk up, but she was so angry she didn't pay any heed to the stunned expression on his face.

'What are you saying?'

She moved closer, her eyes glued to his. 'That my whole reason for being here is built on one of your lies. You duped me into believing I had no choice but to marry you—that my grandmother was such a fire-breathing dragon that she would destroy my parents if I didn't. Shame on you, Max Marchesi, for your wicked deception,' she reproached scornfully. 'If you had really cared anything for me at all, you would have told me my grandmother would have relinquished all claim to me had I not wanted to marry you—and my parents would have been acquitted of any money owing.'

His eyes narrowed and his expression was not without surprise. 'She told you this?'

'Yes, she did. My grandmother may be as tough as old shoe leather, but she is not the harridan you would have me believe. You could have eased my fears and my parents'—had you wanted to. But so great was your desire to get your greedy hands on my inheritance that you let me suffer through the worst time of my life, when I was so frightened I wanted to die.'

Expecting a fresh tirade from him, to her utter disbelief he lifted his brows and gazed at her with an impassive expression for several endless, uneasy moments, then she realised he had moved closer and was offering her his hand. The softening of his features went some way to neutralising her anger, but she was still humiliatingly aware that after releasing her pent-up resentment and anger on Max, she had not seen one gratifying piece of reaction from him. Her pride forced her to look him right in the eye as she placed her hand in his.

As Max drew her towards him, three realisations came to him. The first was that, despite her magnificent show of courage, Christina was on the brink of tears. The second was that the engaging, innocent girl he had met in England had become a young woman of exotic beauty. The third was that her spirit and fiery rebellion were unchanged—and what he found disconcerting was that he was more physically attracted to her now than he had been eight months ago. But if he had hoped to find more submission and obedience in her, he was disappointed. Christina had too much pride and spirit to be cast in the role of dutiful wife.

'Christina, I would like to apologise if you believe I deceived you in England. It was never my intention to do that. I did not lie to you. I truly had no idea that your grandmother would waive your parents' obligation to her. She gave no indication of that to me.'

'It still does not alter the fact that I was just a pawn in your ploy to get what you wanted. I was confused. I now know you are a man who goes after what he wants, yet your method to win seems somehow less than honourable.'

'Christina, whatever you may think, I never lied to you.'

'No? I'm relieved to hear it,' she said, unable to hide a sudden wayward smile.

The smile hit Max like a blow to the head, snapping him completely out of his disagreeable mood. 'It's good to see you smile at last. At least that's a start. Now,' he said, taking her hand and leading her to the door, 'go to bed. We will talk in the morning.' When she was on the point of crossing the threshold, he turned her to face him. Placing a finger gently under her chin, he tilted her face up to his. 'To set your mind at ease, Christina, Francesca is the daughter of a very good friend of mine. Nothing more than that. Be assured that you have nothing to worry about where she is concerned.' Looking deeply into her eyes, he said quietly, 'You look tired.'

'Yes, I confess that I happen to be quite exhausted from a good deal more than my journey from Sienna,' she said, smiling softly.

His lips quirked in an answering smile. 'Then go to your room.'

'There is just one more thing.'

Max frowned, his look wary. She still looked mutinous. 'Now what?'

'The house, Max.'

'House? What house?'

Christina lifted her chin and met his gaze directly. 'I have been speaking to my grandmother about it. She told me about Casa del Sole and naturally I am curious to see it for myself. She also told me you have the keys to the house. If I could have them in the morning I would be grateful. I may go and live there for a while.'

Max's dark brows snapped together over startled blue eyes. 'What?'

Christina gave a delicate lift to her eyebrows. 'I said I might like to go and live there for a while. It was Grandmother who suggested it and I have to say the idea appeals to me. Why not?'

'Because you happen to be my wife and husbands and wives do not live in separate houses,' he snapped, wondering what she was playing at and visibly struggling to keep a tight rein on his temper. 'They live together. What could be more natural?'

A ferocious gleam entered her eyes and her lips curled. 'What more indeed? What you mean is that when one cannot avoid one's fate the only wise thing is to accept it without complaint. I won't, Max. I need time. At least give me that.'

'You can't possibly move into Casa del Sole. It's out of the question, so I do not want to hear any more about it.'

Christina shrugged. 'That's fine. I shall go there anyway.'

'No, Christina, you will not. There's no one there to take care of you. The house needs opening up properly before anyone can even think of living there.'

Resentful of his dismissive manner, Christina's pert nose lifted in a manner of prim confidence. 'I am sure Molly and I can muddle through. I have every faith in my own ability to take care of myself.'

Max recognised the stubborn thrust of her lovely chin and

the glint of determination in her eye. 'I will take care of you. You are my responsibility and the sooner you settle down to being my wife, the happier I shall be.'

'I'm sure you will. But I told you that for the time being ours will be a marriage in name only. I meant it then and I have not changed my mind.'

'I see you have no intention of relenting.'

'None whatsoever.' Her eyes were hard as they locked on his. 'Grandmother told me the house is habitable and comfortable, so I would appreciate it if you would show it to me.'

His expression tightened. 'And I told you we will discuss the matter in the morning.

'Very well, but don't think I'm going to forget about it because I'm not,' she persisted.

His face tightened. 'I'll take you to look at it tomorrow.'

'And accept that I might want to live there?'

'No.'

She smiled, by no means thwarted. The Max who had touched her heart and stirred her emotions in England had changed and in his place she saw a stranger revealed, whose inimical behaviour was totally foreign to her heart. She did not want, and nor would she have, a man who wished to dominate her and bend her to his will.

'We shall see. Goodnight, Max.'

'Apart from unpacking my night things, Molly, leave the rest,' Christina said when she returned to her rooms to find Molly about to begin the process of unpacking. 'We don't want to have to pack it all up again tomorrow when we go to live at Casa del Sole.'

Molly stopped what she was doing and stared at her. 'What? Are we to live somewhere else?'

'Yes—at my grandmother's old home.'

'And has your husband agreed to this?'

'No,' she said, bouncing airily on the bed to test its softness. 'But he will.'

Christina was glad to climb into the huge bed, and when her head hit the pillows her last thoughts were of seeing Casa del Sole on the morrow—and Max.

Christina woke to sunlight streaming in through the wide sweep of open windows. Still half-asleep, she stretched and pushed back the covers, shoving her tousled hair out of her eyes. Refusing to wait for Molly to help her dress, she bathed and debated what to wear for her visit to Casa del Sole, choosing a buttercup-yellow dress, the bright colour suiting her mood, and loosely tying her hair back with a matching ribbon. She was impatient to go out, and after ordering breakfast to be brought to her room—new bread and butter and fresh fruit washed down with tea—she was about to leave the room when the sound of a horse's hooves clattering on a paved drive drew her to the window.

Although the sun-drenched gardens beyond were silent, there was a fountain singing in a pool in the centre of a velvet lawn. A horse and rider were cantering away from the house in the direction of some outbuildings in the distance. There was no mistaking Max. Feeling a twinge of disappointment that he hadn't waited to bid her good morning, she looked round when Molly came in, greeting her with a cheerful good morning.

'I think we'll have to go to the house by ourselves, Molly. It looks as though Max is busy. If we are allowed the use of the carriage, we can take some of the baggage with us.'

Molly shot her a dubious look, strongly suspecting that

Christina's actions might antagonise the count. 'Do you think that's wise? Shouldn't you wait until he comes back?'

'No. He might be gone for hours. I'll go on ahead to the stables.'

Servants were going quietly to and fro about their work. Humming a light airy tune, Christina almost skipped down the stairs in her excited anticipation of seeing Casa del Sole for the first time. She shocked a footman by greeting him with a laughing *buon giorno*, and the man almost gaped when she waved to another. Never had the house had so cheerful a countess—for by now the staff knew who she was and could talk of nothing else. Much bemused, he went back to his work, shaking his head in wonderment.

Christina waylaid the footman who had opened the door to her last night and asked if he would kindly assist Miss Chesterton with the baggage. He frowned, clearly not at all sure that the Count would approve of this, but, seeing the quiet determination in her eye, he complied.

Miraculously, after following confusing directions, Christina found herself at the stables. Asking for the carriage was another matter entirely, for she couldn't make herself understood. Thankfully the footman carrying the bags arrived with Molly and it wasn't long before she was climbing up into a small pony cart.

Max returned to the house looking forwards to having breakfast with Christina. Having given her plenty of time to appreciate the magnificence of Castello Marchesi, he was certain she would have abandoned the ridiculous notion of going to live at Casa del Sole. Handing his horse to a groom outside the house, smiling broadly he bounded up the steps and went in search of her.

Finding no sign of her in the breakfast room, he enquired of the servants if they had seen her. When told she'd left the house to go to Casa del Sole, he was unable to rein in his temper. He wasn't smiling when he strode to the stables, and nor was he smiling when he saw Christina perched on the seat of a small pony cart holding the reins, an uneasy-looking Miss Chesterton beside her and a pile of neatly stacked baggage in the back.

As the pony trotted briskly past him, Max reached out in a deceptively casual move and caught the bridle, jerking the animal to a stop.

Christina stiffened with resentment. 'Max! What are you doing?'

His eyes held a hard menace and his voice was so cold, so soft, that Christina knew a moment of fear. 'Just where do you think you are going?'

Despite her rebellious tone, there was a tiny quiver of fear in her voice when she answered. 'To Casa del Sole. It was hard work making your stable men understand that I needed a carriage, but thankfully one of your footmen came to my assistance. I find it so frustrating not being able to converse with people. I really must make a point of learning Italian.'

'Did I not tell you that I would take you there?'

'I didn't want to put you to any trouble. I thought you'd have work to do.'

His eyes sliced to the baggage and then back to her. 'I will not allow you to live there, Christina. It is absolutely out of the question.'

Tossing her head haughtily and directing her gaze straight ahead, she said, 'I shall make my mind up when I get there. If I don't like the house, then I promise I won't stay.'

'And the cart? Can you drive it?'

Very politely but very firmly, she said, 'I am capable of handling a pony cart, Max—and it's quite a docile little pony.'

'And you know which direction to take?'

She smiled confidently. 'The footman pointed the way.'

'And the key to the house?'

Her smile faded. 'Oh, the key! I quite forgot.'

His smile was one of cruel satisfaction. 'Then you'd better abandon your trip for now.'

'But I really would like to go now,' she protested, sounding desperate.

'Later, I think.'

Her eyes snapped to his. 'Max, I simply cannot understand why you are so set against me going there. What pleasure can you possibly get in denying me something that is important to me?'

'I am not an ogre,' he snapped.

'Then will you please stop behaving like one and go and get me the key?'

Knowing he would get no peace until she had seen the house, reluctantly he conceded. 'Very well. Wait here.'

Another of her smiles appeared, lighting up her entire face. 'Thank you, Max. I would appreciate it.'

Turning on his heel, he strode back to the house, cursing her stubborn refusal to do as she was told. He wanted nothing more than to lay hold of her fragility, to bend her to his will so that never again would she challenge him, argue with and defy him. When he reappeared a few minutes later he was on horseback.

'I see you are coming with us.'

'Of course,' he ground out. 'You might need someone to open the door.'

Max rode behind her, unable to suppress the amused smile of admiration that curved his lips as he watched the pony and cart go bowling down the drive, Christina's good hands on the reins controlling the frisky little beast.

He chuckled low in his throat. He never ceased to be amazed at the effect she always had on him, not just at his natural male instincts to possess, to dominate her body, which he hoped to do very soon, but by the strange, tender feelings in him to protect her, feelings he had shown no other woman.

Casa del Sole was tucked away on land that was invisible from the road, discreetly hidden down a dirt track that snaked through woods for half a mile. Just when Christina was beginning to wonder when they would get there, the view opened to a hundred acres of olives and vines marching in uniform lines like soldiers on parade, watched over by a lovely, impressive old farmhouse built out of local stone with red terracotta roof tiles and with vines sprawling across the outer walls, dripping and looping colour, and cypress trees on either side. The sun illuminated the carefully tended grass in front, and terracotta pots of geraniums and cyclamen added brilliant splashes of colour. A slight haze hid the horizon and there was not a cloud to be seen in the clear blue sky.

Christina fell in love with Casa del Sole at first sight. 'What a lovely place. This is incredible. Is this where my father spent his childhood?' she asked, turning to look at the gently rolling countryside.

'Yes,' Max replied, 'your mother, too, when she married Roberto.'

'It's breathtakingly beautiful—like a timeless patchwork that hasn't changed for centuries.'

Her eyes filled with tears as she looked at the old house. Someone—Max—took her hand and placed a key across her palm. She gazed at him through the haze of tears, her eyes questioning.

'You alone have the right to break the silence that has inhabited Casa del Sole for years, Christina. No one has more right than you to cross the threshold. Apart from the people who come in to clean, no one else has been inside other than your grandmother—although her visits have been infrequent of late. It remains as it was when your mother died and you and your father left.'

Christina took a few steps towards the house, strangely unwilling to use the key. Her bravery having left her, swallowing her nervousness, she turned uncertainly to Max, who stood watching her. 'Will you come with me?'

He nodded, his face grave. 'If you wish. Come,' he said, when he saw her hesitate. 'We will go in together.'

With shaking fingers Christina inserted the key in the lock. It turned smoothly and the door opened.

'Someone seems to have taken the trouble to keep the lock well oiled,' she commented with surprise.

A black cat sprang suddenly from behind one of the terracotta pots and streaked away to disappear round the side of the house. Superstitious, Christina shivered and took a step back.

Max gave her his hand. 'Come.' He pushed the door further open.

Christina stepped forwards with a thudding heart into the gloom of the hall and looked about her. The house was larger than it looked from the outside, the staircase rising in a broad sweep to the upper storey. They moved into the first room off the hall, while Molly wandered off to investigate the domestic quarters. Max went to the window and opened the shutters, flooding the room with rosy evening light. Chestnut beams reached darkly across the ceiling. Everything was gold and gilt—the chairs, the tables and gilt-framed mirrors and pictures—the sofa and rugs of deep rich colours.

'You will have noticed the windows are quite small,' Max remarked, 'which is not an unusual feature of most of the houses.'

'Yes, why is that?'

'To resist the searing heat of the summer and prevent precious warmth escaping in the winter. You will also have noticed how thick the walls are. Unfortunately, by the end of summer the sun isn't strong enough to keep them warm, so fires are lit and warm clothes are a necessity.'

Christina slowly walked about the room, looking about her in awe. The peace of the house reached out to her. The silence was truly golden. There was something quiet and restful about this house, which made her feel much happier than all the luxurious splendours of the Castello Marchesi.

Suddenly she gave a start. Her eyes widened. Over the mantelpiece, staring at her, totally unexpected, was the portrait of a young woman, perhaps nineteen or twenty, her dark eyes exquisitely alive. A little smile curved her lips—sensual lips, Christina saw, the bottom lip full—and her sleek dark hair was drawn back from her heart-shaped face. One of her hands was placed on the silken head of a brown spaniel that had its adoring eyes upturned to her face. She was dressed in a chaste black dress, its only relief a small white lace collar and cuffs and a brooch—a red poppy surrounded with fine filigree, at her throat. To Christina the moment was one of intense emotion and a lump appeared in her throat.

It was a splendid portrait, a fine piece of work.

'It's Lydia,' Christina said quietly, her voice taking possession of the silence. 'She's been painted wearing the same brooch my grandmother gave me.'

'Poppies are very much a feature of the Tuscan landscape, as you will see for yourself very soon.'

'I know. I saw on my journey from Sienna that already they are bursting into bloom.'

Christina stood motionless, her eyes riveted on the portrait. There was a great poignancy in this moment. Until now Lydia, her mother, had only been a ghostly image in her mind and the young woman portrayed here touched her in ways she had never thought possible.

'Your mother was just married when that picture was painted by your grandfather.'

'He was a painter?'

Max nodded. 'A good one.'

'I didn't know.'

'His studio is upstairs. You will enjoy looking at it. I believe it's just as he left it.'

'What was his name?'

'Luciano. Your grandmother hung the painting of your mother where it is now.'

'You have seen it before?'

He nodded. 'Shortly after it was painted your grandfather died and your grandmother married my grandfather.'

'You have been to the house before?'

'Once, when your grandmother invited me. She kept it locked.'

'Like a shrine,' Christina whispered.

'I suppose it must seem like that to you. When Roberto left she never spoke of him, but secretly I think she hoped and prayed he would return here to live.'

'Then that would explain why she didn't rent it out instead of keeping it empty all this time?'

He shrugged. 'I don't think she could bear to think of anyone else other than a Carletti living in it. I think she wanted it to stay like this for ever. What you see is exactly as she left it.'

She looked at him calmly. 'And marrying me means that when my grandmother dies it will belong to you.'

He shrugged. 'I like to think it will belong to both of us. But I do like the house, and you are right, it is an important part of your inheritance that must be preserved.'

'It's such a lovely house.' Christina moved away from the picture into the centre of the room. An expressive movement of her arm embraced it all. 'I can't believe this is where I was born. But for my mother's death, all my youth would have been passed in this splendid old dwelling.' Turning from him, she sauntered outside, standing on the patio and feeling the sun on her face. Max came to stand beside her.

'Now that you have seen the house, are you sure you want to live here?'

'Absolutely—at least for the time being.'

'I am against it, you know that, don't you, Christina?'

'Yes, but I am not yet ready to live with you as your wife, Max.'

'As you keep telling me,' he ground out tersely, 'but you could still live at Castello Marchesi. It is your home now. Is it that you don't like it?'

For a moment surprise left Christina speechless, but anger soon restored her voice. Did Max mean to dictate every single act of her life? All the same, knowing how dangerous it would be to cross swords with him again over this issue, she forced herself to stay calm and even managed to smile.

'I think Castello Marchesi is a splendid house, Max, and I shall look forwards to living there—as your wife. I merely expressed a wish to live here for the time being.'

'Even though it is against my wishes?'

'Yes.'

His expression became one of exasperation. 'Christina, you can come here as often as you please, but there can be no question of you taking up residence. For God's sake, you are my wife. Imagine the ridicule it will create when it becomes known that we are living apart.'

The tone was merciless and cutting. Why, oh, why did there have to be two such contradictory sides to this man? 'I will be sorry if that happens, and I do know that I am your wife, Max, so there is no need to keep reminding me of the fact.'

'You are somewhat apt to forget it.'

Christina spun round to face him, her face flushed with anger. 'How could I forget it?' she said bitterly. 'The property I will eventually inherit—knowing how it has been coveted by you since you were old enough to understand—gives me little chance. I am beginning to wish I were a vineyard or an olive grove,' she uttered sarcastically. 'Perhaps then I would merit some kind of attention from you.'

Max's eyes narrowed and after a moment a laconic smile twisted the corner of his mouth. 'It wasn't just the estate your grandmother had in mind in her proviso, it was the combining of the two families that was important to her.'

'She achieved that herself when she married your grandfather.'

'But there were no offspring, which are important to the continuation of the line. You do want children, I hope—or perhaps you intend making an issue of that like you are about living in my house.'

'I am sorry if my rebellious manner offends you, Max, but I am as I am. I cannot change my nature.'

'Not even to please me?'

'Especially not to please you.' Christina felt the tension increasing between them. Why was Max being like this? 'If it is the servile submission of a slave that you want, it is too bad. I have too much self-respect as a woman to bend to any man's will.' Her eyes did not fall before the hard blue gaze. 'Not even to please you.'

For an instant Max gazed at her standing very straight before him in a dress the vibrant colour of daffodils. The sun fell softly on her beautiful face, which was flushed a delicate pink beneath the heavy helmet of her shining dark brown hair. Her eyes were bright, and in that moment she looked breathtakingly lovely. He had to make just one single movement to take her in his arms, but he was in one of those tyrannical moods that would not allow him to yield to that desire.

Christina sighed, hating arguing with him. 'The combining of the two estates means a lot to you, doesn't it, Max?'

He nodded. 'I have put a great deal of time and energy into the working of Casa del Sole, and I am happy that it is to become part of Castello Marchesi. But I really don't like you living here alone.'

'Don't worry about me. Besides, you're not far away and I have no doubt you will be running my doorstep off on a daily basis—and I intend to visit my grandmother. Now I have met her I would like to get to know her. But I really would prefer to live here for the time being, Max.'

Max looked deep into her eyes. Suddenly he felt himself going back in time while the image of the lovely young woman before him abruptly blended into another image—that of a young girl splashing in a lake, her clothes and hair saturated and her laughing face alive with vibrancy and youth. He felt a pang of nostalgia, mingled with a sense of loss, because the girl in the lake was gone.

Combing his fingers through his hair, he sighed. 'Very

well, have it your way, but I don't like it. I will manage to survive, knowing I will have you eventually—and I will have you, Christina.'

Yes, Christina thought, his indomitable will was going to prevail as surely as night followed day.

'You will need to take on some staff,' he went on. 'Of course there is Lucio and his wife Elsa, who have been care-takers since your grandmother moved out, but they are old and like to do things at their own pace. They live in a small house close by. They have a daughter, Carmel—a sweet girl I can recommend—and I can send a couple of my servants.'

'Thank you. I appreciate what you're doing, Max, but I don't intend being idle.'

'I'd best warn you to expect a great deal of interest. There is no doubt that everyone will be full of curiosity and specu-lation at such an unprecedented arrival in their midst.'

'They'll find out soon enough that I am your wife.' She turned and looked at Molly when she came to join them. 'Well, Molly?' Christina said. 'Is the house habitable?'

'Yes, but where do we get the water from?'

'There is a well in the yard at the back of the house. The water is pumped up,' Max told them. 'There are also stables and out-houses where the wine and olives are processed at harvest, and quite a large cellar with considerable capacity of storage, which you can inspect later. At one time, many years ago, the house had its wine cellar on the ground floor, so that people lived on the first floor, until the new cellar was built outside.'

'How interesting. I can't wait to explore,' Christina said enthusiastically.

'You'll have plenty of time. I'll arrange to have provisions sent down and have someone get you some water. If there's anything you need, send Carmel up to the house—and Christina, if you should change your mind about staying here, you can always come home.'

'Thank you, Max, but I won't change my mind.'

He turned and left her then, angry and frustrated at not being able to persuade her. Perhaps a few days at Casa del Sole with no contact from him and having to fend for herself would make her see the error of her decision to distance herself from him.

When Max had gone out, Christina turned to Molly. 'Well, what do you think, Molly? Can you live here?'

Molly smiled—it was difficult not to do so after looking round this lovely old house with its splendid furnishings, good-sized kitchen and stove and lovely outlook. 'I would be happy to live here,' she said with sincerity. 'It has a good feel to it, but we will need someone to help run it.'

'Max is to arrange all that. Come along, Molly,' she said excitedly, taking her hand and almost dragging her along the patio. 'Let's take a look at the house.'

Walking on to the edge of the patio, she looked out on a view that hadn't changed for hundreds of years. The air was crisp, the sunlight turning the olive leaves from silver to blue. What a truly magical place this was, she thought. How could she not be happy living in this glorious place?

But then she thought of Max and some of the magic began to drift away, and she began to wonder if she was handling this all wrong. Should she be forcing him away from her? She had enough sense to know that by doing so there was a danger that she was inadvertently driving him into Francesca Cantoni's arms all the more. She couldn't bear to contemplate such a thing happening, and if the Italian woman was his mistress, what were Max's feelings for her?

Whatever had occurred between the two of them in the

past, Max belonged to her now, and despite the dispassionate way they had come together, they had made their vows before God. With this thought Christina's naturally buoyant spirit began to reassert itself and she was determined that eventually she would be a good wife to him. In the meantime, it was better that they were friends rather than enemies, and she would do her best to adjust to this strange new life that had been thrust upon her.

Standing on the terrace of Castello Marchesi smoking a cigar, Max looked out on the same landscape that had so enchanted Christina at Casa del Sole, but somehow he didn't see it. Ever since he had left her in England he had thought of no one else, his male body remembering her warmth, her sweetness and yielding in his arms when he had kissed her goodbye, the surprise of her complicit compliance and how she had leaned against him, allowed him to touch her hand, her mouth ready to hover beneath his own.

She had lived in his heart, in the pure agony of his mind and in his soul for so long, and, no matter how hard he tried, he had been unable to wrench her out of it. She had settled there and there she would remain for the rest of his days.

Chapter Eight

❧❧❧

The room was filled with early morning quiet. Everything in it swam with sunlight shooting rays of fire from the glass ornaments and gold-edged candlesticks on the dressing table. Throwing back the covers and climbing out of bed, Christina padded across the floor and opened the French doors. Stepping out on to the balcony, she gripped the wrought-iron balustrade and looked all about her. The landscape was like a sea of olive trees and vines, which fell away to the valley below, and cypress trees stood out like a water-colour painting.

Wrapping a robe over her nightdress, she went downstairs and opened the front door, taken aback to find a lovely, toothless old man, grinning broadly and holding a bunch of cyclamen, which, after bowing his head respectfully, he presented to her.

'Signorina Thornton, it pleases me much to see you and to give you these—from me and my wife Elsa,' he said in broken English.

Realising that this must be Lucio, Christina took the flowers and thanked him, deeply touched by his warm welcome. Wearing a battered old hat, shirt and baggy trousers, he was old—how old it was impossible to say—anything between sixty and eighty. She wondered how he could have found out so soon that she had come to live in the house and how he even knew her name. As time went on, she would realise that nothing remained secret for long about what went on in the neighbourhood.

Behind him appeared a small plump woman dressed in black with rosy cheeks and her iron-grey hair fastened in a bun—she reminded Christina of an apple dumpling. Unlike her husband, she could not speak English, but was able to make herself understood by gesturing with her arms. Going into the house with a confidence of long familiarity, she went straight to the kitchen where Molly was attempting to light the stove.

Elsa and Lucio lived in a small square stone house close by with their daughter Carmel and their son Pepi, a very capable young man who worked in the vineyard and supervised the workers and the harvest of the grapes and in October the olives, which would eventually ripen from tiny buds to glossy green and black fruits. They took both Christina and Molly to their hearts with such warmth and kindness that any apprehensions Christina had had about coming to live at Casa del Sole receded from her mind, but she knew that to make life easier she would have to learn the language to have a better understanding of the people she was dealing with.

Inquisitive to see the house, on the first day she went from room to room. Sitting on the silk bedspread in Lydia and Roberto's room, she had a strange feeling that this empty house was still very much alive. This house that she hadn't known existed until a year ago had become a vital part of her, and she knew that she could never leave it without leaving a wound.

The last room she entered, the room that made the biggest impression of all, was her grandfather's studio at the top of the house—a big room, with lots of windows giving plenty of light, which was essential to an artist.

Even after all these years the overall smell was of turpentine and paint. Sketchpads, pots of pigment and jars of brushes covered the top of a large table, and an easel and canvases of every size leaned against the wall. Some of the canvases were incomplete paintings of the Tuscan landscape, with scarlet poppies staining the countryside blood red, the colours of such vibrancy that they seemed to spring to life before her eyes. It was very much a working room, a room where she imagined her grandfather had spent some the happiest and most creative years of his life, where he would have felt at home with his aspirations, his desires, his own projections. Everything had been left in such a way that it was as if he had just slipped out and she half-expected him to walk in at any moment.

Christina adjusted with astonishing ease to the simplicity of her new life. She missed Max, yet she knew the reason why he didn't come to see her was his way of challenging her to go to him. But she had no intention of relinquishing this small piece of freedom just yet.

The early days were beautiful, golden days, filled with sun, siestas, long leisurely meals on the patio with Molly and leisurely walks in the olive groves and among the rows of vines, getting to know the workers and watching them work, and learning as much as she could about the growing and harvesting of grapes and olives. The estate was well run and grew some fine grapes and olives. The olive terraces were very old—probably dating back to the Roman or Etruscan times. At the back of the house were numerous outbuildings, one housing the large nets, which were spread under the olive trees in the harvest to catch the fruit as it was stripped from the branches. There was also an orchard with several fruit trees.

Lucio told her they were made up of apple, pear, lemon and almond trees, and another would bear a crop of downy golden apricots in June. July would bring cherries, red and white currants and succulent peaches. Molly was delighted and already looking forwards to picking the fruit and making vats of jam.

Things sat quietly at Casa del Sole. Everything had its place, and Christina persuaded herself that for the time being she needed nothing more.

Just one week after their arrival and being left pretty much to themselves, Christina stole out early when the sun was thin behind a pearly white wash of clouds. She could hear the twittering of birds in the olive trees with their twisted trunks and see the dew still sparkling on the grass. She waved and called *buon giorno* to the half-dozen workers who were already at work among the vines. They took advantage of the early morning and the cool of the evening to do their work and to rest during the hottest part of the day, which made sense, but to many Englishmen it would be seen as laziness.

In her blue-and-white-striped gingham dress and a white apron tied about her waist—having removed as many petticoats as was decent because of the heat, free from the constriction of fashionable tight lacing and the metal cage of corset stays and bustles and petticoats, she could move more freely and breathe more deeply—and carrying her straw bonnet, she was sauntering along, feeling a curious sense of detachment. There was much more to this place than she had thought. It was strange and more complex than she had ever imagined.

The tranquillity of her mood was shattered when a voice startled her, coming from the ridge above. She looked up, not expecting anyone at this early hour. The sun was on her and she raised her hand to shade her eyes, and then, as if she was seeing a dream awaken before her, she saw someone standing there who then began to walk towards her, moving with the confident ease of a man assured of his masculinity.

Only Max could move like that. She stood still, waiting for him to reach her, his black hair attractively ruffled and gleaming. At Casa del Sole she could almost forget he was close by and almost erase the memory of his cool welcome—but only almost, for her treacherous mind even now kept remembering the kiss he had given her on their parting in England.

He was smiling, his teeth a white slash in his bronzed face, and his eyes glinted as the sunshine shone directly in them. His smile closed like a fist round her heart and a warm rush of pleasure washed over her.

'Christina.'

At the sound of his voice she experienced a rush of feeling, a bittersweet joy in view of what stood between them. He had appeared too suddenly for her to prepare herself, so the heady surge of pleasure she experienced on seeing him was clearly evident. For one long, joyous moment they held each other with their eyes, savouring the moment, each aware of the powerful sexual force that sprang between them. His just being there sent a message of warmth.

She took a deep breath and tried to stifle her excitement. Max always caught her at her most vulnerable. He was dressed in a white linen shirt, dove-grey trousers and black boots polished to a mirror shine, and she saw how relaxed and at one with his environment he looked. He was darkly bronzed, and in contrast his brilliant blue eyes seemed to shine like bright gems beneath well-defined brows.

'And what brings you to Casa del Sole at this early hour, Max?'

'You. I had a desire to see my wife. Besides, I am always

up and about with the lark,' he replied, hiding his surprise at the changes that had taken place in such a short time. The last time he had seen her she had been dressed like a fashionable young woman. Before him now stood another Christina, vibrant in health, dark, tawny skinned, clad like a bandit princess, her hair tumbled flowing down her back. Here in this rustic setting, stripped of the social trappings that had not so very long ago been a necessary part of her life, the last vestiges of the pampered young woman revealed in her place the resolute young woman who, he marvelled, had rallied to take an interest in one of the largest vineyards in the district.

And yet in a strange way he was disappointed, having hoped she would have become tired of the solitude and isolation and come looking for him at Castello Marchesi. She straightened proudly as he soaked up the sight of her.

'I thought I had better pay you a visit to see how you're settling in—although I would not have disturbed you just yet. I certainly didn't expect you to be out of bed.'

'I am honoured—but you will see I'm not in any proper state to receive visitors.'

'I am your husband, Christina, not a visitor,' he reproached gently, feeling the need to remind her since she was apt to forget it. Warm lights shone in his eyes and he spoke quietly as his gaze swept over her, unconsciously memorising the way she looked, all flushed and fresh and alluring. In the time since he had last seen her she had become a woman, all soft, lovely, eternally female, with a vitality that could not be hidden. 'And you look fine to me. I assure you that dress becomes you perfectly.'

Her flush deepened with embarrassment and she began to walk slowly on. 'Thank you. I'll take your word for it. I wake early most mornings. I always think this is the best part of the day. It's such a shame to miss it.'

'I couldn't agree more. How are you settling in?'

She gave him a sprightly smile. 'Very well.'

A rakish grin spread lazily across his mouth. 'You seem to have suffered no ill effects from your time spent fending for yourself—no scars that I can see—no bruises.' Taking her slender fingers into his, he made a show of examining her carefully tended nails, while Christina watched in amusement before disentangling her hands from his grasp.

'As you see, Max, I have suffered nothing but a couple of broken nails that will soon grow back.'

'I am relieved to hear it. And you still like the house?'

'Oh, yes. It really is appropriately named—the house in the sun. Every morning the sun rises behind it and bathes the valley in warm light, and in the evening it passes over the house, setting beyond the hills. Carmel is an absolute treasure. And Elsa and Lucia are quite excited by my being here and are always coming and going on some pretext or other.'

'You don't mind, do you?'

'No, I like having them around.'

'You sent the servants back? Why?'

'Because Molly and I can manage.'

'You can?'

She smiled. 'Don't look so surprised. I'm not completely useless. I am quite capable of dressing myself and tidying up, and Molly, who has fallen in love with Italian food, has taken over the kitchen completely—once she got the stove to work. Carmel is a wonderful help and is teaching Molly how to cook. The language is posing a problem, but we are both determined to learn Italian.'

'Very sensible. It will help you to communicate.'

They walked on a little way and then she said, 'I've been thinking a lot about Lydia since I came here—indeed, how can

I not when I am living in the house she came to as a bride and her things are all around me? Tell me about my grandfather. Did he buy Casa del Sole?'

'Yes, he did. It was nothing more than a rundown old farm-house when he saw it, but he knew he had to have it—he fell in love with it—it was the first thing he'd ever owned that had nothing to do with his family. He bought it with the money he got from his paintings and completely rebuilt the place. It was also the perfect place for him to paint.'

'I've seen some of them—there are several unfinished canvases left in his studio.'

'And were you impressed when you saw them?'

'Yes. I expected to see poor, amateurish art, but what I have seen is very good. I didn't believe a painter would live in such a remote place. Do you know where he came from?'

'I believe his family lived in Rapallo—in the north.'

'Were they rich?'

'Very. His family owned a marble quarry in Carrara. The white marble is considered the purest marble in the world and they had been dealing in it for centuries. Luciano was the youngest of three sons and two daughters and he had no desire to join the family business. He went to school in Genoa and then on to Paris to be an artist—a very good one too, but not good enough for his name to go down in history.'

'Did he love my grandmother?'

'They were devoted to each other, and she loved the house as much as he did—which you know.'

'What did she say when you returned from England without me? Was she angry—upset, what?'

'She—was disappointed, but it was overcome by the knowledge that she would meet you eventually.' He stopped and looked at her, his expression serious. 'She has been asking after you. There are so many things she wants to talk to you about. You really should go and see her, Christina. In fact, I must insist that you do.'

'I intend to. As I walk about the house I see things—little things—a small stain on the carpet in the room that was probably made by Roberto—ink, I think, and a scratch on the table in the room that was his. I think to myself—he did that, my father, the man I never knew and never will.'

Max grinned. 'Ask Elsa. She'll talk about him till the cows come home.'

'I know and she does—all the time, but I want to know him in a way Elsa could never describe. I want to know him as a child would know its mother—as I knew my mother. Do you know what I mean?'

'I know what you are saying, Christina, but, never having known my own mother, it is difficult for me to understand fully.'

Christina was ashamed of her insensitivity. 'Of course, Max. Please forgive me. I forgot. It was not my intention to upset you.' They walked on in silence and then Christina said, 'I enjoyed meeting Guy. He seems nice. Does he live very close to you?'

'His estate adjoins my own.'

'He grows grapes?' Max nodded. 'How interesting. I didn't expect to find an Englishman owning a vineyard.'

'It was his father who bought it. When Guy's mother died, his father succumbed to the seductive dream to escape London life to a haven of sunny contentment.'

'So he bought a vineyard in the Chianti hills.'

'That's right, even though he could not speak the language and had no experience in growing grapes, but he won through in the end and now Villa Candido is a vineyard to be proud of.' He slanted her a sideways look. 'You say you enjoyed meeting Guy—but, it would seem, not Francesca.'

'No. To be blunt, Max, I did not like her at all and I sincerely hope any meetings between the two of us in the future are infrequent and of short duration.'

Max's face became taut and he looked straight ahead. 'You always were forthright, Christina. I owe a great deal to Francesca's father. When my father died and then my grandfather, Don Stefano Cantoni, Francesca's father, of all my neighbours, was the one person who came to my assistance. He moved from Sicily to Tuscany forty years ago. His family still live there. He is a good man, a fair man, for whom I have tremendous respect. As for Francesca—I have known her all her life.'

'And naturally she has loved you all her life.'

'Perhaps not as long as that.'

'But she does now.'

'In truth, I don't know. One never does with Francesca.'

Christina was silent. She was only just beginning to discover she knew nothing about Max's life before he had gone to England. She wanted to ask what his feelings were for Francesca, but held back. She didn't want to know, for the truth might upset her too much. Emerging from the deep shadows cast by the olive trees, she waved to Molly, who was setting the table for breakfast on the patio beneath trellising interlaced with trailing plants.

'I think breakfast is ready. Have you eaten? If not, perhaps you would like to join us.' She laughed lightly. 'Although I can't promise it will be anything as appetising as what you're used to. Molly was up early cooking some kind of sweet cakes and she has yet to perfect the recipe. Still, I suppose, spread liberally with butter and jam they will be palatable.'

'I'm sure they will be very nice. I take my hat off to Molly for having a go at something different, and, yes, thank you, I would love to join you—at least some coffee would be welcome.'

Molly was pleased there was a guest to eat her sweet cakes— a triumph after several failures. After serving them breakfast, she tactfully disappeared back to the kitchen with the excuse that she wanted to see what else she could concoct now Carmel had arrived to advise her on more delectable dishes.

A warm breeze had sprung up to set astir the slumbering countryside. A bougainvillaea trailing over the trellising threw a violent purple stain against the house, provided them some shade, but Christina enjoyed the gentle caress of the warming air. Sitting in her wicker chair across from Max at the table and feeling totally relaxed and at home as she sipped her coffee, she thought he had a similar ease about him. She saw his eyes grow more vividly blue as he seemed to follow her train of thought.

'I hate to say this, since I would do almost anything to prise you out of this house, but this place suits you,' he said quietly, his gaze settling on her face, strikingly aware of all the endearing qualities that had so intrigued and appealed to him when he had first set eyes on her in England.

'I know.' She gave him a wistful smile. 'I like the solitude. Suddenly my life has become increasingly simple, filled with small tasks that fill me with a sense of well being—getting up in the morning and sitting on the patio drinking my first cup of coffee with Molly, watering the potted plants and strolling through the olive groves. Even the cat's taken to me at last. It follows me closely on my evening walks, always stalking birds and lizards. At night the terraces around the house are alive with bats, and sometimes there are fireflies floating among the vines, looking like illuminated galleons floating in a sea of darkness.'

'You're beginning to sound like a proper Tuscan, Christina.'

'I will never be that, no matter how long I live here. I do wonder what my parents would make of all this. I like to think they are happy for me and wish me well. I shall be eternally grateful for all they did for me.'

'No doubt they will come for a visit very soon.'

'Yes, I am sure they will.'

She stared across the table at the handsome, forceful, dynamic man, and the moment seemed to freeze in time. 'I do know that I can't remain here at the house for ever, Max. I would like to see more of the area. In fact, I would very much like a horse—and a pony to pull a cart I found in the barn. It would be useful for Molly to go to the shops and the market in the village to purchase provisions.'

'Leave it to me. I'll see to it.'

'Would you? Thank you. I would appreciate that. At home in England I was pampered all my life and unable to do anything without having to explain myself. But now that I am tasting the novelty of doing just as I please—'

'Within reason, I hope,' Max remarked, his penetrating blue eyes reminded her of her position.

'But of course. I would not do anything to embarrass you.'

'It is good that you should get to know the place where you live and learn to see it through your own eyes.' He smiled. 'I am biased about the charm and beauty of the place, and I fervently hope that you too will fall in love with it and never want to leave—Tuscany, I mean, not Casa del Sole, since this is only a temporary arrangement.'

'I know that. I realise the honeymoon period can't last. I can't go on living like a peasant for ever. Although I believe I've already fallen in love with Tuscany,' she said, smiling back at him and realising with surprise that it was true.

'Despite our unsatisfactory living arrangements, I am impatient to show you Castello Marchesi. Since it is to be your home, the sooner you familiarise yourself with everything, the better. My winery is located right inside the castle, which I am sure you will find interesting.'

'Yes, thank you, Max, I would love to.'

Placing his cup on the table, Max rose and stretched his long, lean body. 'I'd best be getting back. Thank you for the breakfast, Christina. Since you would like to see more of the area we will make a start by riding into the village this evening.'

'But I don't have a horse yet.'

'I'll bring a spare—and my stables might even run to a pony.'

'It would be wonderful if you could—if not, I think I'll have to take up Lucio's offer of the loan of his donkey. It's a stubborn old beast, according to Carmel and I don't think it appeals to Molly.'

'I think we can do better than that. I'll call for you this evening.'

Christina stood up and watched him walk to where he had tethered his horse and waved when he rode on his way. She was aware that Molly had come to stand beside her, and that she too stood watching Max's retreating figure. They were both silent for a few moments, easy with each other. The special friendship that had sprung up between them was as vital and natural as a friendship could be, and Molly understood Christina like no other.

'Well, that was a surprise—Count Marchesi turning up for breakfast like that.'

Christina's smile was one of quiet satisfaction. 'No, really. I fully expected him to come some time. Although knowing how he is noted for his impatience, I'm only surprised he left it so long.' She smiled, a gleam of triumph in her eyes. 'I think he was hoping I'd weaken and go to him. It must have put him out that I didn't. He'll be back later—early evening he said. He's going to show me the area and then we'll ride into the village.'

'And how will you be going, might I ask? By carriage? Or riding that flea-bitten old donkey that does nothing but bray all night?' Molly complained.

'No, riding.'

'Then we must see you wear your finest habit.'

Christina was ready when Max arrived, riding a beautiful muscled sorrel horse and leading a grey mare and a shaggy-haired pony, which he handed to Pepi to deal with.

Max watched Christina come out of the house, a look of unconcealed appraisal on his face as he surveyed her jaunty burgundy habit and white shirt exposed beneath her open jacket. She had decided against a hat and had fastened her hair at her nape with a ribbon to match her habit, letting her dark tresses fall free.

He studied her, tracing with his gaze the classically beautiful lines of her face, the brush of lustrous ebony eyelashes. She was quite extraordinarily lovely. He had never seen the like of her. Even now she had that untamed quality that had first attracted him to her, running in dangerous undercurrents just below the surface, a wild freedom of spirit that found its counterpart in himself.

'You look lovely,' he said, taking her hand and leading her to the horse.

'It's a change to have the opportunity to dress up—and to ride. Goodness, I've missed it,' she said, stroking her horse's nose in appreciation.

'It's a lovely evening,' Max remarked when they were

mounted. 'We'll take the long way to the village to enable you to see something of the countryside.'

The evening air was sweet scented as they set off. Christina felt wonderfully happy. Everything seemed different when Max was around. She felt happy and carefree as she had not felt in a long time, and reckless—unwisely so, for it would be so easy to give way to recklessness with a man like Max.

He took her on a tour round the vineyards, riding along a labyrinth of paths and tracks open to anyone who wished to use them, sending up a cloud of dust in their wake. He told her about the different grapes that were grown, which grapes made the best wine, how they were harvested and how the Etruscans and Romans and the Medici family and numerous noblemen in Tuscany throughout the centuries had created one of the most recognised wine-producing areas in the world. He answered Christina's interminable questions with knowledge and pleasure, clearly in love with his work.

The village was an enchanting place perched on a hillside, its streets winding and narrow and its towers rising above orange-tiled houses. The piazza, the village's main square, was small, but like other villages it had the church—a baroque church built in sandstone, small and austere with a heavy carved door. The whole of the village seemed to have gathered there.

'Goodness! I never expected there would be so many people out at this time.'

'It's the same every night, in towns and villages all over Italy, when the people come out for a stroll—*la passeggiata*, in and around the piazza—to gather and converse with friends.'

They rode round the edge of the piazza. Christina was engrossed in the scene before her, then slowly she felt a tension evolve inside her. Max was riding so close because of the throng that their horses were almost touching. She was aware of his closeness. His hands holding the reins were brown and strong, the nails cut short. He leaned forwards slightly and the back of his neck was exposed, brown like his hands, his dark hair brushed crisp and smooth into his nape. His back was broad and strong, the seams of his jacket stretched tight, and where it fell open she could see his thighs gripping his horse, muscled and taut beneath the smooth fabric of his breeches.

'I think I would like to get down and walk,' she said, her voice low, for her thoughts had alarmed her.

'Good idea.'

Max jumped down and assisted her, tethering their mounts to a rail. As the large number of villagers idling about the square greeted them, Christina, aware that she was collecting glances as she moved among them, realised that Max was accorded every deference. She heard him call out to several in his own language. The locals were obviously interested in his English wife. It unnerved Christina to see how they paused in their conversations to stand or sit and stare at her. It was as if she was an object of curiosity in her stylish western dress.

'Come,' Max said, placing his hand under her elbow, 'I think some refreshment is called for. A glass of wine is the nectar of the gods. It is generally consumed as part of a meal, but a glass sipped during twilight in good company for pleasure's sake is also part of the Italian tradition.'

'Then how can I possibly refuse when you put it like that?'

'You can't—and I would be mortally offended if you did,' he teased.

He led her to some tables outside a restaurant. Immediately the restaurant owner came to their table and greeted Max effusively. There were polite exchanges between them in Italian. Max ordered the wine and then sat back to wait, resting his foot on his opposite knee, his eyes settling on his companion.

Voices echoed and bounced around the square. A mandolin could be heard above the noise of the crowd and a male voice began to sing. Some of the men sat around tables, talking and playing cards. Reaching inside his jacket, Max leisurely withdrew a silver case and took out a small cigar. Immediately the owner struck a sulphur match and lit it for him and then poured them both a glass of wine. Max turned the glass in his hand, studying the deep red wine, then he took a long swallow and lowered his glass.

Feeling relaxed and enjoying her wine and the smell of Max's cigar, Christina was astonished when someone suddenly pulled out a chair and sat at their table. She was pleasantly surprised to see Guy and her face broke into a bright smile.

'Guy, how lovely to see you.'

His face flushed, his eyes bright, he beamed at her, settling his frame in his seat. Crossing his legs, he rested his riding crop on the upper knee. 'Likewise, Christina. You certainly light up the square with your beauty.'

'You really are charming, Guy,' she replied, smiling graciously.

'I always make a point of being. I have a sister, Caroline, who would very much like to meet you. You must call in and see her—we're only up the hill.'

'Without an invitation?' Christina said doubtfully.

Guy laughed. 'You're in Tuscany now, Christina. Etiquette has its place, but friends should be able to visit one another whenever they wish. Don't you agree, Max?'

'Absolutely,' Max drawled.

'Then Caroline must also call on me whenever she likes. I'd like to meet her,' Christina said, cheered immensely at the thought of having a friend so close.

'How is your Italian coming along? Are you finding it difficult?'

'Very,' she replied, 'although I think you will find a great improvement in Molly. She finds it easier than I do, but then she is with Carmel and Pepi for most of the day and their English is not so good, so she is forced to communicate in any way she can. She insists on learning the Italian name for everything she touches, and repeats it out loud, relentlessly, insisting that I do the same.'

'It's a good way to learn.'

She laughed. 'I promise I shall persevere. Are you here to see someone in the village?'

'I was riding home after visiting a neighbour when I saw the two of you ride into the village. I didn't think you'd mind if I tagged along.' He looked at Max, who nodded curtly. 'The least you could do is to invite me to join you in a glass of wine, Max.'

Max regarded Guy with a sardonic expression. 'Help yourself.' Indicating the bottle, he shoved a spare glass towards him. 'You usually do—although I imagine you've had more than your share already.'

'Just a couple of glasses, Max, no more than that.' Guy poured himself a generous glass, taking a gulp. 'Are you managing to learn anything about growing grapes, Christina?'

'I know as much about growing grapes as the cat,' she laughed. 'I will never be an authority. I suppose when the harvest comes things will be done as they have always been done at Casa del Sole and that under Max's supervision Pepi will be prepared.'

'Pepi is a capable young man and extremely knowledgeable about growing grapes,' Max told her. 'Casa del Sole is a little more exposed to the sun, so that means harvest will probably start a week earlier than most. The workforce will increase when the itinerant workers arrive.'

Christina gave an exaggerated sigh. 'I have so much to learn, I doubt I shall ever know the whole of it.'

'No one does. Time and experience is what it's all about.' Guy grinned as he looked her over carefully, unheedful of Max's face hardening as he witnessed the perusal. 'You really are looking very lovely this evening, Christina,' he remarked in undaunted spirits. Leaning forwards, he braced his elbows on the table, cradling his glass between his fingers. 'Frankly, I'm rather envious of Max's good fortune in meeting you first. I swear if you were not already married to my good friend, I would sweep you off your feet myself.'

Christina laughed softly, light-hearted at his nonsense. 'And I'm beginning to think you're an outrageous flirt, Guy.'

'He is,' Max seconded, carefully knocking the ash off his cigar, 'so don't make the mistake of falling for his charms by thinking he's harmless.'

Guy spread his hands in plaintive appeal. 'I am harmless. Don't listen to him, Christina. Max always was the jealous one.'

'And you're a wicked old rogue,' Max reproached, 'with a string of women lined up from here to Sienna, so kindly stop ogling mine.'

Christina almost choked on her wine and laughter bubbled from her lips. 'Will you please stop it, you two,' she protested, looking from one to the other, totally unable to comprehend Max's mood and the apparent love-hate relationship between the two of them. 'I've seen children better behaved than you.'

'You're mad, Guy,' Max remarked drily.

Guy accepted the biting gibe with a nonchalant smile and giving Christina a broad wink. 'And I'll thank you to keep your comments to yourself, or I might have a few to say myself.'

'Heaven forbid,' Max drawled.

Guy raised his glass to Max in a salute. 'Here's to you, Max. Your taste in women has certainly improved.'

'I'm glad you admire my taste so much. But then, you always did.'

Christina stepped in, unable to resist broaching the subject that challenged her curiosity. 'Do you mind telling me why the two of you are constantly at daggers drawn? You are not only neighbours, but friends too—or supposed to be, are you not?'

'The best,' Guy said. 'And since my good friend is so reticent, I shall put you in the picture. Once upon a time Max and I were raised almost as close as brothers—we were the same age and both our mothers had passed on. When we were eleven we went to England to school together, came back to Tuscany for the holidays together, socialised together…' he looked at Max and grinned '…in fact, we seem to have done most things together don't we, Max? But then Max went on to Cambridge and I stayed at home.'

'Then why all the antagonism?' Christina asked, still unable to understand. And then a thought suddenly occurred to her. 'Does it concern a woman by any chance?' The two men looked at each other and then at Christina.

'Your powers of perception are sharp, Christina,' Guy remarked, laughing softly. 'How is the charming Francesca, by the way, Max?'

'Ah,' Christina said, beginning to understand, and with it came anger. 'Signorina Cantoni!' From the start the Italian woman had become an object of distrust and animosity.

His expression suddenly grim, Guy smiled thoughtfully at his glass. 'Francesca Cantoni—extravagant, spoiled, too confident in her own power—always used to getting what she wants with a snap of her fingers—is that not so, Max?' He was unable to hide the bitterness underlying his words, which piqued Christina's curiosity.

Max's expression turned glacial. He nodded ever so slightly. 'I prefer not to bore Christina with talk of Francesca, Guy, if you don't mind. It cannot have escaped your notice that the two of them did not exactly hit it off.'

As she looked from one to the other, Christina drew back. That Francesca Cantoni was the cause of the antagonism between the two of them was evident and she no longer had any wish to listen to talk about that particular woman.

'Never mind,' she uttered sharply. 'You are right, Max, I don't want to know. It's got nothing to do with me anyway.' She forced a smile to her lips. 'Max is showing me the countryside, Guy. It's very beautiful.'

'Is he, now? Then should his commitments prevent him from showing you more of it, I would be happy to call on you at Casa del Sole—to entertain you in his absence.'

The bright blue eyes considered Guy without any hint of expression, then with slow deliberation Max removed the cigar from his mouth and held it between his fingers, staring at the glowing tip. He raised his eyes, and, had it not been for the coldness in them, his reply might have passed for a flippant remark.

'Then I shall have to adjust my affairs so they don't interfere with my entertaining Christina—or my wife forgetting that her duties lie with me at Castello Marchesi.'

Christina was unable to determine what she saw in Max's face—chagrin or irritation, or both—but she saw the muscles in his cheeks flex and she watched him impatiently tamp his cigar out in the ashtray.

Shoving his chair back, Max stood up. 'Excuse us, Guy. I

think it's time I took Christina home. It will be dark by the time we get there.'

Guy and Christina stood up together.

Uncertainty flickered in Guy's eyes, cutting through his friendly demeanour. 'With any luck I'll see you again soon, Christina. I apologise if I've said anything out of place that might have embarrassed or offended you in any way. Perhaps Max was right and I have drunk one glass of wine too many.'

She smiled warmly. 'You haven't said anything to offend me, Guy. Goodnight. It's been lovely meeting you again. Please don't forget to tell your sister to call on me.'

Dusk had deepened over the land and the west blazed with a brilliance of gilt-framed magenta and pink as they rode back to Casa del Sole.

They rode in silence, neither of them impervious to the throbbing strain of the atmosphere. The encounter with Guy had cast a cloud over the evening, although why it should, since Christina genuinely liked him and enjoyed being in his company, defeated her. She was incensed with Max for his churlish behaviour, and she had found his proprietary manner towards her irritating.

On reaching the house, they rode round the back to the barn. Max was furious and Christina could feel her own anger building by the second.

'There's no need for you to dismount,' she told him coldly and distinctly, slithering off out of her saddle and slapping the reins in his hands. 'Thank you for the loan of your horse.'

Intending to walk away, she pivoted on her heel, then gasped in surprise when Max quickly dismounted and clamped his hand on her arm, jerking her round to face him.

In a voice vibrating with anger he said, 'Do not ever speak to me like that again.'

'I'll talk to you any way I like,' she blazed, shaking off his hand. Her eyes glinted like shards of green glass as they glared at his stone-chiselled features, her expression daring him to attempt control of herself. 'How dare you assume any kind of authority over me? I know it's inappropriate for Guy to call on me alone, but if he happens to bring his sister to meet me, then it has nothing to do with you.'

'It has everything to do with me. You are married to me and I will not have other men calling on you. Is that clear?' Max's face was still, but his eyes were a brilliant, quite dangerous blue. 'I know Guy Saunders. He was looking for an argument.'

Christina sprang immediately to Guy's defence. 'If he was, then from where I was sitting he had just cause. None of it was his fault. All right, he might have had a drop too much to drink, but he meant nothing by what he said. You were boorish and insufferably rude and I'm surprised he took it in good part instead of throwing a punch at you. At least he had the good manners to apologise to me.'

'And so he should. Like you say, the man was drunk.'

'Then his encounter with you must have been a sobering experience.' Christina lifted her head imperiously, throwing back her hair, and Max felt the blood run warm in his veins. Her small chin was squared up to him and her eyes sparked, striking like bright steel in her proud challenge to his authority. 'You were obnoxious. I ask myself how can two people argue like children when they are supposed to be such good friends.'

'We have had our differences occasionally—'

'Differences?' she flared. 'I should hate to be within firing range if war is declared. What on earth was wrong with you?'

Max knew he was being unreasonable, but he plunged on recklessly, combing his fingers through his hair irately. 'That licentious neighbour of mine has lost no time in wheedling his way into your affections. Undoubtedly he has been much attracted to you from the beginning. I will not stand by and watch him trailing after you, showering you with overzealous attentions.' As soon as the words left his lips, Max had the distinct impression that he had just foolishly stirred a volcano and was about to see it erupt in his face.

'Then look the other way,' Christina hissed, seeing his face blanch at her words in the dim light, 'for you will not prevent it if it is what I want. But I will tell you this, Max Marchesi. I am not a pawn to be used by any man for his convenience.'

'You will not see him unless I am present,' he warned softly.

'I most certainly will,' she said firmly. 'Why ever not?'

'Because I ask you not to.'

'You *ordered* me not to, and I didn't like it.'

'Very well. I will ask you,' Max persisted implacably. 'Should he come looking for favours, do not entertain him unless I am present.'

'That will depend on the circumstances. Not even for you will I be impolite and tell him to go away if he comes to Casa del Sole—but I think he has enough sense not to. Should he do so, I promise Molly will be present at all times. Does that satisfy you?'

'No, but I will accept it.'

'Thank you. I happen to like Guy—very much, as it happens—as a friend,' Christina retorted pointedly. 'I may be your wife, Max, but you don't own me. I will respect your wishes, not your authority, and I expect you to respect the same commitments I make to you. And since we are talking of favours, isn't there a woman hoping for favours from you, a very demanding woman, as she made no secret of demonstrating to me on the night I arrived?'

'I am surprised to find you think like a wife, Christina—even a jealous one,' Max uttered scathingly.

There was enough truth in that remark to make Christina flush irately. 'I am not in the least jealous—and I sincerely hope I have no reason to be, although if you really are enamoured of that woman, then our marriage is meaningless.'

'Except by virtue of a signed contract binding you to me—one you will honour.'

The sting of his words reminding her of her duty made Christina's eyes snap with fire. 'I don't think you need worry overmuch, Max. I have little choice but to honour it.'

She took a step back with every intention of leaving him, but he seized her hand and relentlessly pulled her back. Holding her gaze pinned to his, he spoke in a tone of quiet implacability.

'I'm afraid we need to reach a better understanding before I leave, Christina.'

'What is there to understand?'

'This,' Max said as he caught her to him and lowered his mouth to hers.

Christina saw the purposeful gleam in those heavy-lidded eyes and her attention was absorbed by the sensuous male lips slowly coming closer to hers. The warm breath on her face and the masculine scent of his body were all combining to work their spell on her. With desire beginning to course through her veins in danger of setting aside her doubts and fears, she drew in a swift breath and tried to twist her head away.

'Kindly take your hands off me, Max, and don't you dare try to kiss me into submission. I don't want you to—not like this.'

Max caught her chin and forced her to face him, and what

he saw in her eyes was in complete variance with what her lips conveyed; there was a trembling in her slender body that belied any words of denial she might utter. His head was suddenly filled with her fragrance and something wild escaped within him, something too strong to fight. As if he had no will to stop them, his arms tightened around her, gently moulding her to his body.

'Christina,' he breathed, his voice a hoarse, ragged whisper in her ear and it burrowed right down into her soul, unlocking all her forbidden passions. His heavy-lidded gaze dropped to the inviting fullness of her lips, lingering there. 'Why must you fight me all the time? I want to kiss you.' When she tried to pull back, a faint smile touched his mouth. 'Are you not as curious as I am to find out if it is as enjoyable as when we kissed before? I promise you, we Italians kiss very well.'

Christina swallowed convulsively. 'No,' she whispered. 'Besides, you're half-English.'

'My passionate side is all Italian.'

Whatever Christina had expected on returning home, it was not to find herself crushed in an embrace of steel and swept soaring into a dark place where the only thing she could feel was his lips capturing and moving ceaselessly on hers, demanding and ruthless, forcing them apart for the invasion of his tongue.

Swaying a little, for she felt the dizzying, heady aura of his masculinity, Christina moaned in protest and instantly his mouth softened, then began a slow, unbearably erotic seduction, promising far more than this first hungry contact between them, bringing her body to vibrant life in his arms. Her anger subsided rapidly, forgotten in the feverish crescendo of desire. She gave herself up to the magic of his kiss, savouring the difference with a sensual awakening as Max's arms held her captive, her body moulded to his, and yet the longer the kiss continued, the more torn apart she became. It was as if she were two people, one yielding and warm, the other rigid with alarm.

She was aware of his hand stealing up her spine to the back of her neck, caressing, imprisoning her head. Knowing she was playing with fire, she let him go on kissing her, wanting him to kiss her, just this once, to experience again the fleeting joy of his mouth on hers, the disturbing sensations that shimmered through her body. Her arms, which had been fighting to get free of him, stole up his chest and round his neck.

When he finally raised his head and drew back, Christina stood there in a kind of disoriented, bewildered state, looking at the ground. His next words brought her restless spirit plummeting back to earth.

'I did not suspect that you were hiding such a tempest of hungry longing and indiscriminate passion, Christina. Are you thinking I shouldn't have done that?' he murmured lightly, tipping her chin up. Christina lifted her mutinous green eyes to his and his conscience stirred. To master her with his own hard masculine strength had been his initial objective, but the thought had fallen aside, lost in the emotion of their turbulent kiss. 'I think you are. What is it, Christina? Is it possible that I have rendered you speechless at last?'

Swamped with confusion and anger, her face was flushed with shame. She shrank before him. He had won after all. What flaw of passion was it whose aftermath left her like a weak kitten? And why only with Max Marchesi? More than anything, at that moment she wanted to put as much distance between herself and Max as possible.

'I think I would like you to go.' Her voice was a strangled whisper.

'Don't you think we should talk?'

'No—not now—not tonight. I couldn't. Please go, Max.'

He walked calmly away from her. After settling the horse he insisted on leaving in the barn, he did as she bade, telling her he would see her tomorrow. He didn't try to touch her again, but there was a gleam in his eye that told her this was far from over—a promise that he would hold her much closer and much longer in the future.

Moonlight brushed the olive trees as Christina watched him ride away before turning towards the house, trying to understand what had happened and consumed with the emotions Max was able to rouse in her. Her mistake was that, until Guy had turned up, she had enjoyed his company so much that she'd been totally disarmed.

Chapter Nine

All that night Christina found herself thinking of Max. She kept going over in her mind that moment when he had kissed her. What joy that had brought her, what earth-shattering delight that had temporarily obliterated everything else. She knew something unthinkable had happened. She had felt it, she supposed, in England. She had felt it when she had gone to see him before he had left for Italy. There had been some essence of him that had entered into the place that had been sorely hurt by the knowledge that her parents were not who she had thought they were all her life.

Every time they met something had flowed between them, something at that time she did not want. And last night when he had kissed her, she had felt the warmth and masculine vigour of him. She had wanted the moment to go on for ever, for she had experienced a strange languor, warm and deep, cradling her in a most unusual need. He was the most physically attractive man she had ever seen in her life and she greatly feared that she could be overwhelmed by him.

Christina's thoughts turned to Francesca Cantoni, and the barbs of jealousy pricked her deep.

Jealousy!

After giving it a great deal of thought, Christina knew without doubt that this woman believed she had an assured place in Max's life. And just as certainly Christina knew she wanted him for herself. The reality hit her with a jolt, yet still she resisted, trying not to let her foolish emotions overrule her intellect—and yet her foolish notions won and she was happy to be carried wherever they fancied taking her.

Her senses swirled, as if experiencing something way beyond her understanding. Why had she let this happen to her and yet, if she was honest, had she any choice in the matter?

Max called on her early the following morning. In place of the cold animosity that had marked his mood the previous night, his tone was polite, impersonal and businesslike. Relieved but wary, Christina looked at him, suspecting he had decided that it was time that their relationship took a new direction. She was proved right.

'Christina,' he said when they were seated on the patio drinking coffee, 'we have been invited to a dinner party the day after tomorrow. It will be a small gathering and quite informal—just a few friends. Since I have no intention of letting you languish your days away at Casa del Sole, it will be a good opportunity to begin your introduction into Tuscan society. It's high time you were officially introduced as my wife. You—have no objection, I hope?'

'Of course not. I look forwards to meeting your friends, Max.'

'It is also a tradition that the week before the grape harvest a ball is given at Castello Marchesi, so you will have plenty to occupy your time in the run up to it. In the meantime, you will come to Villa Marchesi tomorrow. I want you to see what is to be your home and for you to visit your grandmother. I will also give you a conducted tour of the vineyards and the cellars. I know you will find them interesting.'

The swell of pleasure Christina felt at the prospect of seeing Castello Marchesi again—and being with Max—seemed excessive. She really did wonder what she was doing trying to keep this distance between them. 'Yes—I would like that, Max.'

That day would stand out in her memory. It was so warm and clear that years later she would be able to recall it in every detail. She rose early and was washed and dressed when Max's carriage arrived. Looking cool in a cream linen suit and white shirt open at the throat, he was waiting to receive her outside the magnificent edifice of Castello Marchesi.

Max felt his breath catch in his throat as he watched Christina climb out of the carriage. She looked quite angelic in pale lemon and white and a straw bonnet, her hands holding a folded parasol in front of her, but as he came closer he saw her green eyes held an expression that was vibrant with excitement and anticipation and was anything but angelic. His eyes gleamed as they lightly caressed her.

Christina hesitated as she reached him. It was as if she was seeing her husband for the first time. How tall he was, how blue his eyes. For a moment her thoughts were confused and she found herself wondering why she hesitated, why he seemed like a stranger, a handsome, desirable stranger, but she quickly shook off her strangeness when he came towards her.

Gripping her hands firmly with his cool fingers, he smiled straight into her eyes, drawing her close. 'Welcome to Castello Marchesi, Christina,' he murmured, kissing her cheek. 'And how lovely you look. I thought we might stroll down to the vineyards before the sun gets too hot—that's if you agree.'

Christina sensed his pride for his vineyards. 'I was hoping I could.' She smiled at him obliquely. 'That's one of the reasons why I'm here, isn't it?'

He cocked a sleek black brow and his mobile lips curved in a mysterious smile. 'I fear the nearness of you would completely destroy my good intentions, so it's safer if we are seen out and about. After that, I will show you my cellars where the wine is produced.'

'I would enjoy that very much. I'm sure what you will show me will put Casa del Sole's modest winery to shame.'

'Nonsense. The cellars at Casa del Sole are better than most— your grandmother saw to that. My own cellars have undergone impressive renovations over the years and I have invested heavily in up-to-date vinification equipment. Naturally I am justifiably keen to show them off at every opportunity.'

Christina laid her hand into the one he offered and descended the steps to a lower level of the gardens. Though a smile was in his eyes, he remained silent as he took her arm through his, drawing her closer to his side, leading her along a shaded path that took them to the vineyards, pointing out to her the woods which were a hunting reserve for pheasants, wild boar and roe deer.

They were both unaware of the gaze of the elderly dowager countess, a smile of satisfaction on her lips as she watched them stroll away arm in arm.

Christina began to relax. The day was off to a good beginning. She could only hope that Max's restraint would continue and her resistance would not be tested.

They spent a pleasurable hour strolling along the rows of vines. Broken up with olive groves, the vines were changing colour, with splashes of yellow, orange and deep red. Introducing her to some of the workers, their hair shining with sweat, their shirts damp with exertion, who were cutting down the weeds among the olive trees and vines that had sprouted up after the recent rain, Max proceeded to give her another lesson on growing grapes, explaining how grape yield was a key factor in wine quality, and how it was determined by the severity of pruning in the spring.

'If a vine produces too many grapes, the wine will be thin and dilute, but if the yield is too low, the wine will be unbalanced and concentrated.'

He went on to tell her how the crop could be seriously affected by spring frost and rain, and pointed out the different varieties of grapes, telling her how his great-grandfather had conducted experiments with the blends of different grape varieties.

Christina found it extremely interesting and Max had a wealth of knowledge about it all. When the sun became too hot they headed back to the house.

As they sat beneath a vine-laden trellis on the wide terrace, a servant appeared with cold drinks and delicate cakes.

Christina glanced across at Max and found him watching her in an oddly intent manner, his eyes half-closed.

'When did your family settle in Tuscany, Max?' she asked, sensing where his mind was wandering and considering it in her best interests to direct it along a different path.

'As far back as nine hundred. Castello Marchesi has a chequered history. My ancestors were powerful warriors supporting the Florentines against the Siennese, and Castello Marchesi was destroyed on numerous occasions. The last time it was rebuilt was during the fifteenth century.' Almost at once he smiled and settled back in his chair. 'It's good to sit together like this,' he murmured.

Christina looked up from her drink to find his attention

boldly surveying her face. When she had relaxed against the cushions, her unintentionally provocative position caused the fabric of her dress to stretch taut over the rounded contours of her breasts, providing an appreciative Max with a delightful view, which he was thoroughly enjoying.

Immediately Christina straightened herself and faced his hawkish stare squarely.

'Did no one ever tell you that it's rude to stare so openly, Max?'

The tantalising grin returned and grew wider and his blue eyes were almost taunting. 'Frequently as I was growing up. I was just admiring you.'

'And you are far too bold,' she chided. Strangely, she was not offended; in fact, she felt elated. Relaxing, she found herself looking at him, at his wide, smiling mouth, his masculine throat, his broad chest and strong legs stretched out before him, his hands, long fingered, resting upon his lap. She wondered what it would feel like to have those hands on her bare flesh. She could still feel the pressure of his fingers on her own when he had received her.

'Do you mind?'

'I take heart that you care,' she said, unable to quench the sweet pang of pleasure this caused her.

'And I do care, Christina.'

Those glowing eyes burned into hers, suffusing her with a growing aura of warmth. How could she claim uninterest in a man when his very nearness and the words from his mouth could so effectively stir her senses? His gaze lightly caressed her face, dipping to the low V of her neckline and the soft swell of her creamy breasts. Her breath halted as the kindling fire flared brighter in those bright blue orbs, and then they caught and held her own.

'Just in case you haven't noticed, I am rather singular in my pursuits, Christina. When I first met you I thought you were not only lovely but intoxicatingly innocent, and when I left you that day and I kissed you, I wanted to drag you behind a tree there and then and make you melt in my arms. I had scruples enough to ignore that impulse, but many are the times I have cursed my scruples.'

A treacherous warmth was slowly beginning to seep up Christina's arms and down her legs and gave her reason to hope that he might care as much for her as he did her vineyard after all. 'You thought that?'

He nodded. Across the table their gazes held. Christina's heart began to hammer uncontrollably as Max purposefully came to his feet. Moving towards where she sat he took her hand and raised her up, a deep, velvety softness in his eyes.

'Please don't stand so close,' she whispered desperately.

His eyes smiled, but his voice was quiet and seductive. 'I can hardly kiss you when I am sitting across the table from you.'

Christina swallowed convulsively. Everything was happening too fast. 'You are going to kiss me?'

He nodded. 'That is what I want to do. A man is entitled to kiss his wife from time to time.'

'But I have hardly forgiven you for the last time you kissed me.'

'Then I'm afraid you're going to have to forgive me again,' he murmured, drawing her into his arms and lowering his face to hers. 'Besides, the last time I kissed you, as I recall, you enjoyed it. You did kiss me back.'

His mouth was suddenly there upon hers. The shock of the contact of his lips was electrifying. His hands moved down her spine, moulding her tighter to the hard length of his body. He kissed her deeply, thoroughly and slowly, producing a knot of pure sensation in the pit of Christina's stomach. She shivered as his mouth left hers and traced a molten path over her cheek, her brow, pausing to press gently against the fragile eyelids, before seeking her lips once more.

She surrendered helplessly to the demands of his hands and mouth, and as her pliant young body strained against him, her mind was devoid of everything but the feeling of his parted lips slanting across hers, devouring their sweetness with a ferocity that gave evidence of his starved senses, relentless in its demand.

Until now Max had managed to convince himself that his memory of the passion Christina had aroused in him was faulty, exaggerated, but now the kiss and the exquisite feeling of having her in his arms, the fullness of her breasts pressed against his chest, the taste of her lips clinging to his, surpassed anything he'd ever felt.

He was virile and masculine, a man used to the lusty pleasures that were always available to him, but where Christina was concerned, who was young and innocent, untouched and pure, a woman who had never known the touch of a man's hands on her naked flesh, he would need to proceed with care.

When he finally raised his head and drew back, Christina let her head fall against his chest, her hands flattened against the fine material of his jacket. 'You are a rogue, Max Marchesi, with just one thought in your mind.'

He chuckled low in his throat. 'Rogue? No, Christina. I have only the desire to share a blissful moment and introduce you to the tender touch of passion.'

His voice came as a soft caress and sent an eddy of sensations spiralling down through the core of Christina's being. Gradually her heart slowed to normal and her breathing evened out. Raising her head, she looked up at him and smiled, her lips pink and tender from his kiss.

'Then try to restrain yourself, Max,' she cautioned, softly teasing, drawing away from him. 'I did not come here so you could seduce me, only to see your wine cellars and magnificent house.'

Max's eyes burned like embers behind his dark lashes. 'That was my excuse to get you here. You tempt me sorely, Christina, and I have every intention of seducing you.'

'I sensed as much.'

His gaze touched a quickness within her and Christina quickly averted her eyes. No man had ever set her to trembling for any reason, much less a mere look or words. What was there about this Italian that disturbed her emotions and her senses? Max had the looks and an agile, intelligent mind, and just the memory of his kiss filled her with delicious excitement that made her yearn for him to kiss her again and to go even further.

Placing his hands on either side of her face, he captured her eyes with his own, delving deeply into their depths. 'Do not be frightened by what is happening between us, Christina. Although I think you are not so much afraid of what is happening between us as you are of how quickly it is happening.' His thumbs stroked her warm cheeks as he murmured with tender gravity,

'You know, when you burst into my home that night I couldn't believe you were real. When I saw you standing in the doorway I thought you looked like an angel. I thought if I blinked my eyes you would be gone—that I'd discover you were only a dream.'

'I am very real, Max.'

'Angels are not real.'

She smiled impishly. 'When you kiss me, my thoughts are anything but angelic.'

'So, you do feel something for me.'

She nodded wordlessly. He was right. Everything was happening too quickly. Yes, she had felt the pull of his attraction from the very beginning. She had tried to fight it, but failed. Greatly disturbed by the path her mind was taking, she said, 'Will you show me your wine cellars now?' She glanced away and then peered back at him. 'And will you please promise to behave?'

With a slow, provocative smile he held out his hand. 'I'll show you the winery, which is located right inside the castle,' he lightly replied, making no vow to the latter question.

They entered the cellars through a solid wooden door, locked with quite the largest key Christina had ever seen. Following Max down a flight of wide stone steps, she found herself in a large barrel cellar, filled with countless oak casks stacked in rows, which, Max explained, was where the high-quality wines reached maturity. He showed her the fermentation cellar and the huge cylinders he'd had installed to crush the grapes, where they were then allowed to ferment and gently mature into something delicious and essentially Tuscan.

Christina felt sheltered by the darkness of the labyrinth of cellars that ran beneath the great house and could almost feel the past closing in on her. It was so quiet, like a church. The vaulted ceilings, the brick walls—it was the perfect setting for a confession. It was impressive indeed.

Part of Christina's mind followed Max's words while the rest of her attention centred on the man and what had just occurred between them. Here, she thought, he was in his element. His voice bore an edge of authority, and his manner was sure and confident. Silently she followed him, sensing the pride in his work as he patiently explained the many different processes of making wine, from the picking of the grapes to the finished product, to which he was committed one hundred per cent.

As she listened to him her wonder grew. There was much more to Max Marchesi than she had thought. He was a man who didn't do less than his best. She became thoughtful as she listened, brought back to awareness when she heard him chuckle softly.

'Forgive me. I tend to get carried away when I talk of my work. I hope I'm not boring you. I fear I've given you too detailed a tour of my cellars.' His smile was only slightly apologetic. 'But now you are the wife of the owner of a vineyard, at least you will be more informed and able to answer any question put to you.'

'I never realised there were so many different types of grapes and nor have I been more confused.'

'Come,' he said, taking her elbow and escorting her back to the main part of the house. 'I'll give you a tour of the house and then it will be time for lunch. I am sure we can run to a glass of the best wine Castello Marchesi has to offer.'

The interior of Castello Marchesi, the parts of it she had not seen on the evening she had arrived, was no less magnificent than she expected. She moved through a series of sumptuous apartments and a vast ballroom that shimmered with the dull gleam of gold and was decorated in baroque plasterwork.

Lunch was *bruschetta* topped with drizzles of olive oil and fresh tomato salsa, fresh green salad and cold meats, followed by wild strawberries, which grew all over the hills and roadsides during the summer months. Dipped in sweetened mascarpone cheese and balsamic vinegar, they were delicious.

It was a completely relaxed affair, the wine making Christina drowsy and completely at ease with her companion. She felt the peace and rightness of it settle within her. Never had she felt more light-hearted and carefree. As they talked and ate and drank their wine, she was vaguely aware of Max's appreciative gaze on her animated face and his complete absorption with her, but she was having such a lovely time, she really didn't mind.

'So, Christina, do you like Castello Marchesi?'

'Who could not be enchanted with it? It's like a fairy-tale palace.'

'Your upbringing would have been very different had you been raised here. The English are less formal than we Italians.'

'It makes life easier, I suppose.'

He glanced at her, eyes narrowed. 'When I first saw you at Tanglewood, cavorting in the lake with Peter and James, I remember thinking how uninhibited you were—it was as if you didn't have a care in the world.'

A cloud passed over her face at the memory. 'I didn't.' She brightened and gave him a puckish smile. 'Being uninhibited was a natural characteristic of mine then. I thought you knew that. I am unconventional and have always done things on impulse.'

Max laughed out loud, his eyes glinting with amusement. 'Somehow I didn't quite imagine you allowed convention to dictate your every move. Because of your English upbringing, it must be hard for you to understand the fierce nature of the Italians. It is the Latin blood in us—and although you were born with it, your upbringing has subdued it somewhat.'

She frowned. 'Not that much. My blood often reaches boiling point, and you've felt the full blast of my temper in the past—as you will in the future.'

His lips twitched. 'Now that I do remember.'

'It used to worry me that I couldn't be the sort of girl Mama wanted me to be—you know, death before dishonour, God before king and country, and all the proprieties. I did try, but when I realised I couldn't possibly be like that, I forgot about it.'

'I see,' he teased with a lazy, devastating smile. 'What an unusual young woman you are, Christina, and what a delightful day you have given me. I look forwards to introducing you to my friends as my wife.'

This was true, for Max felt that as soon as she began to integrate into society, the sooner she would realise that her place was beside him. He had taken his grandmother's advice to be patient, and he was prepared to respect Christina's innocence, her naïvety and inexperience, but he had not realised how difficult it would be.

He had fallen victim to his outrageously impertinent girl-woman-bride, who had flatly refused to yield to his authority and blithely incurred his displeasure by insisting on keeping herself apart from him. He had to accept it was the penalty for forcing her into a marriage against her will; in view of how deeply this had hurt her, it was a small price to pay. But he was not prepared to wait for ever.

'Come, I think it's time to go and see your grandmother. She is so looking forwards to seeing you.'

'What happened to Rosa—my nursemaid? Is she still alive?'

'Very much so. She was a much-loved member of the household, but with no children to look after she returned to live with her family in Naples. I wrote telling her of our marriage and she replied saying how very happy she is with the way everything has worked out for us.'

'Then I will write to her.'

He grinned. 'I knew you would.'

The rest of the afternoon passed quite serenely and a stroll through the gardens of Castello Marchesi could not be denied.

They were full of wonders, infinitely varied, intricate and, above all, beautiful, and Christina was content to let her escort lead her along gravel paths with flower-filled borders. Elegant statues and a fountain spouting crystal-clear water high into the sky drew the eye. Max lent himself to a most gentlemanly comportment, making her feel as if she were the only woman in the world.

She sighed deeply, reluctant to leave this beautiful place.

Max turned, his eyes looking deeply into hers. 'And what are you thinking that makes you sigh?'

Just the deep timbre of his voice stirred Christina, yet now that in her mind she had committed herself to him, she felt a certain amount of shyness.

'I was thinking how unbelievable it is that in just a few weeks my entire life has changed—no—not just weeks—from the moment you came to England looking for me. The moment you spoke to me at the lake, my whole life veered on a different course.'

'Do you not believe in fate, Christina?'

'No, not really, although I don't suppose I've ever really thought about it.'

In all it proved a most delightful day and Christina experienced a tinge of regret when the time came for her to return to Casa del Sole. Castello Marchesi was magnificent. It overwhelmed her with a feeling of antiquity, a medieval place; when she had walked through the massive oak door earlier, she had felt as if she was passing into another world.

Yes, she thought when Max took her home and placed a gentle, restrained kiss on her lips before driving off, it had been a most enchanting day.

She watched the carriage disappear up the track. Breathing deeply she turned her eyes towards the horizon. It was a glorious evening, the sky a deep blue and a dozen shades of pink and yellow. She hugged herself and smiled and wondered how she could contain her happiness. Tomorrow Max would come calling and the future would be theirs to shape and share. Was it really possible to be so happy, to feel such joy shimmering inside her?

Still smiling, she went into the house. There was a sparkle in her eyes and a delicate pink flush on her cheeks.

Carmel had gone home and Molly was in the drawing room seated in a chair reading a book. She glanced up when Christina came in and smiled. 'You are positively glowing, Christina—and I don't think I need enquire as to the reason.'

Laughter trembled on Christina's lips as she threw her bonnet into a chair. 'I never could hide anything from you, Molly. I've had the most wonderful day,' she said, wanting Molly and the whole world to know. Never had she believed she could be so happy.

It was a busy few weeks for Christina and she became increasingly happy as they slipped by. There wasn't anyone who had not heard of the English woman who was Max's wife. Who she was and where she came from and what her relationship was to the dowager Countess Marchesi was a mystery that had initially created enormous speculation among the people in the area. But now her heritage was generally known.

She appeared regularly at social events and her popularity multiplied tenfold the more she attended. So did the number of people who clamoured to be introduced. She became an accepted member of Max's circle of friends and found a friend of her own in Caroline, Guy's sister. Twenty-two years of age, she was a tall willowy woman with fair hair and bright, intelligent grey eyes and was extremely pleasant.

On her visits to friends and neighbours, Christina chatted to whoever was seated beside her and thankfully they were unconcerned that she did not speak Italian and conversed in English. The conversation was mainly about the *vendemmie*, the imminent grape harvest, and how everyone hoped the weather would hold out. Heavy rain at this time could mean disaster for most of those present.

Max looked on proudly as some of his friends seemed to find her manners and looks, her direct, straightforward approach quite taking. As her social activities expanded, the experience seemed to have a good effect on her self-confidence.

Max was never far from her side. They were a striking couple, the count splendidly tall and elegantly masculine, smiling a lazy approving smile at his beautiful young wife, who seemed to make him laugh with a delight that anyone who observed it and knew of the circumstances that had brought them together, were made to believe that, in spite of this, they were joined together by more than affection.

When Christina remembered the arrogant, tyrannical and high-handed way in which Max had manoeuvred her into marriage, she was grateful that he respected her wish to have time to grow into their marriage, but she was not unaware of the stormy, tumultuous passion she could arouse in him with a mere kiss and she was in no doubt that for a virile, red-blooded male like Max, this state of affairs could not continue for much longer. He desired her. He told her he was very proud of her—she saw it time and again at the functions he escorted her to, and he did care for her—but he did not love her.

Which brought to mind Francesca Cantoni. Max never

mentioned her and Christina was quietly relieved that she was absent from the functions she attended, but she suspected that she was never far away. Eventually her suspicions were realized.

It was unbearably hot. Christina was returning to the house after taking a young goat that had a partiality for Molly's washing back to Elsa. Wearing a sprigged green dress that was old enough to go on the rag heap, and a wide-brimmed hat with no adornment whatsoever, she was more concerned with keeping the sun off her face than appearing elegant. She knew she wasn't looking her best when two people, a man and a woman, on horseback, appeared on the hill in front of her. The woman was Francesca Cantoni.

Christina could not help but be aware after their first encounter that she would have trouble with the Italian woman, and if she could have found somewhere to hide she would have done. Unfortunately, she couldn't fit behind the gnarled old trunk of an olive tree. And so, taking the bit between her teeth, she walked towards her.

'Signorina Cantoni! Can I help you?'

'That depends. I was out riding and I thought I'd ride by and see how you like living at Casa del Sole.' She spoke with the proprietary pride of one who had lived here all her life, longer than the newcomer, making Christina feel like an interloper.

Francesca's eyes rudely took in every detail of Christina's dishevelled appearance. There was a distasteful curl to her lip and her look made Christina feel so very inadequate and, worst of all, so very vulnerable.

Christina wondered how this woman managed to look so cool in the searing heat. Her hair was piled on top of her head beneath a fetching hat to match her dark blue habit, with a froth of white lace at her throat and a cascade of glossy ringlets at the nape of her neck. Everything about her was precise and impeccable. Even her horse looked as if it had been the model for one of the superb statues she had seen in the gardens at Castello Marchesi: snowy white, flowing mane and plumed tail.

'I like it very well,' she replied in answer to Francesca's question. 'I am flattered that you should have come out of your way to enquire.'

'Not really. I am on my way to the village.'

'Then don't let me keep you,' she said, noticing how her groom, a surly, morose-looking individual, hung back.

Francesca looked down at her, an enigmatic expression in the cool dark eyes. 'You won't,' she said, controlling her restless horse superbly.

Christina looked at her steadily. Was this woman Max's mistress? she wondered, not for the first time. Was she still part of his life? She gave herself a mental shake. There were too many questions for comfort. 'Why have you really come, Signorina Cantoni?'

'No reason in particular, so there is no reason to feel ill at ease by my appearance, I can assure you.'

Christina could detect more than a hint of mockery and rivalry in her eyes. Once again she was surprised at the heavily accented beauty of Francesca's voice. Its pitch was deep and husky. It was a voice that would mesmerise men—they would become trapped by its silken charms.

'I'm not. I'm quite calm, thank you.' Feeling her skin begin to prickle with the heat, Christina looked towards the house. 'It's extremely hot. Perhaps you would care for some refreshment?'

Francesca seemed to consider the invitation and then

smiled and nodded. 'Yes, I would like that. Then we can have a proper chat and get to know one another, so to speak.'

'Why?' Christina knew she had committed a social discourtesy, but the word was out before she could stop it.

Francesca smiled thinly. 'I see that we already understand one another. It is as well that we get to know one another since we have so much in common.'

'We do?'

'Max.'

His name fell between them like an axe felling a tree.

Christina looked at her with unaffected astonishment. 'I see.' And she did see. Very well, in fact.

Keeping Christina at a disadvantage with the inferiority of being looked down on, Francesca did not dismount and rode a fraction ahead until they reached the house.

'I hope you don't mind if we sit inside.' Welcoming the cool interior of the house, Christina removed her hat and shook out her hair. 'I've been out for some time and it's far hotter than it was.'

'Not at all. I too prefer to be inside.'

'And your groom?' Christina asked as the man slouched in a chair on the patio.

Francesca shrugged unconcernedly. 'Bruno will be comfortable where he is.'

'Then I shall have refreshment sent out to him.'

Going into the kitchen, she asked Molly to bring some cool drinks. Molly was always a good judge of character and, seeing Christina's visitor through the half-open door, a look of distaste curled her lips.

'Watch out for her,' she said quietly. 'She'll do you a mischief if she can.'

Christina sighed, brushing back her hair. 'I can only hope she doesn't stay too long.' Pasting a smile on her face, she returned to her visitor. 'Please sit down.'

Francesca gave Christina a sidelong glance, seating herself in a deep leather armchair and resting back against a fat crimson-and-gold tasselled cushion. 'Thank you. What a delightful room this is,' she remarked, her eyes sliding over the furnishings with little interest while giving more attention to the portrait of Lydia above the fireplace.

'Yes, I like it. Along with all her other qualities, my grandmother has impeccable taste.' Christina was aware that Francesca was playing a game with her, like a cat with a mouse. She deeply resented the woman in this house.

Carmel came in and placed a tray of lemon cordial on a small rosewood table between them.

'Please see that Signorina Cantoni's groom on the patio gets some, will you, Carmel.'

Christina poured and handed Francesca a glass, then sat back in her own chair, calmly sipping her much-needed drink.

'Why are you here?' she asked at length, placing her glass down, the resentment heavy in her voice. 'I am sure it was not to discuss the comforts of this house.'

For an instant the atmosphere between them shivered with tension, but if Francesca was disconcerted by Christina's manner she did not show it. 'The relationship between you and Max is a strange one. It has been commented on.'

'Really? In what way is it considered to be strange?'

'You live in one house, Max in another.' Her lips twisted in a sneer of scornful pleasure. 'The situation is hardly conducive for marital bliss.'

'How Max and I choose to conduct our marriage has nothing to do with anyone else, although I am surprised people have nothing more interesting to gossip about. What I am concerned about is Max's happiness and my own without reference to anyone else.'

'Max is an important figure in the area, so it is only natural that he attracts a good deal of attention.'

Christina fought the conflicting rage within her, and with a wistful smile she took a sip of her cordial. After a moment she raised her eyes. 'I understand that you and my husband have been friends for a long time, Signorina Cantoni.'

Francesca laughed softly. 'I like to think so. Max has the right to choose his friends.'

'My husband has many friends, many of whom I have met. I would like to think that his friends are becoming my friends.'

'I am sure they are—I hear all sorts of things about what functions you attend, what you wear and who you talk to, but Max has a right to his own friends. Marriage does not mean a man is in thrall to his wife. If so, it is the surest way of driving him into another's arms.'

Christina met Francesca's eyes steadily, seeing the sparks within their depths. 'You think so, do you, Signorina Cantoni? Is this a common occurrence in your world, because I assure you it is not in mine?'

Francesca picked up her glass. She was beginning to wonder if she had underestimated Max's wife. Holding the glass between her well-manicured fingers so that the light reflected off the cut crystal, she looked at Christina.

'You will soon become accustomed to our ways and enjoy them as we do—with discretion, of course.'

Christina knew then that the Italian woman had shown herself. In those few words she placed great emphasis and implied that it made no difference how she regarded Max. Her position as his mistress was intact and would remain so, and

Christina did not know how she was going to bear it. Feeling her heart sink to the very depths of despair, she chided herself for not being more calm and deliberate in this matter, but she was fighting for something as vital to her happiness as anything she could imagine—her marriage—and no mistress was going to come between her and the man she had married, past or present.

'You know, you are far too young and inexperienced for a man like Max,' Francesca went on. 'Max likes his women more—mature.'

Christina stared at her, her eyes on fire as a slow smile touched Francesca's taunting lips. She could feel the heat of the woman's venom spreading in the oppressive quiet of the room. 'Like yourself is what I think you mean. Signorina Cantoni, you have come to my house under false pretences and I resent that.'

Francesca met her gaze steadily. 'I came to see you in good faith.'

'I don't think so.'

Francesca's eyes narrowed. 'You are too arrogant—just like all you English.'

Christina stood up, clenching her hands to prevent them trembling in her anger. 'I think you had better leave. You and I have nothing more to say to one another.'

Francesca rose slowly, like a sleek cat unfolding itself. Her eyes narrowed. 'I do not believe you are so naïve or so simple that you do not know what a valuable asset you are to Max. You are sitting on something infinitely more precious than your charming self, more precious than gold, something he has coveted for years.'

'Tell me.' Christina was fighting to keep a hold on her composure.

'Casa del Sole. This house and the estate, like a beautiful temptress, have beckoned him for years.'

'I already know that. Max told me when I first met him.'

'You hold him by his indebtedness to you, so do not delude yourself into believing it is you he wants.'

'And you would know that, would you?'

'Oh, yes. It is no secret.'

Christina already knew that Casa del Sole meant more to Max than she ever would. She was painfully aware of the cynical calculation of which she had been the object, and the cold-blooded way in which he had set about playing on her innocence and vulnerability, but having to hear it from this woman's lips was insulting. Even more than the insult was the contemptuous way this woman had entered her house in an attempt to destroy her.

She lifted her head, making a great effort to steady herself. She mustn't let this creature see the full extent of her rage, which grew and grew to become a virulent force. Its power frightened her. She thought she was going mad, but then she realised it generated its own peculiar strength, and the strength enabled her to say to herself that she had to survive. She would not be cowed or play the part of a broken victim.

'Signorina Cantoni, I asked you to leave. Please do so.'

With an arrogant toss of her head, Francesca moved towards the door, where she turned and looked back. 'I will see you tonight at the ball you and Max are giving. I shall be accompanying my father. I look forwards to it.' Without another word she swept out, the scent of her expensive perfume lingering in the air.

Scarlet faced with anger, Christina opened her eyes, which she had just closed to shut out the vicious face of Francesca Cantoni, feeling the full force of the wreck that she had brought about. She was alone in the midst of a ruin, too dazed to think, too numb to feel, but she could still hear, over and over again, the brutal, vicious words the Italian woman had uttered, as she had tried to shatter the image of the man she adored.

A sharp pain in her chest told her that anger and disappointment were not enough to kill what she felt for Max. He fascinated and repelled her. The feelings she had for him were like a damaged plant, which she was determined to tear out by its roots, even if her heart was ripped apart in the process.

At that moment Christina really needed someone to talk to. Going in search of Molly, she found her in the kitchen preparing another tasty meal. The table was cluttered with tomatoes and fresh vegetables and herbs, which were also hanging from the ceiling in bunches, along with onions and garlic, and there was a lovely smell of oregano and mint coming from a pot bubbling on the stove.

Sensing everything was not well with Christina, Molly removed her apron and went with her to the drawing room where Christina poured out everything Francesca Cantoni had said to her. All the while she was impatiently pacing the carpet, unable to contain her anger. When she had finished she flung herself in a most unladylike fashion on to the sofa, so insulted by the Italian woman's visit that her heart pounded until she could scarcely breathe.

'How can I possibly face the party tonight with that woman present? I feel so angry and insulted that I will be bound to say something I shouldn't and make things worse.'

Molly stared at her. This was the first time since coming to Italy that Christina had shown any signs of anger or bitterness. She told Christina in no uncertain terms to ignore the words of a vicious, jealous woman. But Molly was angry at the way Signorina Cantoni had stirred the seeds of doubt in Christina's mind and was disappointed in Christina's reaction, and there wasn't any way she was going to allow her to skulk away.

'Why, I would never have taken you for a coward,' she admonished. 'What excuse will you give if you decide not to go? That you have suddenly developed a violent headache and taken to your bed with your salts? That isn't like you. If you don't show your face tonight you'll have an extremely furious Count Marchesi knocking on the door in no time at all.'

Christina sat up and looked at her. With the thought of action, her head went up and her shoulders went back.

'You're right, Molly. I will go and I will show Signorina Cantoni that I am Max's wife—Countess Marchesi—and I intend to sparkle as never before.'

Molly smiled broadly, glad to see Christina more like her old self. Her eyes were feverishly gay, eyes that looked like the naughty girl of old. 'Sparkle? But you have nothing that sparkles to wear.'

'Oh, yes, I have,' Christina replied with a triumphant smile, springing into action.

Taking Molly's hand, she almost dragged her upstairs and proceeded to go through her wardrobe for something suitable, knowing the moment she drew out the sapphire blue that she had found it. It was a beautiful dress, low cut over the bosom and nipped in at the waist. She held it out, running an appraising eye over the fine silk embroidered with silver thread.

'This will be just perfect. No modest creams and lilacs tonight, Molly. My flag must be nailed securely to the mast for all to see.'

Christina stood staring at the dress, her sapphire blue. Reaching out, she trailed her fingers over the soft material. This dress more than any other evoked so many memories. A lump of emotion clogged her throat as the past year rolled away.

'Oh, Molly. Do you remember when I wanted to wear this dress to impress James? I only chose the colour because he told me it was his favourite. Mama wouldn't let me wear it.' Her lips curved in a wobbly smile. 'She said it would upset the vicar's wife.'

'Quite right, too. There's a time and a place to wear that dress, and in my opinion tonight is the appropriate occasion.'

'There's a little less of it than I normally wear,' Christina said with a twinkle in her eyes, 'but Max can't fail to notice me.'

Molly chuckled and agreed.

Chapter Ten

Christina had not felt so excited, apprehensive or frightened at the prospect of a ball since she had left England. She had been at Castello Marchesi for most of the afternoon, helping with the flower arrangements and making sure everything would be ready for when the guests arrived.

With Molly and Carmel fussing around her she paid great attention to her *toilette* and dressed with care in the most revealing gown she had ever worn, completing the look with a diamond necklace and matching ear drops. She turned from the mirror to face Molly, and their eyes met with the gleaming look of successful conspirators.

'You look lovely, Christina. Your husband will not be able to resist you when he sees you.'

It was sunset when Max called to collect her. In a rustle of sapphire silk she swept into the drawing room. Max was pouring himself a drink, his tall, muscular frame resplendent in an exquisitely tailored black suit, his neckcloth dazzling white. He looked unbearably handsome. He also looked absolutely furious as he came to a complete halt and his blistering gaze raked her from head to toe before freezing on the daring display of tantalising flesh swelling above the bodice of her gown.

Moving closer, he loomed over her like a hawk. Standing head and shoulders above her, he looked down at her from the advantage that his height gave him. He had a very pleasurable view of what lay beneath her less than demure bodice and whenever he chanced to glance her way—which would be often, the high swell of her luscious breasts was a tantalising sight for any man, who would certainly enjoy the treat.

'Go and change it,' he said in a hard tone that Christina had never heard before.

Christina stared at him in stunned disbelief. 'What?'

'I asked you to change your dress.'

'But—there is nothing wrong with it,' she protested, managing to look extremely innocent despite the seductive allure of the gown.

'If we were to dine alone, then I would have no objections to you wearing it, but if you think I am going to allow you to display yourself in such wantonness tonight, then you are mistaken. You will have every male present after you like a pack of dogs. Go and take it off.'

Christina's colour rose with indignation. 'I most certainly will not,' she burst out furiously.

Max's jaw hardened as he suddenly realised she really did intend defying him and wearing that dress to the ball. 'Damn it all, Christina, are you trying to provoke me?'

'No, of course not.'

'Tonight you will dress as befits a Marchesi,' he said impatiently. His haste to return home to greet their guests drove all caution from his mind and he forgot the fate of dealing firmly with Christina. Her sudden angry glare should have warned him.

'Max Marchesi,' she snapped, 'I will dress as befits myself. I have no intention of changing. I reveal no more than any other woman who will be at the ball tonight, and I cannot for the life of me understand why you are behaving like this.'

'Can you not? Then I will tell you. Italian woman are more modest in the way they dress and would be highly critical of a woman seen exposing so much bare flesh. You are also my wife and I will not have every man present ogling and fantasising about what it would be like to bed you when I have yet to do so myself.'

Christina sighed, her anger abating, but she would not relent. 'I can see that you are angry—'

'How observant of you,' he mocked curtly.

Ignoring his sarcasm, Christina persevered in what she hoped was a reasonable tone. 'I will not take it off, Max,' she said, taking a white silk shawl and draping it around her shoulders, hiding the two offending orbs from her husband's angry gaze. 'I don't like it when you order me to do things and I wish you wouldn't. If you think you married a complaisant, silly female who would willingly do your bidding, you didn't get one.'

'I am beginning to realise that. Consider very carefully before you think of defying me, Christina,' he said in a silken voice.

'Why, Max? What will you do? Beat me?'

'Don't be ridiculous.'

Max gazed at the beautiful young woman before him, her eyes flashing like angry jewels, her breasts rising and falling with suppressed fury, and his anger gave way to reluctant admiration for her having the courage to stand against him. She had grown up since she had come to Tuscany and become more beautiful, arrestingly so, with her dark burnished tresses artfully woven into a swirl of grandeur, the colour contrasting vividly with her sun-tinted flesh, her brilliant green eyes and soft rosy lips.

Looking down at her, he was unable to find any trace of guile in those flashing eyes or her belligerent upturned face. Within him, he felt a pang of nostalgia for the laughing girl in the lake. Furious with his inner reluctance to see her for what she had become, he turned on his heel and headed for the door, where he turned and held out his hand.

'Come. We don't want to be late for our guests.'

Picking up her small reticule that matched her gown, Christina moved towards him, swamped with conflicting emotions, including amazement and relief that, having stood her ground, she had won. Sadly she didn't feel all that triumphant as she followed him out to the waiting carriage.

As the carriage, open to the soft evening breeze, began to move on, she looked at his stern profile. 'Max, I'm sorry about the dress. Truly. But do you have to be so angry? Tonight is important to me and I really do want it to go well.' She did her best to smile, to make her voice sound light, treating the matter of her gown as though it was of no importance.

He turned and looked at her directly, and she felt the need to recoil from the expression in his eyes. They were as hard as rock. There was nothing in them of the lively warmth, the good humour that had lit up his face of late when they had been together.

Max stared at the tempestuous young woman in the provocative sapphire-blue gown. When she'd come to Italy she hadn't known what to expect and of late she had tried so hard to integrate with his friends and come to terms with what was expected of her as his countess.

The fury within him died abruptly and, as he looked into her glorious eyes, his stomach clenched at hurting her further.

'We both want it to go well, Christina, which is why I am concerned with what you wear.'

'To be displayed like some possession of yours?'

'One of the duties of a wife is to perform as hostess for her husband.'

'Which I intend to do to the best of my ability.'

'I know you will and I am proud of you. But there is just one thing you have to do before we reach the house.'

'There is? And what is that?'

'Kiss your husband.'

Christina's breath caught in her throat at the husky timbre of his voice and the desire in his eyes. He held out his hand to her and, without realising what she was doing she lifted her hand and gave it to him, waiting for him to make the next move.

Max noted her hesitation and his sensuous lips curved in a slight smile. 'Come over here,' he said quietly.

Some small, insidious voice in her mind urged her to obey, reminding her that, after her earlier defiance, Max was entitled to a kiss. Another voice warned her to stay where she was. She swallowed, looking at the space on the seat that separated them. 'Couldn't you meet me halfway?'

The sweetness of the question was almost Max's undoing, but he managed to shake his head. 'I want to kiss you, Christina, but after your disobedience, if you want me, then all you have to do is slide along the seat.' He lifted an eyebrow, his mouth curving sensuously. 'Well? It isn't too great a distance.'

Too naïve to know how to hide her feelings, Christina lifted her green eyes to his, and her longing for his kiss was in their soft depths. 'I—I don't think I know what I want,' she whispered touchingly, 'but right now I really would like you to kiss me.'

As if drawn by a will stronger than her own, feeling the

gentle pull of his hand, Christina moved towards him and almost fell into arms that closed round her with stunning force. For one breathless moment his smouldering eyes studied her face while the pressure of his arms increased, and then he bent his head and placed his lips on hers, his sensual mouth claiming hers in a kiss of violent tenderness and touching desire, while his hands slid over the sides of her breasts. Lost in the heated magic, Christina felt all her resistance and her will begin to crumble. She fed his hunger as his mouth moved urgently against hers, desire pouring through her.

A shudder shook Max's powerful frame as his dormant passion exploded, and the same uncontrollable compulsion to have her that had seized him when he had first laid eyes on her was in danger of overtaking him. As she returned his kiss with such gentle innocence, until now he had managed to convince himself that the memory of the passion that had erupted between them in England was exaggerated, but he was wrong. His passion for his lovely wife surpassed anything he had ever felt.

What seemed to be an eternity later he lifted his head, just as the carriage was drawing up in front of the house. Kissed into insensibility, drawing a shattered breath, Christina gazed up at him. His brow was furrowed, his eyes slumberous, knowing and lazy, a thoughtful smile hovering about his mobile mouth. How was this man able to strike such fire in her blood? she wondered as her heart began to thump with a sweet wildness that stirred her very soul.

The next thing she knew his lips were on hers once more in a surprisingly tender kiss. When he raised his head, some-where in the depths of those knowing blue eyes smiling down at her, she saw something deep and profound and quiet. It held her captive, promising her—what?

That was the moment she knew that she loved him. She had loved him for a long time, perhaps from the beginning, but only now did she realise it.

She swallowed, trying to keep her voice from shaking in reaction to his kiss. 'I think we had better stop now, otherwise we are not going to be in any fit state to greet our guests.'

'Agreed. Kissing is something we can continue later.'

The green eyes were wide as they looked at him. 'You would like this to continue?'

He frowned at her. 'And why not? I look forwards to knowing my wife as a husband should, Christina,' he said, tenderly brushing her cheek with his finger. 'It is time the bargain was fulfilled. My patience is not endless. Have you no idea how the merest sight of you tortures me?'

His voice was low and husky in her ears, and Christina had to dip deeply into her reservoir of will to stop the shattering of her defences. 'It was never my intention to cause you pain, Max, but now is not the time to press me.'

In the gathering dusk his face was in shadow, but his eyes seemed to glow with heat. 'No, you are right. We will continue with this discussion later. We must think of the evening ahead. Tonight is your night, Christina.'

'I am apprehensive.'

'You'll carry this off without a hitch. A lesser woman might fail, but not you.'

Christina digested this for a moment and then slowly inclined her head. 'I will try not to.'

'I know you will,' he murmured, squeezing her hand encouragingly.

Climbing out of the carriage, together they walked up the steps and went inside, just as the glittering carriages of Tuscany's elite began to arrive.

* * *

The whole place was ablaze with light, with flowers and garlands everywhere. Glass doors stood open and the gardens were alight with coloured lanterns, and tables and chairs had been placed on the terrace and covered walkways, where guests seeking respite from the dancing could gather and talk, and for those not inclined to dance there were rooms set aside for whist and faro. The overall effect was stunning.

On entering the house, Max went to have a word with the footmen at the door. The dowager countess, attired in a plain black gown, its only relief being a rope of creamy pearls around her throat, glided across the marble-tiled floor to her granddaughter. By appearing at the ball, the dowager Countess Marchesi, one of the most illustrious and influential personages in Tuscany, was putting her stamp of approval on the union of the Marchesi and Carletti families—along with giving her granddaughter some sound advice.

'My dear, you look quite radiant, and that colour does justice to your colouring. This is going to be the most enjoyable evening I've had in years. However, I would like to instruct you to put yourself on good terms with everyone, to treat everyone the same—even those you would rather ignore.'

Looking into those shrewd eyes, Christina knew her grandmother was referring to Francesca Cantoni. When she visibly balked at the idea, the old woman smiled and tapped her arm with her fan and said in her regal voice,

'I may be old, but I am not a fool, and I can see when something unpleasant is in danger of developing. Don't let it. You must rise above it, Christina.' She paused, waiting for a comment from her granddaughter, but Christina merely regarded her in non-committal silence. 'Had Max shown the slightest partiality for any one woman,' she continued quietly,

'I would be extremely concerned. But he has not. So,' she said, smiling at Max as he came to greet her, 'enjoy the ball.'

Christina stood by Max's side, trying to appear calm as they received their guests. She looked exquisite set against a backdrop of unashamed opulence, waiting to receive some of Tuscany's privileged class, some she already knew, others she was looking forwards to meeting. The dazzling radiance of her smile had everyone in thrall.

Max bent his head towards her. 'I do believe I am the envy of every man present,' he murmured.

'And I believe I am the envy of every woman present,' she replied, smiling into his eyes.

No man watching her as she moved to the rustling of her silk train, could have said whether their admiration was given to the perfection of her smooth features, the diamonds that lay shimmering against her skin, or the curve of her sublime smile.

Conversation became muted as all eyes became fixed on this fabulous creature who had appeared within their midst. Max Marchesi was as enchanted as all the gentlemen present by the wide-eyed beauty of his wife. There was something remote and detached in her attitude and everyone stepped forwards, eager to be greeted by her.

The kiss had left a sultry brightness in her eyes and a flush of colour across her cheeks. Feeling the way she did, vigorous and exhilarated and positive in a way she had never felt before, Christina believed she was capable of anything tonight—until the footman in stentorian tones announced Don Cantoni and his daughter Francesca.

Christina stiffened her spine and watched the Italian woman draped in a gorgeously provocative crimson gown sweep across the floor. Without so much as a glance at Christina, she went directly to Max, which made Christina's blood boil. Francesca was playing one of her clever social games, designed to keep Christina firmly in her place, the subtle snub calculated to disarm her hostess by reminding her that she had first claim on Max.

Aware of the snub to his wife, his expression grim, Max took Christina's hand and drew her forwards. 'You remember Christina, Francesca.'

Francesca turned her head and looked at Max's wife. Her eyes were hostile and her heart cold, but with a practised smile she drew herself erect and smiled. 'Of course. How charming you look, Christina, and how nice to see you again.' Her smile did not falter though the reminder of their earlier unpleasant encounter was on both their minds.

'Why, thank you for the compliment.' She smiled at the Italian woman as one would an amusing child. Max looked bemused at her confident reply, but Christina was determined that no one would intimidate her tonight.

Watching Francesca and Don Cantoni move away to mingle with the other guests, Christina's instincts warned her that she was under threat. She must not allow herself to be disadvantaged on her own territory. At all costs Francesca must be prevented from embarrassing her before so many witnesses waiting speculatively to receive the latest society scandal.

Christina was pleased when Guy and Caroline appeared.

Max greeted Caroline warmly. When he looked at a smiling Guy, he gave him a steady look. 'I thought you wouldn't be able to make it.'

'I didn't think I would be able to, but I couldn't let business get in the way of an invitation to dance at Castello Marchesi,' he replied in jovial humour. 'And neither could I resist the opportunity to dance with your beautiful wife.'

'You will probably find that most of her dances are taken,'

Max said drily, his eyes hardening as he observed Guy's gleaming eyes pass over Christina in interested perusal, while sliding his arm around her waist, claiming her as his possession.

'I'm sure she has saved one for me—is that not so, Christina?' he said, placing a gallant kiss on the back of her hand.

Christina nearly broke into laughter at the outrageously lecherous leer he gave her—feigned to rile Max more than anything else, who never failed to take the bait. 'I would love to dance with you, Guy, and I do believe I have one or two not taken.'

Although Max and Christina spent the early part of the evening interacting with their guests somehow they became separated. Everyone seemed to want to talk to Christina. After a while she looked around for Max. He was speaking to Don Cantoni across the room, and Francesca had positioned herself between them. Never had Max looked more handsome. And to make everything worse, Francesca was more haughtily attractive than Christina had realised when she had come to Casa del Sole earlier.

She watched Don Cantoni move away and Max and Francesca continue to converse. The way Francesca looked up into Max's eyes, with those flashing provocative glances, and the pouting red lips that blatantly invited kissing, was too much for Christina to bear. She knew she was being cursed with the most vicious attack of jealousy she had ever known, but she couldn't rid herself of it, and she resented the time Max was spending talking to Francesca. Feeling the touch of someone's hand on her arm, turning, she saw it was Guy, his expression uncharacteristically grave.

'Don't let her get to you, Christina. It's not worth it.'

'Is it that obvious?'

He nodded. 'I'm afraid it is. Would you care to drink a glass of Max's finest wine with me out on the terrace—or some champagne, perhaps? There we can watch the fireflies and admire the rather splendid sunset together.'

Christina stifled the urge to request a full bottle. Across the room her eyes met Max's briefly, but, pulling her emotions into a tight knot of pride, she looked quickly away. Moved by some feminine impulse that lurked deep in every woman to deal blow for blow and return hurt for hurt, she placed her hand on Guy's proffered arm and favoured him with her most dazzling smile.

'Why, it would be my pleasure,' she replied, deliberately turning her back on Max and Francesca. 'I am beginning to think you are an outrageous flirt, Guy Saunders,' she said sweetly.

'I do my best,' he answered.

As they walked away Christina didn't miss the jolt of tension that stiffened Max's long frame, nor the gaze that burned between her shoulder blades as she went. The image she took with her to the terrace was of Francesca linking her arm easily inside his and together they walked towards the dance floor. The musicians were playing a waltz. Christina watched Max take a laughing Francesca in his arms and swirl her across the floor to the strains of the music, and she was unprepared for the stab of pain that penetrated her heart.

If Francesca Cantoni had been heir to Casa del Sole, she might well have been Max's wife now. If it hadn't been for her grandmother's whim for the Carletti and Marchesi estates to be united, this Italian woman might legally have been sharing Max's bed and his life, as Christina strongly suspected she had been doing for a long time.

On the terrace where a marble-topped table had been set out with drinks, one of the footmen handed her a glass of fruit punch and spooned in some crushed ice. Sitting at a small table sipping their drinks, the warm night air heavy and sweet with summer scents, Guy and Christina began making small talk. Christina had to force her attention not to wander. Guy was an agreeable enough gentleman, but he did not warm her or challenge her wits. He was not the sort of man who would rip her heart in two with a smile or burn her flesh with a touch of his hand.

Their table was positioned to give them a good view of the ballroom through one of the open glass doors. Christina noted that Guy seemed unusually quiet and preoccupied. Following his gaze, she was surprised to see him looking at Francesca. Understanding dawned.

'Why,' she exclaimed, 'you're in love with Francesca yourself, aren't you, Guy?'

Guy's whole body tensed at the words and then he looked down at the glass in his hand. Keeping his gaze averted, with a dry laugh, he said, 'You have no idea how much I would like to say no to that question, Christina.'

'I can understand that. Francesca is not a very nice person and she does not deserve to be loved by a man as wonderful as you.'

'Thank you, Christina, but I wouldn't let Max hear you say that if I were you,' he quipped at an attempt to sound jovial. But immediately his expression reverted to what it had been a moment before. 'Although Francesca sometimes has a sharp tongue and says things she doesn't really mean, I would spend the rest of my life with her if only she'd let me,' he said quietly.

'Have you told her how you feel?'

He shook his head. 'And humiliate myself? No.'

'Guy, I'm sorry. I really am. Have you—asked her to dance?'

'No—but I will—if only…'

'If you feel like that,' Christina said quietly, her gaze

searching his face, 'how can you justify the fact that you're out here and she's in there?'

Guy looked at her steadily. 'Dancing with your husband.'

Christina looked downcast. 'Yes, dancing with Max.'

She knew it wasn't the done thing to question Max's old friend, whose loyalties might well be divided, but as far as she was concerned, the niceties didn't come into it. She had to know.

'Guy, Max and Francesca have known each other for many years. Just how well does she know him? Is—Francesca my husband's mistress?' she asked hesitantly, her gaze unwaveringly on Guy's face.

'The truth, Christina, is no—at least, I do not believe so, and I sincerely hope for both our sakes that she isn't. Francesca has aspired to be Countess Marchesi, that I do know, which is why she is resentful of you, but she was more in love with the kudos this would bring rather than being Max's wife.' He paused, looking over at the dancing couple. 'Francesca is the daughter of a nobleman who just so happens to be Max's close friend. Max respects him and knows better than to dishonour his daughter by making her his mistress.'

'Then that makes her respectable.'

'As you are, Christina, and you have to respect Max. It is not my place to interfere in marital relations and I would not dream of doing so, but don't you think it is time to repay the man who gave you his name by at least showing some respect for that name?'

Christina blanched as the brutal truth of his words hit home, words she had not expected to come from Guy. 'Why, to hear you, Guy, anyone would think I chose my own fate. And how have I failed to respect it?'

He shrugged. 'Max lives here while his wife lives at Casa

del Sole. Don't you think that speaks for itself? What kind of message do you think you are sending to Francesca?'

Christina was silent. It was true, it was time she moved out of Casa del Sole. It would be a beginning to her new life, and an end to the old.

When the waltz ended, Max drew away from his partner, having danced what he considered to be a duty dance to please her father. He was impatient to claim his wife, but, reluctant to let him go, Francesca firmly looped an arm through his.

Seeing Christina and Guy emerge from the terrace, he approached them, effectively having to disengage himself from Francesca.

'Excuse me, Guy, but I think it's time I danced with my wife.'

'I agree, Max.' Guy looked at Francesca. 'It's high time you did. Perhaps you would like to partner me in the next dance, Francesca? I waltz quite divinely and promise not to step on your toes.'

Francesca looked at Max, her mouth coming open to vent her objection, but he was already moving away with Christina. She turned to Guy and smiled haughtily. 'I suppose I might as well. And then if you are available, Guy, you can take me in to supper.'

Everyone was being drawn back on to the floor by the strains of another waltz. Max drew Christina into his arms and let the music carry them away. He was poised, sure, sweeping her across the floor in a swirling rhythm that dazzled her and made other couples seem clumsy. As the dance progressed Christina noticed that he kept the larger part of the dance floor between them and Guy.

When she had seen Max come towards her, looking breathtakingly handsome in fastidiously tailored black evening attire that hugged his wide shoulders and long legs and contrasted beautifully with his dazzling white shirt and neckcloth, her heart had seemed to stop, checked by the potency of his dark stare. She had wanted to go to him, to tell him what she had decided, to declare herself his for the taking, until she looked into her husband's face, which was a brooding mask, and seen Francesca hanging on to his arm.

'You are being obvious,' she cautioned him.

'Obvious?' He looked down at her. 'Do you mind explaining what you mean, Christina?'

'Why are you so determined to avoid Guy? He is quite harmless.'

'I'm not avoiding him.'

'Then could it be his partner you are avoiding?' she asked hopefully.

'I know Francesca isn't one of your favourite people, Christina, and I am merely trying to prevent a collision between the two of you.'

'Very wise, Max, and I appreciate your consideration,' she said quietly, lowering her eyes.

Suddenly tired of talking about Francesca and having no wish to get into an argument over her, Max looked down at his lovely young wife, his irritation caused by the time she had spent on the terrace with Guy melting. She was as unaware of her beauty as she was unaware of its effect on him.

'You know, I was wrong when I told you to change your gown. The colour is delightful, Christina. It suits you.'

Startled, she looked up into his face. 'You think so?'

'Of course I do.' There was something in his eyes, something intense and passionate. 'I never say things I don't mean. You should know that.'

Christina could feel herself shaking inside. She was afraid of facing his passion just now, afraid of how much it would hurt her in the future.

'And you dance very well too,' he commented as he spun her round in a dizzying whirl. 'I'm glad to have you dance with me at last, for you have kept me on tenterhooks as I have watched you dance with every male present.'

'To dance with the guests is my duty, Max—as you know. However, it was never my intention to cause you such suspense,' she countered. 'You should have asked me yourself.'

'Yes, I should, and I'm sorry I didn't.' His expression softened as he studied her. 'Are you happy, Christina?'

Surprised by his question, she frowned. 'Yes—I suppose I am. Are you happy, Max?'

He nodded. 'Happy—and disappointed, for I was hoping your feelings would have taken a different direction before now—towards fulfilling your vows,' he reminded her pointedly.

Feeling as she did about him there was nothing she wanted more than to share his life, but she still could not forgive him for forcing her into their marriage.

'I will—soon, Max. I promise.'

'And in the meantime I must content myself with every scrap of favour and attention you cast my way,' he retorted, unable to moderate the bitterness of his tone.

'Please stop it, Max. All this smacks of insincerity. It's not like you.'

'I speak honestly and truthfully—not that I blame you for keeping yourself apart from me. I have come to care for you deeply, but I have done little enough to prove it. I have not been the most articulate of suitors, I know, speaking of duty and obligation, when I should have been talking of passion and romance, sending you flowers.'

'I don't want flowers, Max. Flowers would make no difference to the way things are between us.'

His brows lifted. 'The way things are? And how are things between us, Christina?'

She looked away. 'Not now, Max. Can we not simply enjoy the dance and forget about everything else?'

When the music ended, Max took Christina's arm and led her into the supper room, where people were already dining and an army of servants danced attendance on the guests. Guy was leading Francesca to a table, where she haughtily sat to be waited on.

It was a truly impressive affair. The supper dishes were elaborate and delicious and served with all the pomp and splendour one expected at Castello Marchesi.

Francesca was rarely out of Christina's sight. Having spoken to Guy, she felt no better about the Italian woman and felt sick with anger and despair. She seemed to be caught in a world of half-truths more damaging than the truth itself.

When she saw Francesca look at Max or talk with him, sit across from him at the supper table or merely tap him on the shoulder with her fan in passing, Christina felt ill inside. If she were secure in Max's love, she would not be unduly worried, but as things stood it was enough for her merely to see Francesca look at Max to know that, despite what Guy had said, she was his mistress.

As Max watched Christina, he realized she belonged here at Castello Marchesi—this was her world, where she glowed and reigned like a young queen. It was the world she obviously loved. But something was wrong. Not since they had left the supper room had he seen her glance his way, even though his gaze was constantly drawn to her.

Unaware of her husband's increasing disquiet, but following her grandmother's advice to be charming and sociable to each and every one of their guests, by the end of the night Christina had become a success.

'Congratulations, my dear,' the dowager said to Christina when she had just said farewell to a party of guests, having stayed on the periphery of the festivities while remaining a keen observer. 'You have won the hearts of everyone here tonight. Have you enjoyed yourself?'

'Oh, yes,' Christina said. 'It's been a wonderful evening.'

'I know you will understand when I say that in the days ahead you are likely to be under siege at Casa del Sole from visitors wanting to know you better, which, as Max's wife, is not appropriate.'

Christina looked at her. 'What are you saying, Grandmother?'

'That it is time for you to come to Castello Marchesi—to Max, and for the two of you to begin married life.' She paused, watching Christina very closely, waiting for her answer as if it were of momentous importance.

Christina looked desperately away from her grandmother's shrewd and penetrating gaze, as if searching for some means of escape. Her grandmother didn't know what she was asking of her. The old woman's brows lifted a fraction. 'I sincerely hope you have considered it, Christina. You should not expect Max to wait for ever. Now, I see he is waiting to whisk you away. We should all take a good night's rest after the evening's excitement.'

Christina breathed deeply the sweet-scented air. The moon hung heavy in the sky as the carriage swept away from Castello Marchesi. She stared silently ahead, hearing the familiar night sound of crickets.

From the moment they had pulled away from the house, Christina had treated Max with polite cordiality, albeit with a trace of ire. Suspecting the reason for this, he was determined to have it out in the open.

'Christina?' Max said with quiet determination after several silent minutes.

'Yes?'

'When are you going to tell me what is wrong?' When she looked at him, a wry smile curved her soft lips. Max read her face and knew full well that anger was simmering in her beautiful head. For the sake of caution he waited for her to speak.

'Wrong? There is nothing wrong. Why should there be?' she said, looking the other way. 'I've had a lovely evening.'

'Has this got anything to do with Francesca, by any chance?' His voice was strained and strangely tight.

Her head spun round and her eyes fastened on his. 'Yes, since you ask, it has everything to do with her. She is too persistent.'

His lips curved in a mocking smile. 'And what little time you have with me, you are loath to share it with her. Is that what you are trying to say, Christina?'

The green eyes flashed. 'Yes, if you like. I do resent the time you spend with her. She is too arrogant, and I protest the careless flaunting of herself when she is near you. In short, I protest the woman herself, and I decry the fact that my husband does nothing to dissuade her.'

The severe frown that accompanied her outburst surprised Max. He leaned back better to see her face. He was surprised that this capricious young wife of his had such a jealous vein in her otherwise flawless character.

'Why, what's this, Christina? Are you jealous of Francesca?'

Christina glowered at him. She had put to the back of her mind Francesca's earlier implication that she was Max's mistress, but her face burned with the scalding memory, and that same woman's presence at the ball and constant attention to Max had struck a violent note in Christina. The fire in her mind was not quickly cooled.

'As soon as I set foot in your house—'

'Our house,' he amended coolly.

'Whatever. It really doesn't matter,' she flared irritably. 'It didn't take me long to realise that she was potential trouble. Guy is hopelessly in love with her—has been for years, apparently. Have you any idea of the torment he has been made to endure, watching the two of you together?'

Max stared at her in disbelief. Clearly this was news to him. 'Good Lord! I had no idea. The poor devil. But there was no reason for him to be—tormented, I mean. I've told you, Christina, there is and never was anything between Francesca and me—but Guy?'

'You would have seen it for yourself had you taken time off from your pride and your explosive Latin temper and talked to him. Signorina Cantoni is extraordinarily attractive and she is no one any woman would like to find interested in her husband.'

'She is attractive, I grant you, but you are the most attractive woman I have ever met, Christina.'

'And you have known many to measure me by,' she retorted before she could stop the words, feeling mean for not accepting the compliment for what it was.

'Several,' he informed her bitingly, not bothering to deny it. 'I am no saint—but there has not been a woman in my life since I became officially betrothed to you.'

'You must have been very young, for you were betrothed to me when I was still in the cradle,' she retorted scathingly, knowing she was going too far when she saw his jaw tighten, but seemingly unable to stop.

'I considered the betrothal official when you were made aware of it in England and agreed to it.'

'I see. And how many of those other women were present tonight?'

'None. Christina, stop this and take that martyred expression off your face. This is neither the time nor the place for an argument. Your jealousy is unfounded, unworthy of you, and in bad taste. For better or worse you are married to me, and, since you are to spend the rest of your life in Tuscany, you would be better employed making friends, not enemies.'

Despite the icy tingle of alarm his silken voice caused in her, Christina lifted her chin. 'I shall, but don't ask me to sanction your affair with Signorina Cantoni.'

'If I were having an affair with any woman, there was not a man present tonight who would blame me, since my wife prefers to live elsewhere. You should have paid more attention to the vows we made, when we both affirmed the sanctity of marriage.'

'Yes, I spoke my vows and I meant every word, but how can I ever be sure of you, Max? I was not there when you spoke yours. You saw to that,' she accused heatedly.

'Pressure of work prevented me from travelling to England at that time. We each need to trust one another that our vows were uttered in faith and sincerity, Christina. Marriage is nothing without trust.'

'And it appears that marriage is a far more complicated state of affairs than I imagined.'

'It needn't be. It is what you make it. A husband and wife should live together and sleep together. That equation seems perfectly logical to me. Not, apparently, to you; bound by some obscure feminine impractical ideal, you want to keep yourself apart from it. I am not known for my patience and definitely not used to being given the run around by any woman, so the sooner you accept the binding vows you made the happier I shall be. I am not having an affair with Francesca, but since your mind is made up and closed to all reason, I will not waste my breath denying it further.'

Having arrived at Casa del Sole, Christina climbed out of the carriage before him and marched to the door, but Max was hard on her heels. Taking her arm, he halted her before she could open the door, pressing her ardently to the wood at her back. He was about to claim her lips, but she wouldn't allow it. Turning her head away, she struggled free, though her treacherous female body was ready to curve into his to accommodate him. Opening the door, she went inside the house. He strode after her.

Max frowned and looked down at her. 'Christina? What the hell is the matter with you?' he demanded to know, his voice harsh and shaking with anger. Just when he thought everything was going to be all right, that she was to agree on what he had always hoped for, planned for, she had turned truculent, and all because of Francesca.

Christina averted her eyes. Max's belief that she would respond to his warm, moist mouth and searching hands made her livid. Ever since coming to Casa del Sole she had been living in a fantasy world, a world where dreams would become fruition if she was patient, a world where Max's attention had lulled her into a false belief. How could she have been so stupid—such a credulous fool?

'Christina, do you mind telling me why you are behaving like this? Why are you fighting me? Am I to assume you do not welcome my advances?'

'Your assumptions are correct.'

Max's face hardened into an expressionless mask, but his

eyes were probing hers like daggers, looking for answers, as if he couldn't believe what she was saying.

'Like hell you don't. I do not believe you.'

This time their eyes met, Max's dark with anger and contempt, Christina's glittering with rage. She turned from him, but he caught her by the shoulder and spun her round. In the dim light from the lamp Molly had left burning his face was suddenly grim, his dark eyebrows drawn together in a straight line.

Christina recoiled instinctively. 'Let go of me,' she cried. 'Max, please take your hands off me.'

But Max, his self-control sorely strained, was too far gone, too incensed to listen. Before she could guess what he meant to do, she found herself imprisoned in a grip of steel, her lips sealed by a hard demanding mouth that bore down relentlessly on hers. She struggled furiously, but Max held her fast, and for all her frenzy she could not escape.

Temporarily robbed of the anger that had fortified her resistance, Christina's traitorous body lost its rigidity and her struggles grew weaker and ceased. The scream of warning issued by her mind was stifled by her pounding heart and the shocking pleasure of being held in his arms. She was aware of his hand stealing up her spine to the back of her neck, caressing, imprisoning her head.

Knowing she was playing with fire, she let him kiss her, wanting him to kiss her, just this once, to experience again the fleeting joy of his mouth on hers, the disturbing sensations that shimmered through her body. Her arms, which had been fighting to get free of him, went round his neck and held him to her.

For a brief moment when both of them had ceased to think, to consider what they were doing, they allowed themselves to rejoice in the ferocity of their desire. They allowed themselves to live, to think wholly for themselves, knowing there could be nothing more wonderful than this.

And then, abruptly, Christina found herself released and stumbled backwards, standing alone while the world swayed round her, while Max's mocking laughter sounded in her ears.

'There is one thing you must know about me, Christina. When I set my mind on having something, I am not easily dissuaded from that end. And I want you. Remember that when you try to pit your will against mine. My thanks for your co-operation.'

Her face scarlet with shame and her body trembling with furious indignation, striding to the door Christina held it open. 'Please go, Max.'

Max forced down his ravenous lusts with an iron will and strode angrily past her and out into the night. She banged the door shut behind him, almost bringing it off its hinges, then, sinking to her knees, she wrapped her arms around her waist and began to cry broken-heartedly. Feeling two strong arms enfold her and raise her up, she gave herself up to Molly's loving embrace.

In his bedroom at Castello Marchesi, Max removed his jacket, flinging it into a chair. His waistcoat followed. Removing his cravat and loosening the top buttons of his shirt, he stalked over to the window and thrust his hands into his pockets. His eyes were colder than an icy winter sky and there was a thin, white line about his mouth. He was furious.

Just when he was beginning to think Christina was all grown up and ready for love, he had discovered she was as unpredictable as ever, as wilful, stubborn and fiery as she had been at seventeen. What was it about his wife that made him unable to get her out of his mind?

When she had turned her back on him and disappeared on to the terrace with Guy, laughing up at him as she went as though she had not a care in the world, it had crucified him. He had wanted to shake off Francesca's cloying presence and stride after them.

Dear sweet Lord, what was wrong with him? How could he let a woman affect him as this one did? When he had held her in his arms he had felt the glory in her and the beauty, not just in her face, but in her heart and soul. He had been encouraged to hope. But tonight she had denied him and sent him away.

Chapter Eleven

Deeply affected by her argument with Max, Christina woke with a dreadful headache the following morning, having cried herself to sleep. She had tried to provoke him and she ought to congratulate herself—she had succeeded admirably. But never had she seen Max so angry, and she hated herself for being the cause of it. A kaleidoscope of misery, despair and self-castigation hurtled through her mind, and there was only a fragile hope that he would forgive her.

The day of the *vendemmie* had arrived. Christina walked down the long, green tunnels of vines with steep banks wet with dew to one side and roofed in by trellises that supported the vines, which seemed to be groaning under the weight of the bunches of grapes.

The tables and ladders were set up and the vats and each worker would be given a basket and a hook. Some of the workers would be cutting the grapes, others carrying the full boxes to the sorting tables, where the grapes would be subjected to further scrutiny and cleansing.

Pepi as usual was responsible for the *vendemmie*, much to

Christina's relief, although Max, whom she had not seen since the night of the ball, could often be seen among the workers, making sure that everything was going according to plan.

He was impatient to get on with it in case the weather broke. Sometimes in September quite suddenly the sky would cloud over and the thunder would rumble behind the peaks, and those who had vines prayed that they would be spared the *grandine*, the hail, which could destroy an entire crop of grapes in a matter of minutes. Much to Christina's relief there wasn't a cloud in the sky, so with any luck the grapes would be harvested without a hitch.

By mid-morning, when the workers had been working for three hours in the lower fields, stripping vine after vine like locusts, exhaustion was beginning to set in. It was therefore a welcome surprise for them when Carmel and Molly appeared on the scene with hampers of food and wine stacked in the pony cart.

It was a happy scene and a colourful one, the women and girls in colourful skirts and headscarves. The big straw hats they usually wore in the open fields when the sun was hot were no good under the trellising as they kept getting knocked off by overhead branches.

When everyone had eaten their fill the remains of the picnic were packed away and work resumed, and before long it was more food and siesta time. The boxes of grapes were carried up to the troughs in which they were trod, the treaders' feet having been scrubbed clean. At Casa del Sole they observed tradition. Everything was conducted in the same way as it had been done for hundreds of years. Christina watched in fascination as their feet sank deeper and deeper into the purple juice, a process that would go on for hours.

They worked until the sun went down in a blood-red orb when it was time for dinner. Long trestle tables with white cloths were set out under a pergola, and lights from lanterns strung between the trees flickered in the warm evening air. Molly and Carmel had been working non-stop for days to feed the workers and the meal was delicious. They ate ravioli, freshly baked bread, meat and chicken and cheese and there was a lot of wine drunk, red and white, and singing of folk songs and dancing and lots of laughter.

Christina thought it was simply wonderful.

It was her laughter rising on the warm scented air above the drone of conversation and music that Max recognised. Christina was waltzing under the lanterns, whirling round and round to a jaunty melody, and she was enjoying herself in a way Max had never seen before. The young man she was dancing with playfully linked her arm and they spun around on the grass in time to the frenzied music, exposing the long flow of bare calf and ankles above her well-shaped feet, gleaming beneath the fast swirl of frilled petticoats.

On seeing Max, Christina stopped, breathless, her eyes shining, her heart hammering in her chest. She watched him approach her, gazing at the dark, austere beauty of his face, noting the authority, the strength held in check as he walked. Her pulse raced with a mixture of excitement and trepidation. So many conflicting emotions roiled inside her, fighting each other. She had missed him dreadfully, and now, as he came towards her, he was more attractive than ever, more desirable, and the need to be even closer to him was more vivid than ever before.

Whatever his reasons for marrying her she had set them aside because quite simply she loved him. She had to believe that if there had been something between Max and Francesca it was over, no matter what suspicions the woman herself might put into her head in the future.

For a moment Max was speechless. He hardly recognised her. Dressed in a plain gown the colour somewhere between blue and green, her hair unconfined and flowing thick and curling in glorious disarray to her waist, her cheeks crimson with her exertions, her bright green eyes shining with enjoyment, she looked magnificent. Her bare feet, long and slender, gleamed white, her sleeves had been pushed up above her elbows to reveal the soft flesh of her arms and the neck of her bodice was unbuttoned almost down to the high, full curve of her breasts.

Max gave her a long, thoughtful stare, and then lifted one eyebrow and smiled that lazy, familiar smile she had come to love so well.

'Well, Christina? Am I welcome, or are you still angry with me and going to show me the door?'

His voice, rich and too hypnotically deep to belong to any other man, sent a tiny shiver coursing through her. Unable to harbour any ill feeling towards him on a night such as this, she smiled back at him. He was casually dressed in fawn breeches and tan boots, and she was all too aware of the strong arms where the white shirt had been rolled up to the elbows, and of the small area of chest exposed by the open neck.

'That would be impossible, since we are not in the house. Of course you are welcome, and I apologise if I made you feel that you would not be. Are you very angry with me?'

His eyes shone wickedly. 'That depends on your method of making amends.'

'Perhaps you would you like something to eat? Molly and Carmel have made enough ravioli to feed a regiment of hungry soldiers.'

He shook his head, a wicked gleam in his eyes. 'I had something other than food in mind.'

Christina laughed lightly. 'I thought you might, but you'll have to cool your ardour, Max.'

'For now, perhaps. I've already eaten, but some wine would be nice.' He glanced at the crowded table. 'Shall we take a walk first and find somewhere less boisterous?'

Although there were people milling around them, who were unfazed by the presence of the illustrious Count Marchesi in their midst, Max was aware of nobody but her.

'Will you walk with me, Christina?'

Christina put up no resistance when he took her hand and placed it into the crook of his arm. He guided her past the table littered with food and bottles of wine and people conversing, some of them in mellow mood. Casa del Sole had come alive with the *vendemmie*, and Max's arrival had given it an added boost. As they strolled away from the happy workers she almost believed that something magical was about to happen to bring her face to face with her destiny.

Poised and inwardly relaxed and cloaked in the comforting glow of the wine she had consumed, secretly there was nowhere Christina would rather be at that moment, and yet she suddenly felt extremely vulnerable and strangely apprehensive about being alone with him.

When they had strolled far enough and the sounds of people were softer, Max paused and looked down at her. Smiling up at him, she stood motionless, feeling the warmth of his gaze.

'You look very beautiful tonight, Christina,' he said softly, his voice oddly ragged and his eyes brilliant with what he felt for her.

Christina felt herself relax, every tired limb settling into its everyday posture. Emotions swept over her as she remembered the kiss they had shared and the intense passion he had roused in her. She enjoyed hearing him say she was beautiful. His compliment brought a flush to her cheeks.

'How is that possible when I am dressed as a peasant and look like one, with grape juice all down my skirts?'

'You look as though you've been picking the grapes yourself.'

'I have—at least for a while. I never realised it could be such hard work.'

'It's because you're not used to it.'

'I know. Never in a million years did I envisage myself picking grapes.'

'And how much wine have you drunk?'

'Probably more than I should have,' she declared with a happy smile. She sighed, leaning back against a tree with her hands behind her and gazing into the murky darkness. Pinpoints of glimmering lights glowed from myriad tiny fireflies flitting in and out of the olive trees. She took a deep breath of the fresh night air. All around them the undergrowth was alive with sounds of nocturnal creatures. 'I feel so different from what I used to be that I cannot believe I am the same person. Sometimes I have to pinch myself to make sure. I feel more alive now than I have ever been before.'

Max agreed. A peculiar inner excitement touched her cheeks with a flush of delicate pink adding a special sparkle to her eyes. 'I think you have adjusted very well. Are you missing Tanglewood?'

She smiled ruefully. 'Tanglewood is a long way away. I do miss it, but not as much as I thought I would.'

'You never cease to amaze me,' Max said, his voice soft and warm. 'I salute your courage and your boldness, Christina. You are undeniably brave, beautiful and one hell of a reckless woman.'

'Life touches everyone with a hard hand at times. I am no different, only some are able to deal with it better than others. I've done my best.'

'From what I know about you, Christina, I think you are seduced by the drama, irrationality and passion of Italy, and that you enjoy the kind of emotional disruption that has turned your well-ordered world upside down.'

Christina looked at him steadily. How well he knew her. His powerful masculinity was an assault on her senses. She was unable to resist him. 'Yes, I was looking for all that, but I was also looking for something else.'

Closing her eyes, she became silent and lifted her face to a warm breeze scented with wood smoke. Images rushed into her mind, prompting memories of a man with hard, firm hands and a touch and kiss that lit fires inside her. Was he really here with her now?

'A penny for them, Christina?' Max asked softly, perching his hip on a low stone wall and folding his arms across his chest.

She opened her eyes and looked at him, her body awakened by her thoughts. 'A penny?'

'For your thoughts.' Max was watching her, his eyes half-closed as he gazed at her face.

'Why did you bring me here?' she asked, not looking at him but continuing to stare out blindly into the distance.

'I wanted to talk to you.'

'What do you want to talk about? I thought you and I had said everything there was to say to one another already.'

She pushed her heavy mane of hair back from her forehead and Max watched her, bemused by the loveliness of her.

'I want to talk about us, Christina.' His answer was slow in coming, but it did not surprise her.

'Yes, I thought you might. I think you're going to ask me when I'm going to give up living at Casa del Sole. Am I right?'

He nodded, continuing to watch her closely. 'Right.'

Her eyes were drawn to his, for no matter how a man looked, stern and firm, the eyes have a will of their own and cannot be fixed. There was a light in them now, warm and compelling. 'I intend moving out some time during the next few days—when the grapes have been harvested. Does that suit?'

'Perfectly. And it's about time. I was beginning to think that the only way I could get you out of here was to drag you into my bed.'

'You should learn to be more patient. If I have taken too long in deciding, it's because I have liked living here.'

'And seeing me suffer,' he said, pulling her against his chest. 'You're a sadist, Countess Marchesi. I knew you were going to be difficult the minute I laid eyes on you.'

She laughed lightly. 'Mama was always scolding me for being so, but I can only hope that I will improve with age.'

'Do you always intend being rebellious towards me?'

'Always, for I don't think you would approve of a new me.' She smiled serenely and, standing on her toes, placed a featherlight, tantalising kiss at the corner of his mouth, her eyes warm with laughter. 'You're not cross with me, are you?'

'No,' he laughed. 'It's good to see you gaining in confidence.' He kissed her neck, then added in mock threat, 'But don't let it get out of hand or…'

'Or what?' she whispered, placing another kiss on his lips.

'I'll think of something,' he said, capturing her lips and kissing her long and deep.

When he raised his head Christina met his gaze, her eyes slumberous. 'Have you ever made love to a woman out in the open, Max?' she queried, casting her eyes sideways and thinking the grass looked soft and inviting.

'There will be a better time and a better place than this for us to make love, Christina. Come, let us get back to the others.'

Too dazed to do anything else, when Max took her hand she allowed him to lead her back along the path to the house.

They were so engrossed with their thoughts they failed to see the two horses and riders, one a woman, watching from the undergrowth out of sight. The hatred in Francesca's face raged almost out of control, swamping the shine in her eyes to the murky depths of an old, neglected pond.

The workers were already beginning to drift away to their beds. Tomorrow would be another long and arduous day.

Christina entered her room, knowing beyond a shadow of a doubt, from the moment she had first met Max, that she would become his wife in every sense had been inevitable.

She thought she would fall into a dreamless slumber of the exhausted, but she was too disturbed to sleep. Going downstairs on to the patio and sauntering beyond among the olive trees, she looked out over the Tuscan countryside shrouded in darkness. The night was still and serene. She stood very still to absorb her silent, undisturbed possession of Casa del Sole.

That was when she smelled the smoke. Alarmed, she looked towards the house in the distance, unaware that she had walked so far. Seeing a rising thick column of smoke and a lick of flame shooting skywards, she gasped. Voices were already shouting and people were leaving their caravans and running up the hill. Christina ran with them, her main concern being that Molly was in the house.

Everything seemed to be happening at once. Flames became higher and fiercer as the fire took hold of the furnishings, announcing the conflagration to all who could see it for miles around.

As Christina ran, her mind emptied itself of all thought. A blackness took over. When she had still some distance to go, her attention was caught by a man behaving oddly. Instead of running towards the house to help, he was running away, but kept turning to look back over his shoulder. He had been up to no good and Christina was surprised when she recognised the man as Bruno, the groom who had accompanied Francesca when she had visited Casa del Sole.

She dismissed him from her mind as she became caught up in the drama. People began forming a human chain from the well, frantically passing pails of water from one to the other to douse the flames which were greedily feeding on the furnishings.

Christina ran about in a frenzy, trying to find Molly—and there she was as part of the chain, raw fright on her face, with Pepi behind her.

'Molly! Oh, Molly, thank goodness you're all right,' she said, gasping for breath, the smoke getting into her throat and making her cough and her eyes water.

'Pepi raised the alarm. I looked for you, Christina. Where were you?' Molly's voice was sharp with concern.

'I couldn't sleep, so I went for a walk. But how has this happened, Molly? This is simply terrible.'

'I have no idea how the fire started—but for now we must try to salvage what we can.' When Molly had been alerted to the fire she'd had the presence of mind to save as many of her own and Christina's possessions as the time allowed.

Christina joined the chain of workers, passing buckets of water to the person in front and hearing the hiss of steam as the liquid met the flames.

* * *

Max had been about to go to bed when he had been alerted to the fire. For a moment he'd turned to stone, his face ashen, and then, his heart thundering in alarm, he'd set off for Casa del Sole, more frightened than he had been in his life. The vision of Christina, his love, caught up in the fire set his mind alight.

Max and Guy appeared almost at the same time, having seen the flames and bringing more people with them to help.

'Guy! Where's Christina?' Max had to shout over the roar of the fire.

Guy shook his head. 'I haven't seen her. I've only just got here. Good Lord! How did this start?'

'How the hell should I know? I haven't been gone from the place more than an hour. I must find Christina—make sure she's all right.' His eyes did their best to split the smoke that rolled around them and the frenzied mob of people trying to quench the flames. 'I won't believe she's...' But Max's resolve was weakened as the anguish that threatened to overwhelm him savaged his body.

Guy placed a firm hand on his shoulder. 'Don't even think it, Max. She'll be all right. Let's take a look round the back of the house. Water's being drawn from the well. We're bound to find her there.'

Everyone was working frantically to put out the fire. For Christina the blurred minutes passed without definition, counted by the pails of water that passed through her hands, unable to tear herself from the nightmare. Graceful fingers trained to etiquette now gripped the heavy receptacles, unconsciously clasping the wooden handles as one might cling to a branch in the middle of a raging current.

She didn't see Max until he was close, and then she stopped

abruptly and fell out of the chain. 'Max! Oh, Max, thank God you're here,' she cried, in a voice of utter exhaustion.

She ran her wrist back and forth over her soot-smeared forehead and Max thought it was the closest to collapse he'd ever seen her. Forgetting that discretion was needed in front of others, he mindlessly snatched her into his arms and buried his face in her hair as he hammered his will into iron self-control. For a full half-minute they clung to one another, both ready to weep at the relief each of them felt, to weep at the emptiness of their lives without one another in it.

'Christina—*caro*—' he said, his voice harsh and angry. 'Thank God you're all right. I was beginning to think… I can't tell you what I was beginning to think. I thought I'd lost you. Don't you ever frighten me again like that.'

Her body stiffened. Was he censuring her, or was his anger simply out of relief for her? She didn't know and she was too weary to work it out. 'I'm all right, Max,' she whispered, pushing herself away from him and looking up into his haggard face, forcing the moment of weakness away. 'As you can see. No one is hurt.' She disengaged herself from his embrace. 'I must get back. We have to put the fire out—we have to save what we can.'

Having already assessed the situation and the damage so far, Max took one look at the burning house and knew it was useless.

The constant roar of the fire rattled windows and sent things crashing down inside. When it became obvious that there was no stopping the flames, everyone stood back in apathetic, bewildered silence and watched it burn.

The charred ruin of Casa del Sole, the house that had looked out over its vineyards and olive groves with dignity for decades, had soon become a smoking ruin. There was a hideous, haunting stillness over everything.

Standing beneath the walnut tree, its branches scorched from fire, Christina felt sick at the sight of it. This desolation went to her heart as nothing she had experienced. Here was her grandmother's pride, nothing but ashes. This was the end of the lovely, lonely house that had welcomed her to Tuscany, where for a short time she had lived. It was only by tremendous effort she kept from bursting into tears of fury and exhaustion.

Knowing there was nothing else they could do, people began to wander off, back to their beds. Max moved towards Christina. Though she had borne up bravely since the start of the fire, her shoulders were slumped as she stood staring at the smoking house and crystal tears slipped silently down her cheeks. Max felt his heart turn over. He wanted to put everything right. He'd do anything to take that weary look from her face, that droop from her slender shoulders.

'Christina.' His voice was soft. She turned her head and looked at him and he was shocked by the pallor of her face. The lovely light in her eyes, the light that he knew to be the recognition of what was between them, was gone.

She came to life with an abruptness that took him by surprise. Turning from the ruin, she walked slowly away, wiping her face with the back of her hand.

'Don't look so worried, Max,' she said with a flat kind of bitterness. 'I am shocked by what has happened, but I'm all right really. There is nothing to be done. I wasn't meant to live here—just to savour a taste of it, and now it's over. Being here has been like an interlude in my life, part of the healing process. I saw everything for what it was and it's over, gone, done with. I'm sorry for the loss of the house.' How irritating it must be for him to find part of her inheritance had gone up in flames, she thought bitterly.

Mechanically Max dragged his arm across his sweating

brow, pushing back the damp hair, trying to smooth away the terror that had taken hold of him when he'd seen the smoke and the orange glow in the sky and thought Christina might be in danger.

'How did it start? Does anyone know?'

Slowly she turned and gave him a hard, direct look. 'Oh, yes, Max. I know how it started.'

Christina coldly told him that she did not think it was an accident, she had seen a man she believed was called Bruno running away.

Max became quiet, his face like cold granite, his mouth so tightly clamped he could barely speak. 'Is that so?' he managed to say icily.

'Bruno is Francesca's groom. You might have met him on occasion. Perhaps Signorina Cantoni can shed some light on what her groom was doing at Casa del Sole at the same time as the fire started.' Christina was unable to hide the anger that was gathering force inside her, for she was certain Francesca was responsible for the fire.

The resulting suspicion was far fetched. Yet the moment it presented itself Max knew he couldn't rest until he had proved or disproved it. The rage he felt at the mere suspicion that, out of spite, Francesca might have endangered Christina's life was so powerful, so great, he could feel it thicken in his throat. His face hardened and so did something inside him, something that now felt it could do murder on her behalf.

'I cannot imagine why Francesca would want to do this.'

Christina fixed him with a fierce gaze. 'Can't you? I can.'

Max looked at her without speaking for a moment, and then he said, 'No matter what you think, Christina, I swear that Francesca was not my mistress.'

Christina sighed and shook her head wearily. 'It may

surprise you, Max, but I do believe you. But that does not alter the fact that she wanted to be.'

'And I cannot be held responsible for the way she or other people think.'

'Burning the house with me inside it are the lengths she will go to to get me out of her life—and yours. Her malevolence knows no bounds.' She lifted her head. Her eyes were bleak, their brightness quenched. She did not weep now, but she felt like it. She was a fighter, and she would not let the likes of Francesca Cantoni get the better of her. 'That woman's hatred has cost me almost more than I can bear.'

Max took her hand, his face grim with the knowledge that he had been unable to stop this fiery ravishment of Casa del Sole. 'So it would appear.'

'I was thinking that love sometimes makes people ruthless in a way that hatred doesn't. When it comes to love, some people find it easy to stab someone in the back when they're not looking. In Francesca's case, in her way she must love you very much and I was in the way. Thank goodness Molly smelled the smoke and got out in time, otherwise she could be looking at a charge of murder.'

Releasing her hand, Max turned from her in an attempt to bring his thoughts into order, before looking at her, his face hard and uncompromising. 'Proving it would be difficult. We won't speak of it now. In the morning will be soon enough to discuss what's to be done.'

'But—'

'In the morning, Christina,' he told her firmly.

Too weary to protest, Christina nodded.

'In the meantime you must come with me,' he told her in a sharp authoritative voice that normally quelled anyone who heard it.

'Yes, I know. I really don't have a choice in the matter any more. I believe Molly has managed to salvage a few of our things.' She would be happy when she realised that, among other things, Molly had thoughtfully rescued her mother's trinket box and the small bear Max had given her, and she had even asked Pepi to save the portrait of her mother, knowing it was the only likeness of her she would have. 'Perhaps you would be so kind as to put them in the cart. Molly will show you where they are.'

After everything that had happened tonight, Christina was impatient to be by herself for a while, to be given a place of quiet to mull it all over, to think what it meant and what she was to do in the light of what had happened.

Christina's first conscious thought on waking was for Max, and her second for Casa del Sole. Opening her eyes she looked around the strange room, forgetful at first of where she was. It was quiet, the silence a balm to her wounded heart. She must move on from this. She must accept and live for the moment, and yet it was so very painful. Not so long ago she had been happy to come to Tuscany, but now those dreams were fading. Nothing seemed clear to her any more.

Not even Max. He had done things to her mind and now all she could think of was him. How could she be content now that she knew the heartache of real love?

When she had dressed she went to see her grandmother. The dowager Countess had been told about the fire and was naturally distressed about the loss of her old home, but relieved no one had been hurt. When she had enquired into the cause, knowing she would be satisfied with nothing but the truth, Max had told her what Christina had seen and that there was a strong suspicion that Francesca had had the house burned out of spite.

The dowager was quiet. If Francesca was responsible for the fire which could have resulted in taking Christina's life— the young woman who had become the child of her heart, then she would see to it personally that Don Cantoni would hear of it and act appropriately.

Having risen at first light, Max rode his horse long and hard over the Tuscan landscape, but was unable to dispel his black mood. Coming to Casa del Sole, he stared at the blackened ruin for a long time, his thoughts turning to Christina. The fire had hit her hard and when he had taken her home she had been so distant, so far removed from him that he could hardly get a word out of her.

For the first time he was being forced to face a situation that had been thrust on him, and he was seriously beginning to think his marriage was a mistake. Christina had been a girl, too young, and she should never have been forced to marry him. But, dear Lord, he loved her. He scowled darkly at the thought, but he admitted the truth of it. He loved her, and he wanted to fill her days with joy. After twenty-eight years of life and several amorous affairs, he had fallen victim to a tempestuous, outrageously impertinent and lovely young woman who incurred his wrath and enjoyed flouting his authority at every turn.

And now he would have to consider letting her go.

He had never expected her to care for him, or to return his love. In the beginning he had deeply resented her decision to live apart from him, and he remembered how he had seethed with frustration each time he had left her, simmering with rage every night he slept alone.

Before the fire she had told him she was ready to be his wife, but not because she loved him, he knew that, but because it was her duty. Duty! The joining together of any man and his wife. But you're hardly a woman, are you, Christina? he thought, while tapping his riding crop against his leg. Not you. Not yet.

And nor would she ever return his true feelings, and with the destruction of Casa del Sole, the chance of her remaining in Italy looked bleak. But by God, he didn't want her to go. Christina at Castello Marchesi in any circumstances was better than no Christina at all.

He kicked a tuft of grass viciously. Of all the things he had done in his life, all the people he had known, he laughed to himself ironically, and it took a slip of a girl to do this to him.

The workers were picking grapes as though nothing had happened when Christina dismounted at Casa del Sole. They nodded their heads in solemn greeting. On leaden legs she slowly drifted towards the charred and blackened ruin that had been her home for such a short time. Her throat was clogged with tears as she realised just how much she had come to love the old house.

'Christina.'

The name was spoken softly. She turned and nearly crumpled to her knees in relief as she recognised the tall form of Max. She could see that his hands were clenched, as if he were holding himself very much in check. She was shocked to see how strained he looked, as if he had gone through a great ordeal.

Struggling to control the trembling that threatened to reduce her to tears, with a wobbly smile, she said, 'Good heavens, Max! Do you have to creep up on me and scare me? Couldn't you have made your presence known in a noisier fashion?'

'I came to take a look at the damage.' He looked quite desolate as he gazed at the ruin, kicking a charred piece of wood with his boot. 'How damned unfortunate. What a waste of a perfectly good house.'

Christina felt her stomach twist. She knew exactly how important the property had been to him.

'Max, I'm sorry.'

'Sorry?'

'About Casa del Sole. You must be feeling mortified. I realise what its loss must mean to you. It was an important part of my inheritance. You must feel I am turning out to be a poor investment,' she said deliberately.

Frowning darkly, he looked at her. Her face was absolutely without expression, and in his own sorrowing heart he wondered whether it had been brought about by the fire or something else. 'Investment? What makes you say that?'

'Because that's how the terms of our marriage have made me feel. I know very well that, were it not for what I would bring to this marriage you would not have married me.'.

Comprehension dawned in his face, comprehension and a hint of dismay. 'Did I really make you feel like that? I had no idea, Christina. It meant so little at the time.'

'So little to you, perhaps, but so much to me.' She was too angry to care that it would serve no purpose to go over these things now, but she had to let him know how she felt. 'Do you really have no idea how it felt for you to speak of marriage to me—with all your talk of terms and settlements and—and this,' she flared, referring to the ruin with a sweep of her arm, 'and no personal regard or respect for me behind them? Have you really no idea how insulting, how humiliating it was for me? And if you had known, would you have really cared?'

Something in his chest gripped him and he had an urgent

need to reach out, take her in his arms and comfort her, but he dare not. 'As a matter of fact, I care for you a great deal, Christina. But if you'd had any choice in the matter, what would you have done at the time? Would you have gone ahead and married me?' Max waited for her to answer—it seemed like a life time, and when she did his heart clenched in his chest.

'No, Max, I don't believe I would.'

'I see. I assure you that wounding your feelings was never my intent.'

'Then what was your intent, Max?'

'To fall in love with you. Since our meeting in England I have developed a strong attraction for you that can only be described as a form of madness.'

'A temporary madness, I hope.' She smiled grimly. 'You do not have to soothe my pride, Max,' she said, unable to bear to hear compliments now. 'It isn't necessary.'

'Damnation, Christina! I appreciate the wrong I have done you, and perhaps when I tell you what I have decided, some of your pride will be restored and you will be relieved.'

Turning his back on her, he took a couple of slow steps forwards, looking down at the ground. 'It grieves me to have to say this, Christina, but to be fair to you I must. If it is what you want, I will set you free. Our marriage has not been consummated, so there are grounds for an annulment. It shouldn't be too difficult to obtain. It offers you a way out of a situation that is clearly not an agreeable one to you, and it will enable you to return to England—to your parents.'

Appalled, Christina stared at his stiff back. He could not be saying this to her—an annulment—and that she could go back to England? No, oh, no, surely not. How could he do this? She was unable to bear it. The thought of him sending her away, of losing him now, hurt more acutely than any physical pain could.

'Excuse me.' Without more ado she mounted her horse and with a flick of the whip was galloping back to Castello Marchesi.

Chapter Twelve

A torrent of conflicting emotions battered Christina—disbelief, misery, loneliness and despair tore through her mind. She couldn't bear the thought of leaving Castello Marchesi. How could she, loving Max as she did? Yet, deep down, she knew he didn't want her to. She spent the rest of the day in her room pacing to and fro, rejecting all Molly's attempts to cheer her, until she could stand it no longer.

And so, her heart hammering wildly, she walked swiftly along the landing to Max's rooms.

He was standing by the long open window, looking out at the night sky. He had removed his jacket and his necktie was pulled loose. He held a brandy glass in his hand. Light from the candles flickered across his face, one moment enhancing his handsome features, the next lending dark shadows to them to suggest overpowering wickedness lurking within.

Christina stood in the doorway, uncertain now she was here. That Max was aware of her presence she knew.

In a quiet, husky voice, he said, 'Come here, Christina.'

His words inexplicably beckoned her to him, and she came and stood before him, facing the inevitable. She held her breath as he put down his brandy glass and reached his hand towards her. The flickering light brought her dark hair alive and turned her skin to a silky golden glow.

'I am glad you have come. If you hadn't, I would have come to you. I am grieved that you should have thought all those things you accused me of earlier. I have been torturing myself ever since. How could you bear the weight of such cruelty without hating me as I deserved? It was true that I wanted the two estates to be one, but when I realised that Casa del Sole was on fire and that you might be inside, everything else became meaningless. I have never known such fear, such a deep sense of loss as when I thought what my life would be like without you in it.'

'Max—are you saying that you don't want me to leave after all?'

'Dear life, Christina,' he said, moved by the tears shining in her eyes and the intensity. 'Of course you don't have to go—that was never what I wanted. I want you to stay with me more than anything, but after everything that has happened it was only right that you should decide for yourself.'

'Do you mean it,' she whispered, looking deep into his eyes, 'that you don't want me to leave here…?'

He placed a finger on her lips to still the words. 'Hear me out, Christina. Please believe that I have nothing but regret for making you feel that you were second-best. To give you that impression was cruel and thoughtless, and I realise you must have been deeply hurt, but listen to me—my beautiful, tempestuous wife. I swear to you that Francesca was never my mistress, and when I went to England and found you again, there could never be any other woman for me. I thought that unspoken link between us had told you that.'

Christina stared at him, a softening coming to her eyes as

the heady words penetrated her brain. 'I loved you then, Max,' she confessed without shame, 'but to hope you would one day love me back was just a wild dream.'

'Good God, Christina, of course I love you. I love you so much I couldn't bear the thought of losing you. I love you more than my own life, and when I saw the fire and I knew what might have happened to you, I wanted to die with you. It wasn't the thought of any house I was concerned with. It was you, Christina, only you.'

Christina's throat was clogged with tears, her mind stunned as she tried to believe he was saying these things to her.

'God, but you're lovely,' he said, his voice oddly ragged. Taking her hand, he drew her towards him. She looked like a wild young temptress with the candle light gleaming on her hair. 'You are all that I want.'

'I want you too, Max. I cannot help the way I feel. In all humility, quite simply I am throwing myself on your mercy.' She looked up into his eyes, trying to read his expression. There was a cynical lift to his eyebrows.

'What? You could not be humble if you tried. Without doubt you are a most impulsive creature.'

He was amused. His mobile lips crinkled at the corners. Christina shook her head, having no way of knowing what his thoughts were. 'You know the extent of my feelings, and now I feel quite helpless.'

'The hell you are. Helpless be damned. A woman who has gone through what you have and can still lift her head with fire in her eyes is not helpless.'

His voice was so soft, so tender, so deep and warm. How was she to resist it? How was she even to look up at him, see his eyes shining with what she hoped was an expression he had given to no woman but her. He was so close she could feel the heat of him. She sighed and melted and felt a languorous magic drift through her.

Feeling the dizzying aura of his masculinity, the strong pull of what she knew was his attraction for her wrap itself about her, when she swayed against him he gathered her into his arms in an act of possession. She lifted her face; when he placed his lips on hers, gently, barely more than a touch, she moaned softly.

'Max,' her mouth murmured against his, and she could feel the hard muscles of his powerful body. She loved this man more than she had thought it was possible to love another human being. She wanted him and that was enough.

The exploration of his hands stroking her neck, her back, her breasts, and the deeper kiss he gave her left her purring and glowing. She could smell the odour of his cologne, the smoke of his cigar, the taste of brandy. His mouth became more demanding, taking hers with an unleashed passion that sent giant waves of desire crashing over her, and she returned the same stormy passion that he was offering her.

Max groaned with rampaging desire and plunged his hand into the thickness of her hair, holding her mouth to his before dragging it away and lavishing scorching kisses on her face, her eyes, her neck. His control was beginning to snap.

'You are going to drive me out of my mind, do you know that, Christina?' he murmured thickly. But Christina didn't answer because his lips had recaptured hers, and she was drowning in an ocean of pleasure. Tearing his mouth from hers he held her head between his strong hands, looking intently into her eyes. 'Want me, *caro*, want me as much as I want you—more than anything else.'

'I do,' she whispered in a tortured breath as he ran his tongue over her full bottom lip. All she knew was that she was bursting with love and that she wanted, needed, him to know how she felt and how wonderful that feeling was. 'I do want you. I love you, Max, I love you so much.'

Max became still. Her words struck a strange chord of intense feeling deep within him. Raising his head, he stared down at her. He already knew many things about his wonderful wife—that she was beautiful, intelligent, sensitive and witty—and he had also just discovered that she was hopelessly naïve. He smiled. There wasn't a woman of his acquaintance who would tell a man she loved him. A huge constricting knot of tenderness and desire tightened his throat and, snatching her into his arms, he buried his face in her fragrant hair.

His finger touched her chin, tipping her face up to his. Its purity was striking. He smiled into her glazed green eyes. 'I have already told you that I know exactly what I want. And I want you, Christina. Very much,' he whispered.

Christina saw his eyes darken as if his thoughts were lifted in some eager anticipation. The steady eyes, the resolute, beautiful mouth were so close. She remained still, drawn into those eyes. She must have him, this handsome Italian she had not wanted to fall in love with.

'I love you, Christina Thornton, and I have done for a very long time. Of all the women I have known, none can hold a candle to you. I will show you just how much.'

With a movement Christina had not anticipated, he dragged her back into his arms. She made a move to step back from him, but he held her firm, and when his lips found hers once more with a fierceness that paralysed her and flamed with a fiery heat that warmed her whole body, she wrapped her arms about his neck, to hold him even closer, finding the place where she was meant to be.

Christina's eyes closed and the strength of his embrace, the taste of brandy on his lips, the hard pressure of his loins and the firm, rippling muscles beneath his shirt made her all too aware that this was a strong, healthy man, and that he was treating her like a woman.

His kiss was overwhelming and she felt the instant awakening of what she knew to be desire. His lips parted hers and his tongue caressed and sought and found the honeyed sweetness of her mouth. He put his hand to the back of her head, entwining his fingers in her hair. She lifted her chin and his lips slid beneath it and along her jaw, gasping her name as he took the lobe of her ear between his lips.

With a groan they both sank to their knees as though the strength had left them. She held his head as his mouth slid to her breasts, his hand deftly unfastening the buttons to release the fullness of them, white and soft, taking the hard rosy nipples in his hungering mouth. She was moaning deep in her throat as he laid her down and knelt over her, finding her lips once more, at the same time loosening her clothing and his own and flinging them off until they were both naked.

Picking her up in his strong arms, he carried her to the bed, laying her down, and then he was beside her. Christina clung to him—it seemed he was the only real thing in her swirling world. She shivered as his hand caressed the bare flesh on her ankle and calf, slowly moving up her leg to its goal. Following his lead, gradually she gave a little more of herself, her heart telling her in a small whisper that surely this man must truly love her to be doing this.

Max's male body, hard and eager, yearned to go on, to satisfy itself with nothing less than her total submission, and it was only her innocence and trust that had held him back so far. But he was delighted to find she was as eager for him as he was for her.

Christina wanted him with a fierceness that shocked her, that had her sighing and stretching and moaning in his arms, her treacherous female body ready to arch itself to accommodate his. She could not deny that she loved him, that it was a live and burning thing inside her that would not ease. She took no time to think about it, to dwell on the possible consequences of what she was doing, as his flaunting manhood quested between her open thighs, making her realise there was no going back, no escaping what was to happen, what she wanted to happen, and there was nowhere more appropriate to become a complete woman—Max's woman—than in his bed at Castello Marchesi, beneath the dark Tuscan sky.

Max did not take her gently and nor did she let him as she wrapped her legs about him, glorying in the hurt he caused her, surprised when his mouth sought out her lips and he kissed her with a long, leisured thoroughness until the ache of the intrusion began to subside. His loving and the throbbing heat of him brought her to new levels of pleasure, and each level was so completely filled with joy she was sure she could go no higher.

He devoured her and she knew that nothing would ever be the same again. He attacked not only her body but her senses, and she began to respond to his wild, ardent passion that made her incapable of reason. Lips and bodies were merged in a fiery fusion that touched to the depths of their soul and left them spent.

In the aftermath they lay together, replete, not speaking, their hearts gradually slowing to a regular beat, Max's face against her tangled hair, as he sought to hold fast to this moment lest he lose some portion of it to the awareness of time. The ecstasy he had just experienced was a marvel to him, for, having made love to many women, he thought there was nothing new in making love. But he realised there was. He was the first man Christina had known. He knew it and his body rejoiced. She was his now. He had put his masculine mark on her and she was his for all eternity.

Christina sighed and melted and felt a languorous magic drift through her as she lay nestled against his warm, hard body. For the moment all was quiet around them, all was perfection. Nothing in her life had given her the pleasure that Max had just given her. Nothing else had mattered but her body, which had been alive with need and awash with feeling.

Max watched the emotions flitting across her face. She had never been able to hide her feelings. She had been a warm and willing participant and had welcomed him into her body and he rejoiced in that. Slowly, deliberately, he reached out and gently touched her cheek with his finger.

'It was wonderful, Christina. What we did—the first time for you—will remain with you for ever.'

She looked at him. He was right. There was no feasible way either of them would forget what they had done. Their eyes held. His so blue, hers so green, remembering, already beginning to imagine the possibility of a next time.

On a warm day in October, when the grapes and the olives had been harvested, smiling serenely and with a great tranquillity of heart, Christina stood beside Max in the lovely little Italian church where Lydia and Roberta had been married and had worshipped. The pews were filled with family and friends and beaming villagers. Her papa and mama and Peter, her grandmother and beloved Molly, looked proudly on.

Guy was there, putting on a brave face, for he was saddened by Francesca's departure, but when Max had told him what she had done he was determined he would purge her from his mind if it killed him. She had left for Sicily in disgrace immediately after the fire, where she was to live with relatives indefinitely. Both Max and Christina knew that following her visit to Don Cantoni, the dowager Countess was in some way responsible for Francesca leaving, but she kept a discreet silence.

Casa del Sole was in the process of being rebuilt, and would be very much the same as how it had looked before the fire. Molly, who had loved the old house as much as Christina, had expressed a wish to live there, and Christina didn't think it would be long before Pepi proposed to her and the two of them set up home together.

Christina moved closer to her husband and placed her hand in his, to have their marriage blessed.

Max gazed down at the beautiful woman attired in ivory silk, holding Lydia's prayer book, unable to believe this had come to pass. His expression was soft, rapt as though he looked at an angel, his love for her shining through the brilliance of his blue eyes. Memories of…

Christina as a baby, when he was ten years old, flashed before his eyes.

Christina cavorting like the happy girl she was in a lake in her petticoat, her adorable green eyes glowing with merriment.

Christina arriving at Castello Marchesi and creating mayhem.

Christina lying in their bed beside him—provocative, irresistible temptress—the memory of this still very much alive.

And now Christina, his wife, turning her face up to his. Joy exploded, pouring through him until it was almost past bearing.

Love tightened his throat as she held out her arms to him. What he felt was so exquisite it pained him to draw breath. He wanted to give her the world because she had given him so much.

'I love you so much. Today you look the way every woman

should look on her wedding day, *caro*, radiantly happy,' he whispered huskily.

'But it is not our wedding day.'

'It is to me. It is as it should have been, and I regret it not being so.'

Christina took a step closer. 'I am very fortunate to have found you, Max.'

'After eighteen years, when you were such an adorable, perfect baby, who would have thought we would come to this.'

A smile tugged at the corners of her mouth, broadening and deepening until it reached her eyes. 'Who, indeed.'

On sale 5th December 2008

THE OUTLAW'S BRIDE
by Carolyn Davidson

When an outlaw meets an outcast!

Shunned by her tribe, Debra Nightsong simply wanted
to tend her farm alone – until a mysterious stranger arrived.
He *said* he meant no harm, yet his brooding presence
unnerved her – perhaps there was pleasure to be found in
the arms of this outlaw…

On the run and in search of a hideout, Debra's farmhouse
was just perfect for Tyler. He vowed not to take advantage
of the mesmerising beauty, but he soon regretted his words!
Could they both have finally found a place to
belong…together?

Celebrate 100 years of pure reading pleasure with Mills & Boon®

To mark our centenary, each month we're publishing a special 100th Birthday Edition. These celebratory editions are packed with extra features and include a FREE bonus story.

Plus, you have the chance to enter a fabulous monthly prize draw. See 100th Birthday Edition books for details.

Now that's worth celebrating!

September 2008

Crazy about her Spanish Boss by Rebecca Winters
Includes FREE bonus story
Rafael's Convenient Proposal

November 2008

**The Rancher's Christmas Baby
by Cathy Gillen Thacker**
Includes FREE bonus story *Baby's First Christmas*

December 2008

One Magical Christmas by Carol Marinelli
Includes FREE bonus story *Emergency at Bayside*

Look for Mills & Boon® 100th Birthday Editions at your favourite bookseller or visit
www.millsandboon.co.uk

FREE

2 BOOKS AND A SURPRISE GIFT!

We would like to take this opportunity to thank you for reading this Mills & Boon® book by offering you the chance to take TWO more specially selected titles from the Historical series absolutely FREE! We're also making this offer to introduce you to the benefits of the Mills & Boon® Book Club—

* ★ **FREE home delivery**
* ★ **FREE gifts and competitions**
* ★ **FREE monthly Newsletter**
* ★ **Books available before they're in the shops**
* ★ **Exclusive Mills & Boon® Book Club offers**

Accepting these FREE books and gift places you under no obligation to buy; you may cancel at any time, even after receiving your free shipment. Simply complete your details below and return the entire page to the address below. You don't even need a stamp!

YES! Please send me 2 free Historical books and a surprise gift. I understand that unless you hear from me, I will receive 4 superb new titles every month for just £3.69 each, postage and packing free. I am under no obligation to purchase any books and may cancel my subscription at any time. The free books and gift will be mine to keep in any case.

H8ZEE

Ms/Mrs/Miss/Mr...Initials ....
BLOCK CAPITALS PLEASE

Surname ....

Address ....

....

....Postcode ....

Send this whole page to:
The Mills & Boon Book Club, FREEPOST CN81, Croydon, CR9 3WZ